P9-ARK-443

The Stones of the Abbey

Fernand Pouillon

The Stones of
the Abbey

Translated by Edward Gillott

Originally published in England under the title
The Stones of Le Thoronet

A Harvest/HBJ Book
A Helen and Kurt Wolff Book
Harcourt Brace Jovanovich, Publishers
San Diego   New York   London

HBJ

Copyright © 1964 by Editions du Seuil
Translation copyright © 1970 by Jonathan Cape Ltd

All rights reserved. No part of this publication may be reproduced or trans-
mitted in any form or by any means, electronic or mechanical, including
photocopy, recording, or any information storage and retrieval system,
without permission in writing from the publisher.

Requests for permission to make copies of any part
of the work should be mailed to: Permissions,
Harcourt Brace Jovanovich, Publishers,
Orlando, FL 32887.

LIBRARY OF CONGRESS CATALOGING IN PUBLICATION DATA

Pouillon, Fernand.
The stones of the Abbey.

Translation of: Les Pierres sauvages.
Reprint. Originally published: New York Harcourt,
Brace & World, c 1970.
"A Helen and Kurt Wolff book."
1. Le Thoronet (Abbey)—History—Fiction.
2. Cistercians—France—History—Fiction.
3. France—History—Louis VII, 1137–1180—Fiction.
I. Title.
PQ2676.079P513   1985   843'.914   84-22440
ISBN 0-15-685100-8 (Harvest/HBJ : pbk.)

Printed in the United States of America

Originally published in France under the title *Les Pierres sauvages*

The architectural drawings are taken from a book on the Cistercian abbeys
of Provence by the same author, published by Editions F. De Nobèle.

First Harvest/HBJ edition 1985

A B C D E F G H I J

To Joséphine, Violette, Fernand,
to my children,
to all those who fought
for me, with me.

Illustrations

The Stones of the Abbey

Third Sunday in Lent

The rain has soaked through our clothes, the frost has hardened the heavy stuff of our habits, congealed our beards, stiffened our limbs. The mud has bespattered our hands, our feet and our faces, the wind has cloaked us in sand. The motion of walking no longer swings the frozen folds on our emaciated bodies. Urged along in the pallid half-light of this mistral-blown winter, following our own distorted shadows, we look like three saints in stone. We have been walking now for weeks, making our way down the valley of the Rhône towards Avignon, and thence to Notre Dame de Florielle in the diocese of Fréjus, on the estate of my cousin Raymond Bérenger, Count of Barcelona. On this fifth day of March 1161, in the thirtieth year since my coming to Cîteaux, I am once more directed to build a monastery. My orders came from our abbot.

St Zachary, thirteenth day of March

Today, after four hours' walking, we have arrived at Le Thoronet: a forest, peaceful and sombre, and a green valley, narrow but not deep, through which a stream runs eastwards. All three of us have a holiday feeling; the day is cool, sunlit; since the first light we have been pacing to and fro, in every direction. We approached the site of the abbey from the east; a road in poor repair, rain-furrowed, climbs steeply in two loops through a thick forest of oak and pine. To anyone arriving by this route, the abbey will be revealed suddenly. The site of the monastery slopes gently towards the stream; the thought at once came to me that this situation would lend itself to interesting arrangements of levels. In the evening we climbed the slope which faces north, and sat down on the first ridge. Scanning the hills as far as the eye could see, we glimpsed not the smallest farmhouse or hut. The site, or what we can make out of it, looks like a nest of the softest moss: in fact the 'moss' is really thorn scrub a yard high.

When we arrived the brothers were assembled at an open space on two levels, situated to the south of where the abbey was to be. Their welcome was reserved. We learned that this terrace was known as the Field. Along its westward edge the Field is extended by the first attempts at cultivation. The ground has been broken, and streaks of red and grey suggest that crops will be meagre.

Far off, on the northern slope, we noticed traces of cultivated plots upon which the forest had encroached. Stepped walls (*bancaou* in Provençal), crumbling and lost amidst young pines, were bracing huge, exposed olive trees that seemed to have writhed to escape stifling. We decided to give them space without delay. Against all these greyish and dark greens, the branches of some handsome oaks, which we shall retain near the abbey, stand out blackly. The course of the stream, a reversed S, is outlined by soft colours – at present yellow, brown and straw: doubtless willows, hazels and honeysuckles. In a few days all the light greens will sing, for everywhere about us we can hear the stirring of spring; leaves unfolding, branches growing, seeds splitting, buds bursting. The sap is rising after this warm day of clear sunlight, and the song of the birds as they settle for the night no longer has the plaintive and fearful note of winter evenings.

Our journey went badly. On the day of St John of Damascus, March 7th, we halted at Montmajour for a rest. The abbot gave us the news of the region. Henceforth, owing to the defeat of the Balz faction last year, we shall be subject to Count Raymond; my brother, Hugues Balz, rightly continues to press his own claim to Provence. It seems right that our family, which has never left this county, should govern it. Ever since the time of Count Leibulfe and Louis the Blind, more than three centuries ago, the silver star given to us by the Wise Man Balthasar has been shining over Provence. Only once has the star left this place, and that was with my ancestor Guillaume, at the time of the First Crusade. Yet Frederick Barbarossa, an unworthy emperor, remains our suzerain. It seems that to please him and to keep his protection, my brother supports Victor, the antipope; to regain the county at this price would be an infamy. This is very bad news for me; despite the cloister I remain attached to my family and to its traditions. It is hard for me to endure the rule of my cousin, Raymond Bérenger, a Catalan, a foreigner. Yet, alas, it is he who upholds our Pope Alexander, and who thus fights to end this dreadful schism. Meanwhile, Christians are once again at odds, and humble folk are bewildered. The Abbot of Montmajour also told me that my mother was still alive: she is almost eighty years old. I was troubled to be so near to her without going to pay my respects. But suddenly the wind, which for three days had raged against us, died down. In order to rid myself of any temptation to revisit my family, I ordered our departure for Aix and Saint Maximin, our last stage. We were at the limit of our strength, sustained only by eagerness to arrive at Notre Dame de Florielle at the earliest possible moment. We hastily took our leave of the good abbot.

Towards midnight we came to the Alpilles, clear weather and a full moon guiding our steps as if it were broad daylight. There our misfortunes began. First we saw horses tethered to a pine; from their harnesses we knew they belonged to men-at-arms. Then a few steps farther on we saw some men whispering together. As we passed them we greeted them with a 'The Lord be with you,' in the most natural manner. Less than an hour later we heard the horses approaching behind us, and gaining steadily on us. We were already walking quickly; fear made us lengthen our stride. When they had overtaken us they surrounded us, and told us to follow them. We obeyed. They then set off up a fairly steep mountain road. Like us they were silent; their seizure of us poor monks made them uneasy and ashamed.

An hour later they drew up a few paces from a well-sheltered farmhouse, built like a stronghold. Bernard and Benoît, knowing our total wealth, were not worried. The older of the two men, bearded, rough, tall and heavy, with a squint which made it impossible to guess which way he was looking, said to me, 'Give me all your money and the valuables that you have on you.' Without further ado I raised my habit and emptied into his hands a few small coins that were intended, in case of need, to procure our subsistence. He looked at them with contempt and shoved us roughly towards the house. We entered a low room. A stench of corpses, of burnt flesh, of vomit gripped our throats. The darkness was complete. One of the men lit a lamp, but we dared not look about us. We were made to strip off our habits and tunics. When Bernard refused we were beaten cruelly. Benoît was bleeding profusely from a shoulder wound. A misshapen creature carefully searched every one of our garments. When they realized that we carried nothing except a letter for the Abbot of Notre Dame de Florielle, they threw us naked into the courtyard. Pain prevented our feeling the biting cold.

Several hours later, the oldest of the bandits came for us. Again we entered the stinking room. We were ordered to bury some corpses. I agreed on condition that our garments were restored to us. The filthy task consisted of dragging five mutilated and rotting bodies into a near-by field and then digging a great hole to bury them in. By the dawn light we recognized the remains of three men and two women, their bodies grotesquely deformed by torture and putrefaction. We were left alone for a moment to pray for the dead, but we took cowardly advantage of it to flee after a hasty prayer.

The sun, although hidden behind great grey clouds, was already high when we halted near a pond to wash our wounds and to sleep for a while. The noise of a cart awoke us, and we concealed ourselves in the undergrowth. A shaggy russet mule was drawing a covered cart along the rocky road. A woman lay on it among furniture and utensils. The pallor of her face and the strange jerking of her body led me to suppose that she was dead. A peasant now dragged at the mule, now helped the wheels along. We then revealed ourselves. As soon as he saw us he looked frightened, and ran ahead without taking his eyes off us, tugging at the animal, and beating it wildly. What could we do? For some time we watched the cart bouncing over the stones, the mule's neck outstretched, its thrusting muzzle held by the man's clenched fist as its vigorous hooves tore at the uneven ground. Beneath the lowering, luminous sky, a flight of crows wheeled about the cart. Sadly we went on our way.

On the day of the Feast of the Martyrs we reached Saint

Maximin. It was the tenth day of March. Fasting, the hard stones of the roads, exhaustion and cold had been our travelling companions. We were greeted by sunshine, clear skies and almond trees in blossom. On the morrow, St Eulogius' day, Abbot Paulin received us at Notre Dame de Florielle, ordered us to rest for two days and expressed his impatience. He had been a companion of Abbot Bernard of Clairvaux, and had entered the Order very late after an adventurous life. Notre Dame de Florielle is to be his final abode.

St Cyriacus, sixteenth day of March

The clearing of the forest has begun; eleven lay brothers already live here. On our arrival, they improvised a dry-wall dorter-workshop, roofed with foliage.

The abbot has delegated his authority to me. In future I alone, in my capacity as master builder and cellarer, will be responsible for discipline. As soon as the dorters are finished, the community will establish itself here. In the meantime we are subject to Notre Dame de Florielle, whence I shall receive my orders and to which I shall submit my reports.

St Patrick, seventeenth day of March

My anxiety equals my impatience. I am conscious of doubt — creation is like a miracle, and doubt is a consequence of the uncertainty of the miracle.

After a thorough inspection of Le Thoronet, I have ordered changes to be made in the work schedules and the discipline, and have devised an overall plan. Life here will be hard. To our observance of the Rule will be added the demanding work of building. I shall ask the abbot for a more ample diet and less rigour in times of fast. I shall make great demands on the lay brothers. Shortly, ten brothers are to enlarge our group, and experienced craftsmen are to teach them their trades.

I have drawn up a list of rules for the lay brothers and for us which completely transforms the customs practised before our arrival. It all begins with mental discipline, that ultimately results in a timetable.

At the third hour we shall rise, and the lay brothers, having set all in order, will say a prayer at the oratory and then go to the building site. At the eleventh hour, assembly at the spring, ablutions and first meal; that will take an hour. In the evening, we shall leave the site at the nineteenth hour; the lay brothers will clean and put away the tools, go to the spring and have their last meal. After prayers we shall retire at half past the twentieth hour.

Distribution of the work force will be organized on Thursday of each week. On Saturday, two hours will be set apart for the upkeep of garments.

All the lay brothers and monks of Le Thoronet will receive the full allowance of fish or meat and the extra allowance of bread. During Lent fasting will be obligatory until the twelfth hour.

Canonical hours will be rung: Matins and Lauds at the third hour, Prime at the fifth, Tierce at the eighth, Sext at the eleventh, None at the fourteenth, Vespers at the seventeenth and, finally, Compline at the twentieth.

On the first Friday of each month the infirmarian of Florielle will examine the lay brothers and treat the sick. The abbot will fix the day for blood-letting.

The lay brothers are advised to consume one pint of olive oil per table per day, and as much garlic as possible; it fortifies the body against epidemics, infections and chills. The maintenance of strength is a duty imposed on our community. Abusive fasting, self-chastisement and vigils, likewise the use of hairshirts that give rise to sores, will be considered serious offences and severely punished. The lay brothers are responsible for guarding their own health and that of their brothers, and will report anyone who conceals sickness.

Henceforth I shall exact strict obedience to these rules. I have authorized talk during working hours so as to simplify our tasks.

On Sunday, Mass will be celebrated by a monk from Florielle. For the rest of the day, I shall allow much freedom; the brothers will be able to rest or sleep in the afternoon until Vespers, go for walks with Bernard or Benoît, collect herbs, or gather fruit or mushrooms under the supervision of Brother Gabriel, who knows the poisonous species.

As for my two brothers, I have set down some recommendations. Three offices only are required of them daily: Lauds, Vespers and Compline. The others will, as far as circumstances permit, be performed at their place of work. They must therefore carry their diurnals. I have asked my brothers to assemble for the obligatory offices at the chapel.

Even in Lent, I require them to be meticulous in observing the rules, except during Passiontide, when exemplary fasts, self-chastisement, contemplation and prayer will be permitted. Each week, the rules will be read out by Brother Bernard at the eleventh-hour meal. Next, I entrusted Brother Benoît with the allotment of tasks for rainy days; he seemed at a loss. So far we have no workshops. What was to be done? Seeing his perplexity, I suggested that a shelter be put up quickly where the woodwork could be turned out with rough tools.

I must also make decisions about our clothing. Eight months of isolation, poverty and no discipline have made our lay brothers look like serfs. I mean to see them all clothed in the tunic and scapular, drawers and stockings required by the Rule. Their incongruous finery will be worn out on the site. Garments contrived out of sheepskins will be made into bed coverings. The abbot certainly has no knowledge of all these irregularities. He will have to furnish me with the necessary woollen cloth and linen. It seems that from this year the cowl is to be worn during non-working hours. The General Chapter has so decreed—in my view, foolishly: all this dressing-up takes too much time. Last year, the same Chapter forbade the wearing of gloves. On my last work site it was a disaster; the lay brothers' hands were so cut and damaged that they would not heal. I raised a protest, whereupon mittens were authorized. I had some made which so closely resembled gloves that the Order was obliged to prescribe their shape in great detail. It also specified which craftsmen were allowed to wear them. Thus blacksmiths, who work in heat, may have them, and carpenters, who generally work in the open, may not. Those who concern themselves with such regulations are usually precentors rather than overseers.

Eve of Passion Sunday

A day of preliminary work. We are marking out the various levels on the ground and deciding where the axis of the church is to be; later this will give me a basis for my designs. We are also arranging the schedule for the coming weeks.

It seems that work began here eight months ago. The results so far consist of a quarry excavated to the east of the monastery – in my view, too near the stream; we shall, I am sure, abandon it one day. To the west, on a raised foundation, a long hut has been constructed out of planks – an incredible waste of wood bought at high prices: it is a folly. At one end it houses the implements and the refectory, in the middle the dorter – still useless, because the roof has not been finished – and at the other end a wet, exposed space: the oratory. On Sundays a monk celebrates Mass in this shed which is unfit to shelter animals. A layman from Fréjus preceded me here; he left a few days before my arrival. The only well-chosen site is that of the hut in which Bernard, Benoît and I are living. By making some improvements we shall make it comfortable enough to work in. Set high up, near the source of the stream, on a raised foundation, it overlooks the entire work site. The quarry is hidden by trees, but we can keep watch on the coming and going of the brothers without seeing the long hut. I shall have some oaks felled to give a clear view of the terrace on which the lay brothers have their lodging. At the foot of the slope, less than fifty yards away, lies the Field; along its edge the south wall of the church will be built.

Although the lay brothers' permanent dorter has been started on, the only plans I have found are fragmentary and useless. The monastery site has never been cleared of brushwood. No borings of the ground have been made. For months great disorder prevailed. Nothing was done methodically. The lay brothers slept where they liked beneath shelters of branches and earth, and prepared their food like nomads. They wasted their time in useless tasks and had acquired bad habits; for instance, they formed groups of two or three, following their inclination, and in the evening talked in undertones. Sometimes they reached work after Tierce, so difficult was their physical life, and wasted two hours in cooking between None and Vespers. They ate too much but not well. Wine had been allowed the previous winter to help against the cold; now that the weather was fine, they continued to drink. One month they were very poorly supplied with grain and vegetables, so they went hunting. For ten days I watched and said nothing; today's assembly surprised them, although I noticed some signs of approval among them.

Nothing is ready, that is our difficulty: only the plan of cultivation seems practicable, only the farming implements have been thought of. The initiation and organization of a building project must inspire by demonstrating superb ability. Before next winter I aim to see walls already rising, order everywhere, a complete supply of tools, a forge, lime kilns, brick kilns, suitable buildings for the implements as well as for the men and animals. First and foremost, a chapel. Everyone has taken to this hermit life—they seem to forget that they are Cistercians. By assembling in church every day they will regain their awareness of communal life.

During the assembly I spoke as simply as possible. I laid down a work schedule, and declared that next year we should set up an altar in the roofed apse in time for the Feast of the Virgin.

They watched me, their eyes blank, disheartened before they begin. The discipline does not seem to satisfy them; as for confidence in the project, they have none. They think they will be long dead by the time the monastery is completed. They are aware of the habitual slow pace of our building, know there is no money, that Notre Dame de Florielle barely survives. Why was it decided to change the location of the monastery? I still do not know, nor do they. Why give up a place already organized and an abbey already built, in favour of this little valley, in which every foot reclaimed from nature requires considerable effort? The ground is all slopes and rain-furrows; each acre needs dozens of cubic yards of supporting masonry. The stream is shallow in summer, the hollows are too wet, the slopes dried out. To install a system of irrigation would be folly: even after great expense of labour and material, water would always be lacking in time of need. I told them that ten years hence over a hundred monks and novices would live in this valley, to the glory of Christ and the Virgin. They went away, nodding their heads and murmuring. Bernard and Benoît were touched by these folk, and said nothing. Frowning, I wrote before them, reading each sentence aloud:

'After marking out the sites: clear the level areas of scrub, peg out the chapel, dorter, workshops, forge. The siting of each of these buildings will be decided after the spaces have been cleared. Thus the extent of the level areas will be the determining factor in our decisions. Surrounding the spaces intended for huts, dry walls will be constructed with graded quarry waste. The best stones will be kept for stepped field-walls (*bancaou*), the poorest to raise rubble and earth foundations beneath the temporary wooden buildings. The dry-stone facing of these walls will be given a slight slant, so that driving rain will not seep into the rubble and earth mixture. Storms in this region are extremely violent and are always accompanied by a strong east wind. Felling of resinous pines will be carried on, in a place near the site, the selected trunks to be transported by hand. Consequently trees over a foot in diameter will be avoided. Borings will be undertaken on the site of the monastery. Others will be made to find new quarries and limestone. Benoît will make inquiries in the locality about the clay-pits nearest to the work site.'

I wrote a long letter to the abbot, requesting him to send a messenger to Cîteaux. From there I want some craftsmen whom I know well, and a team of carpenters from the Beauce. As for a smith, there is no point in asking the abbey for one, they have not enough.

We have discovered that the lay brothers, for the most part, are skilful, but few of them are craftsmen. They have learned how to extract and square the stone, but it is pitiful! For one cubic yard of usable blocks, they make twenty of fragments.

Passing through Arles the messenger will look up a certain Master Paul. I do not know him; I have heard much good of him … and much ill.

St Benedict, twenty-first day of March

Moving from the whole to the detail, from the material to the immaterial, from the defined to the undefined, my thoughts and my instincts will inspire methodical action, and my brain and my heart will pass from trance to practical detail without my being able to control them to any great degree.

For the moment, my principal preoccupations are the positioning, the general shape, the orientation. There is one serious obstacle: the layout was determined before we arrived by the foundations already begun for the lay brothers' dorter. Now I want to alter the direction of the church's axis, so that it points directly towards the east. At first I was tempted to abandon the work so far done; today I decided against this on account of the time and labour that would be wasted. The irregular angle will show on the plans. Will this basic fault matter? I cannot yet make up my mind. If I had been here at the beginning it is certain that I would not willingly have drawn an obtuse angle on the site where the cloisters were to be.

As I was writing, the noise of the quarry gave way to silence. The lay brothers have ended a day of apprentice work. This sudden quiet set me thinking about the stone, about the quarrying, shaping and appearance of it. I have examined this material closely; no saw can get a bite on it, and under the chisel it shatters like bad glass. We shall make something out of it. Freshly shaped, the stone is a light, warm, yellow ochre; in time it will become a golden grey. Light seems to lay on it in turn all the colours of the prism, so that the grey is compounded of and impregnated with sunlight. The raw blocks torn from the ground, measured and scored, become noble material; each stroke, each visible flash of light bears witness to energy and perseverance. Are not we Cistercian monks like these stones? Torn from secular life, scored and chiselled by the Rule, our faces illumined by faith, marked by our struggles with the Enemy? Enter into the stone, and be yourselves as living stones raising an edifice of holy priests.

During the night I read the Abbot of Clairvaux's *On Consideration:*

Consideration purifies its own spring, that is, the very mind which gives it birth. Moreover, it moderates the passions, regulates action, corrects excess, forms morals, puts good order and honesty into life; lastly it confers knowledge, as much of the human as of the divine. This it is which unravels what is tangled, draws close what tends to wander, assembles what is dispersed, penetrates what is secret, follows truth everywhere, passes through the sieve of examination what are only vain appearances, tracks down both real intentions and false semblances. This it is which settles in advance what must be done; reviews what has been done so that nothing shall remain in the mind that has not already been amended or that needs to be amended even more. This it is, lastly, which in fortunate times foresees trouble, but which appears quite unaffected when it comes; the first case showing the working of prudence, the second, that of strength. It is right and proper here to draw your attention to that perfect accord of the virtues, to that harmonious connection which links them one to another. As you have just seen, prudence is the mother of strength; but a bold action not born of prudence is the daughter of temerity, not of strength. Now it falls to this same virtue of prudence—intermediary and to some extent arbiter between the pleasures of the senses and the needs of nature—to delimit exactly their respective zones, to assign to the latter and provide them with the necessary, to deprive the former of the superfluous.

St Victorianus, twenty-third day of March

The dream is beginning, I shall wait, I shall receive. Twenty years and more of fleeting visions, well stored in my memory, are there; I feel them, restless and manifold, like a mount trembling under me.

Though one is very often rightly amazed by the slow progress of a project, sometimes it happens that a considerable task will be planned quickly. The longest part for me is the waiting, and later all the time I have for reflection. These periods once past, the method of work once settled, the practical details can be arranged in a few days. Why? The question touches on everything that the art of creation owes to one's accumulated knowledge. Every artist at work has in his leads, his brush, his graver, something that links his movements not only to his mind, but also to his memory. The stroke that seems spontaneous is ten, thirty years old! In art, knowledge, labour and patience are everything, and what may appear in a moment has been years on the way.

St Hugh, my brother's patron, first day of April

Tomorrow is Easter Sunday; two days of rest and holiday after an exhausting week.

After Sext, I attempted to verify my conjectures, to match them against the terrain. As always, fact rearranges one's ideas without completely destroying them.

Now, alone in my hut, I wait and I live my inner light. Like a flash of light, the vision of the apse crosses my mind; if I could only seize it, I would be able to define it better. Then, that vision that came to me on the day of my arrival; from low in the valley I saw the steeple; it thrust boldly upwards, yet I was unable to draw it.

There is a sore on my leg which is spreading; I must have been wounded that night in the Alpilles, and did not attend to it. I shall consult Brother Gabriel or the infirmarian.

St Clotarius, seventh day of April

'The tangible is the ultimate state of things.' Isaac de l'Étoile

This undertaking will be dedicated to successive generations of brothers; the atmosphere of the inhabited place will have its origin in the initial inspiration, whose substance is impalpably contained in the finished building. The more, at the outset, intensity and power of thought compound with generosity, purity, piety, with affection and hope, with courage and pride, the more will be reflected in my brothers' souls the harmonies, the emotions perceptible and appropriate to each of their sensibilities. In cloister or chapter house, through sun, mist or wind, by day or night, the harvest of visions, sombre or radiant, will exalt the least receptive monk—just as the novice, prostrated in prayer, learns without effort the harmonies of the sacred songs. In the vaults of a church cool in any season, a place where sounds rise, break, multiply in measured resonance, the soul will be illumined

23

as much by the enchantment of a paradise of stone as by out-
pourings of prayer.

St Fulbert, tenth day of April

Matins will shortly be rung. I woke before the first hour of the
day, body unusually rested, mind calm to the point of indifference,
of detachment. It is a good thing to retrace one's steps. First of all
I must examine the site afresh, try to absorb the shape and to feel
it as a whole; the architecture of a monastery is not made up of a
collection of buildings – it is one complete, massive block, like a
sculpture.

The plan, a two-dimensional drawing, is not a basis for judgment; it depicts the outline of an incomplete concept, like a guide
to an imaginary walk. It is impossible to create without at the same
time deciding height and breadth, without defining everything
from the smallest elementary detail to the whole. There can be no
architecture without evoking the fourth dimension, the trajectory:
the perception of the building as dynamic. The completed work is
rarely an unmoving mountain or horizon; it changes ceaselessly
as our gaze wanders over it. Its bulk turns on the pivot whose
fixed end is our eyes. Architecture moves, in the sense that our
steps beget the movement of shapes, our swivelling heads tilt
lines, and our eyes perceive the endless mobility of reliefs. It is the
business of us master builders to create what comes before, to
precede the image, to live in the plan, to set up house in it, to move
our beds into it, to tear down walls, to shift the weightiest blocks,
to defy equilibrium and gravity, to envisage at once the rotations,
the tiltings, the swiftness of successive images, and their im-
mobility in relation to each other.

'What is God? He is at once length, breadth, height, and
depth. These four divine attributes are the objects of as many
contemplations.' Bernard of Clairvaux.

St Leo, eleventh day of April

I have spent the whole day at Notre Dame de Florielle, and have
resumed my former relations with the abbot. I told him for the
first time since my arrival of my many cares, my sufferings, my

weaknesses. He did not believe me, and so our discussion produced none of the results I had expected. On the other hand, I managed to settle a number of important practical questions. For our provisioning, he decided that in future a lay brother from Notre Dame should bring the supplies by cart. Until now we had been fetching them ourselves, thus wasting a day for six of my brothers, who got back exhausted, loaded like mules. For the labour force, we agreed on posting six of the abbey's lay brothers to the work site. I promised him that next year we should be largely self-sufficient, with the aid of our newly cultivated fields. I submitted my regulations to him. He did not seem very pleased with all the expenditure on clothes. He hesitated, walked about in thought for some time, then, to my great relief, spoke of other matters. For implements and animals he counted out gold; each coin as it fell on the table was transformed in my eyes into materials, carts and tools. At sunset, the purse hanging at my neck, I insisted on returning. My wish was that Benoît should set out without a day's delay to buy what was needed to build the abbey. With the gold I knew that now nothing would be held up; the work site was really there on my breast. I set off on the paths that would be visible for three more hours of the long twilight: but fatigue and pain overwhelmed me on the way. That imprudent decision nearly cost me dear. At nightfall I had covered three leagues and could go no farther. I was not far from the highroad to Lorgues, on the heights of Sainte Foy Wood. Like a lost child, I was afraid, I imagined footsteps, I hid in a thicket. There the sleep of exhaustion brought release from my sufferings and my terrors. The chill morning aroused me, and I went on my way, fearful at the thought of an unlucky encounter. At one league from Le Thoronet, just as I had crossed the Argens at the ford, I heard Bernard calling.

St Paternus, fifteenth day of April

For the last two days our community has been in a commotion; at mealtimes the lay brothers exchange knowing glances, laugh at the least incident. At every unaccustomed sound they listen, stop chewing, silently suspend every gesture, concentrate for better hearing, look vacant. On the sites, at the quarry, they abandon their tasks, climb the rocks, watch the farthest turn of the road, then thoughtfully resume the interrupted work.

At last they came; it happened today halfway through the meal; by dint of waiting, the lay brothers had learned patience. From this morning they had hoped with serenity. They ate slowly, calmly, in polite silence. Normally their clumsy movements at mealtimes set up a racket of bowls, spoons or knives which, though not deafening, is disagreeable.

First of all came a distant cry, a creaking noise that transfixed us, then sounds of sand flattened and of pebbles crushed by wheels. Then, for some time, nothing more. A flight of disturbed birds, joyful rather than frightened, passed screeching over us. Now there could be no more doubt, they were there: cries, heavy rumbling – they must be starting the ascent. Almost everyone rose or straddled the benches. I rapped hard and quickly on the table, but as I raised my hand imploring looks were turned towards me, and I could not help smiling. Like a horde of devils they ran off, knocking benches over, jostling each other. I remained alone with Brothers Gabriel and Thomas who, not having dared to disobey, waited as usual for me to rise first. Quietly, we went over to the Field.

In the harsh glare of the midday sun, some of the lay brothers were unloading the carts; some were patting the sturdy beasts which were restless, harassed by gadflies and covered in white foam. Luc gave them his bread. Thomas ran his hand carefully over their necks. The tall Antoine inspected the carts. Thibault, crouching by a mule, wanted to see its shoes and waited for the animal to paw the ground. Hugues, mounted on the largest, played the knight. Bruno lifted the lead, put the hemp aside, counted the tools, stroked the anvil, sorted the implements. The entire load was placed on the ground, carefully but in great disorder. Gabriel stepped quickly from one mule to another, looking at everything. Philippe fingered and examined the harness, ran a hand under back-strap, breeching, traces, collar, appraised the thickness of the leather, the workmanship. Despite the dust, all was brand-new, well greased, freshly painted. In the midst of the general gaiety, I roughly unhooked the harness bells and walked up to Benoît, who, wearied by the journey, was sitting in the shade at the foot of the bank. 'Why this needless expense?' I asked.

'They were a present,' he replied; 'at the market they would not let us leave without them.' I had the three rows of bells in my hand; a moment before, I could have flung them away. I went back and attached them again to the breast-straps of the three mules. Those who had not understood my action thought it was a ceremony, and grouped themselves about me, some making the Sign of the Cross.

The construction of the monastery, which for the majority had been an unreal task, became, with the arrival of mules, carts and materials, a pressing matter. The minor jobs, performed for almost a year with apathy and in hope of reward in a better world, belonged already to a distant past. Benoît had recovered. He gave a series of rapid commands, had the scattered material reloaded, organized its storage in the dorter. The mules were to be unharnessed, groomed, fed and watered immediately.

Long ago, with Benoît's help, we had chosen our men: Luc for the animals, Antoine for the tools. When we sent for Luc and informed him of his office he paid no heed to our instructions but repeated over and over, 'They are mine, then,' and clapped his breast with his hand. We chatted until Vespers and deliberately ignored None.

In the evening we were startled by an unexpected visit. A horseman, habited and armed like a nobleman, halted on the Field; he was brown-skinned, covered in dust and mounted on a dark, wild-eyed horse with quivering hooves. He addressed us haughtily in a strong Provençal accent. As soon as he learned who we were, he dismounted and walked with a slight roll towards us. 'I am Paul, of Fontvieille and of Les Baux, master quarryman; I bring you the homage of the count your brother and am at your service. Where are the quarries?' Which will prove the greater day, that of the three mules or that of Master Paul?

St Mark, twenty-fifth day of April

Since the arrival of the mules, my brothers and I have been accepted by the lay brothers. I can now recount what has happened here since the twentieth day of March, after my regulations came into effect. On Monday, work was slowed everywhere, rebellion was in all hearts. Two days later, three recalcitrant brothers were absent from communal prayer, took no meals and remained in front of the oratory. Fearing further disobedience, the consequences of which would be serious, I had all the tools carried at night into our hut. At daybreak Bernard and Benoît went out to fell trees and clear the scrub. I settled myself at my table before the open door and kept watch on the tools. When we went to the refectory, four brothers out of eleven were at table, the others were waiting at the far end of the hut. As the kitchener had prepared nothing, we ate raw vegetables.

Immediately afterwards, I ordered the four brothers present to bring me a brother whom I had picked out after some thought. We waited. I was very worried; if I did not succeed in settling this business on my own, I would be obliged to report to the abbot. When all hope had vanished, I requested my brothers to go to their work without me. Sadly I walked by the long front of the hut towards the oratory. There I found the four poor lay brothers standing before the one I had sent for and repeating patiently, 'Our brother cellarer wants you to come to the refectory.' As I had not yet decided what to do, these words gave me an idea. I had deliberately chosen the most stubborn of the lay brothers, the one from whom obedience was least to be expected.

'Will you answer my questions?' I asked.

'Yes, Brother.'

'Who, after the abbot, is responsible for discipline in the Order?'

'The prior.'

'After the prior?'

'The cellarer.'

'What is the chief function of the cellarer?'

'To direct the lay brothers.'

'Am I cellarer here?'

'Yes,' he replied.

Knowing already that I had won, I went on, 'What vows have you made?'

'Those of poverty and chastity.'

'What promise?'

'The promise of obedience.'

'What is your offence in refusing to follow your four brothers?'
He lowered his head.
'Will you accept the punishment I enjoin?'
'Yes, Brother.'
'One hundred strokes of the discipline.'

To receive one hundred strokes given by a monk is a terrible ordeal. By requiring him to inflict the penalty himself, I knew that his own strength would set a term to his sufferings. Then, turning to the stricken brothers who had gathered, 'You, all of you, deserve the punishment which your brother alone has accepted! Go and collect the tools stored in our hut. Your first duty is to till the soil, your second, to build an abbey. I do not intend, because of your offence, to diminish your bodies, to waste the strength that you owe to our community and to the Order. Your brother will expiate the disobedience of all.' The wretched lay brother disrobed. At the first strokes, I went away. Overwhelmed, the brothers followed me. That evening I ordered an end to the punishment, having learned that the brother had thrice re-commenced his torment and had finally dropped at the fiftieth stroke.

When the mules came, the unfortunate brother was ready to resume his work. I mean to forget the names of those who disobeyed.

St Frederick, twenty-seventh day of April

What I shall call the revolt of the lay brothers was followed by unexpected results, for my brief speech delivered in front of the oratory after decreeing the harsh punishment spurred them on to unusual efforts.

Discomfited at escaping punishment, conscience-stricken by the sufferings of a brother who was, as they well knew, particularly irresponsible, the lay brothers felt obliged to punish themselves, and no doubt me also, by frantic and mortifying labour. The ringleaders, I knew, had incited them to disobedience chiefly on the grounds that the morning meal and the serving of extra bread and of meat or fish were not, in their opinion, in accordance with the spirit of Lent. Lay brothers always attempt to follow or to surpass monks in mortifications and prayer, and although some do so out of real piety, others force themselves, without knowing it, from a desire to imitate or emulate. Now the prescribing of both meals plus the extra bread and the meat seemed to them, despite the example set by ourselves, contrary to the Rule, especially in a penitential period. They did not realize that the diet previously in force during their irregular nomad-like life was, in quantity, much more plentiful than that prescribed by the new ordinance. The majority thought that if they had one meal after a day's work — necessarily half-hearted owing to their weakness from fasting — they could eat their fill in the evening without depriving themselves of the merit of abstinence. I firmly believe also that, although they were unwilling to confess it, the withdrawal of wine until next winter aroused their dissatisfaction. Whatever the truth of the matter, they felt neither affection nor loyalty towards me, and thought to make up for the mortifications of which they were thwarted by excessive zeal in the obedience they owed me. They realized that only their work afforded a possibility of satisfying their need for physical or moral suffering. The coming of the mules made us trust each other for the first time, and when Lent was over, each man continued to do the work of three with a dash and an ardour whose primary motive was already half forgotten. The immediate consequences of this excess of zeal are amazing. Never have I seen such results in such a short time. Despite the lack of specialized tools, of materials and of professional training, the place has assumed the appearance of a real building site. A new quarry has been discovered. Some limestone found near at hand at the foot of the eastern slope is already in place on the foundations for a kiln. At a league's distance from here two lay brothers are at work with an elderly local potter, restoring a disused clay-pit. Yesterday the first loaves were proudly presented to me by the one I used to call 'the unfortunate brother'. In his simple way he had fashioned them in the shape of monks, which caused us both to exchange affectionate looks. This was not merely a promise of obedience, but another, the fairest of all promises: that of friendship.

I should never finish this evening were I to speak of all the changes that have come about since the twentieth of March: the beginning of temporary buildings, the chapel, the test borings, experiments in the extraction and dressing of stone, the tree-felling, the construction of *bancaou*, the channel from the spring, dug out to improve its flow, the installation of a washing place on the bank of the stream, the final roofing-over of the dorter, the embellishment of the oratory. Finally, the soil of the abbey site has been cleared away down to the rocks, which now stand out clearly, revealing the physical difficulties I must allow for. The time now seems distant when only the lay brothers' building, lost amidst the brushwood, showed the beginnings of sketchy, amateurish foundations made, for want of limestone, of roughly shaped boulders.

St Robert, twenty-ninth day of April

Travellers are rarely met with here. The new road that passes through the demesne is little known, although it is appreciably shorter for those coming from Entrecasteaux or Carcès and making for Fréjus. On many routes it also cuts out a crossing of the Argens when it is in flood.

In the surrounding region it is generally known that the 'White Brothers' are going to build an abbey. We have a good reputation as tillers of the soil; moreover, in the unanimous opinion of the humbler folk we bring good luck. In these early days of our settlement we need the peasants, for they can help us and tell us about the region.

We are usually welcomed and quickly accepted. Gradually we become masters of the region. Numbers, labour and frugality always result in the production of wealth. The peasants therefore assume that we were wealthy when we came, and that our Order is generously supplied with prebends or donations. This is rarely the case, however, and our beginnings are always difficult. Even with the indispensable support of powerful men, great privations are still necessary. It is certainly due to our unremitting toil that we become affluent farmers. The modesty of our needs results in abundance. Providence at first brings a rush of enthusiasm; our faith, our simple confidence, call forth generosity. But there comes an end to that; once the walls are up, we must rely on ourselves alone. Donors dislike seeing a community decay after it has been established with the help of their money and on their land. That is understandable. Nevertheless, we are often thrown back on our own resources at the time of our greatest need. The completion of the whole or of the greater part of the church is the occasion of a celebration; our benefactors consider that after this ceremony their part is finished. It is a difficult period for us. Often half the abbey has still to be built, and the farms, mills and most of the cultivation have yet to be tackled. We ought to be cunning and put up the apse at the last minute. But then Cistercians cannot, should not, calculate; we are loved and helped for our faith and our candour.

The building of our monasteries, the creation of our demesnes won from the forest, are impossible undertakings without help, support and charity. Afterwards it is our turn to repay a hundredfold, to multiply our generous gifts. We must prosper in order to be bountiful.

As I have said, it is rare that we encounter strangers on the Field. In the course of the last two months, events that are still being talked about have changed the rhythm of life here: first we came, then the mules, then Master Paul. We realized from the impression produced by the second event how much the first must have struck the community. We know that some travellers cross the demesne and that usually the brothers do not remark on it. For months they have been aware of these regular visitors coming and going, always for the same reason. Peasants or pedlars, their visits have no other object but to obtain food for gossip at remote farms or in the neighbouring villages.

'How are the monks of Le Thoronet getting on?'

'Oh, they're scraping about here and there, they don't seem to be making much progress.'

Or, 'It seems that some monks have arrived and they have already cleared all the ground and are felling timber.'

Obviously they can have little to relate for the time being. These people, known to all our brothers, give a shy greeting, halt for a moment at the spring, water their beasts and, having had a momentary look all round, feel that it would be improper to remain longer. They take either the downward or the westward path and pitch their camp at a distance.

Three days ago, we had just come back to our hut after

Compline and were about to set to work. The night is all that remains for writing and for drawing up accounts. My brothers retire early, but for my part I sleep only when my strength is exhausted.

That evening, as Luc was leaving the makeshift stable near the road, he heard slow steps coming down the path that runs by the stream. He waited for a time, and a man of huge stature appeared, taller than Brother Philippe. This giant halted by the spring and drank deeply. He then calmly covered himself in the short cloak which he had carried in a roll on his back; minutes later he was peacefully asleep in a corner of the Field beneath the great green oak. Luc flew to our lodging, apologizing. Obviously it was a piece of news worth telling. 'A man with a quiet conscience', said I, 'can always go to sleep like that.' Brother Benoît went back with Luc. On his return Benoît reported, 'He is a giant; I did not see his eyes but he had a fine head. I wanted to wake him up, so I touched his hand, it was like taking hold of a ram's horn.' Then Benoît and Bernard went to sleep.

Curious, I went down to the Field. The moon was already high, and in the darkness beneath the oak some rays of light came through the wintry foliage. The stranger lay on his back: fair skin, black beard, serene countenance, long, fine nose, smooth young brow, eyes (probably small) very deep-set. For a long time I contemplated that face: a moonbeam crept slowly towards his brow, and when the cold light outlined his head, I marvelled at creation.

Next day we were busy all morning with the new quarry. Paul is lending us his tools, but they were not made for our stone and the master quarryman is in a temper. Earlier he was in an unusually good humour because during the night his tests had produced the hoped-for results. He had cleared a bed of stone four feet high and separated from it a block of two cubic yards by a method that was both clever and safe. Into rounded holes two inches across by four inches deep, made in lines along the desired edges of the block and not quite a foot apart, we pushed round pegs of very dry oak, fitting them as tightly as the unavoidably irregular shape of the holes would allow. Next, by means of a clay gutter leading from a small spring about a hundred yards from the quarry, a thin stream of water was channelled to the bed of stone, where it dispersed in trickles or tiny cascades. The water did its work; the wood swelled and the block broke cleanly from the bed in one movement. Further cutting up is to be attempted by a process which is still Paul's secret. I believe it entails placing wedges along the length of the bed in order to detach from the mass the thickness of one course of masonry. When this is chocked up on flat iron bars, its weight—helped by grooves that provide lines of least resistance—causes a split. By these means the slab is broken down into stones which the lay brothers can dress. We were engrossed by the quarry until the hour of the first meal. It was as if we stood before a mountain of gold, anxious and stirred by greed. Alas, in dealing with this heap of rock we shall have only one weapon—patience—and one hope—skill.

After Sext, when I asked if anything further were known of the previous evening's traveller, Benoît replied, 'What? Don't you know? He stayed at the spring.'

'What is he doing?'

'Nothing; he seems to be waiting.'

'Has he said nothing to you?'

'No, and we dared not go too near him. When he realized this, he moved away from the spring and sat facing the site, so that the brothers could drink. He seems not to see us.'

On the way back to our cabin, I caught sight of him; he was walking with bowed head, seemingly deep in thought, but I saw no sign of nervousness in him. This strange visit was odd in that it disturbed no one, made no one afraid. I decided that the beauty of the place and the presence of the spring justified his prolonged stay. However, as I was working I tried several times to catch sight of him from my bay. 'Either the foot of the bank and the brushwood are concealing him, or he has had to leave,' I told myself. The thought saddened me: a man so tall, so strong, with hands hard as a ram's horns, in this region where the stones are so heavy, the trees so far away. Then I once more saw his profile outlined by the moon.

I had to meet the old potter before the evening meal. I was eager to settle him at the foot of the slope near the face of the lime quarry. Various reasons inclined me to take this step: first, it was logical, because of the kilns; second, it was right on moral grounds, because of the man's character—drunken, talkative, choleric, rowdy. We did not cross the Field to reach the refectory, but came back along the path by the stream. So I did not know whether our giant had left us. I was unable to eat and unwilling to inquire about him during the meal. I rose before it was over, instructing my brothers to take charge of evening prayers. Alone and free, I climbed slowly towards the Field. I lowered my eyes to maintain my composure and to justify any appearance of surprise. He was still there. When he realized that I was making my way towards him, he rose to await me.

'Good evening,' I murmured.

'Good evening.'

'Are you ... waiting for someone or something?'

'Yes.'

'What?'

'Someone from here to speak with.'

'Whom do you wish to speak to?'

'To the one in charge.'

'I am he.' My heart was beating more quickly.

'I am very pleased,' he said.

'What do you want?'

'To work.'

'As what?'

'I am a smith.'

Thus it was that Providence sent us Antime. He is unmarried, a good Christian, stronger than any three men. I realized that his chief characteristics were discretion and silence. He waited for two days without food and with the utmost calmness.

Fourth Sunday after Easter, twenty-eighth day of April

I have had news from Cîteaux, an announcement that Master Edgar, Master Étienne and a certain Master Jean, who is unknown to me, are coming. This is no surprise, but if they had refused it would have been a great disappointment. I have a stock of poor quality wood for them.

After consultation with Master Paul I shall draw up a plan of action as soon as they arrive. Except for the hands needed at the quarry, everyone will be set to building the forge, and then the chapel. In this way, one by one, the huts will be finished within the shortest possible time. If these decisions are not made, the temporary buildings might easily continue to serve for months and delay all our installations for preparing materials. On work sites there are always two alternatives to juggle with: whether to carry out the various tasks simultaneously or successively. Each method is the right one in its turn, the choice being sometimes guided by nothing more than feeling.

My brothers are growing thinner; no question now of abolishing the meat allowance. Now I can smile at those unhappy memories. The warmth of our mutual affection grows like that of the approaching summer; everyone is distressed by my sufferings, by my lameness. And that evening when I turned up at the refectory on two sticks, there was gloom and sadness in the customary silence of the meal.

St Stanislaus, ninth day of May

I embraced Edgar and Étienne on their arrival; Jean is a small stocky man with a kind face. I am happy to see my old friends once more, my faithful fellow workers. Today I am in too much pain to write more.

St Solange, tenth day of May

Every day, like a hen with her chicks, I make a tally of my lay brothers. It is hard to keep track of them. Lively discussions are carried on with Benoît.

'We should press on with building the kiln, complete all the clearing and make a start on uncovering the stone required by Master Paul; put three lay brothers on each of these jobs.'

'Where am I to find them?' asks Benoît. We begin to count. Benoît puts up his left thumb and starts, 'We have Joseph and one lay brother, plus the one at work at the clay-pit. For the lime, one lay brother, enough for the time being; shortly we shall need two. Antime needs one lay brother, at least. Two lay brothers with Étienne and Edgar. Jean, as foreman, needs a whole eight-hour shift, that is, five lay brothers, working full time, to put up the huts. For the gardening, one ...' And Benoît goes on counting, now with the left hand, now with the right. 'As for Master Paul, ordinarily we should give him fifteen men; we can scarcely manage ten — five for stone-dressing, five for quarrying. Quite insufficient. For cooking, one; for the fields, two, where there should be ten. For transport, looking after the beasts and loading, there should be five, where we can provide three only. For stock-keeping, one, half-time. Look, I have got up to over thirty. As we have twenty-five, when no one is ill or injured, the work force at its lowest falls short by about half a score. So, elder Brother, how shall we manage?'

'Yes, yes,' I replied; 'I shall see the abbot this week; however, there may be a way. The days are long. If we were to work sixteen hours, we should create two shifts. That would be the same as two teams of twenty-five, each working eight hours. So, let us increase the hours of work and the food allowance: let me see, it is daylight at ... ?'

'Five,' said Benoît.

'Full daylight, yes; but enough to work by — four o'clock?'

'Yes.'

'From four to twelve, eight hours, and from twelve till twenty, eight hours. Everyone in bed at twenty-one hours, and there are seven hours left for sleep.'

'No, six,' objected Benoît.

'Why?'

'Because of the time for getting to sleep and for the time for rising and getting to the site.'

'All right then, six; I do not sleep longer than that, and it has not killed me. On Sunday mornings we shall have Mass at nine; in the evening, they will retire at seven. That makes two long nights of sleep each week, feast days not included.'

'But, dear Brother, what of their prayers? Clothes? Hygiene? The discipline? The lay brothers are as much Cistercians as you and I!'

'That is true, I had forgotten prayers; never mind, do as I say, they can pray as they work.'

'And if these prayers distract them from their work?'

'You will punish them severely.'

'What punishment?'

'Two hours' overtime!'

'Very well, dear Brother. Tell me – before I leave you – will you tell me why you are so concerned about time? Why are you in such a hurry?'

I looked at him sadly. He went away without another word.

Whitsunday

This countryside is no richer in fine trees than our community is in gold. Bernard is getting ready for a journey to Fréjus; we are so poor that he will have to beg for supplies. Our abbot relies more on God's help than on the liberality of the bishop.

The stone-dressing is devouring our picks; we are setting up the forge. Eight brothers are in the quarries and will soon be able to shape the corners like true craftsmen; they work with care and have had a thorough training. Interior ornamentation and mouldings hold no secrets for them.

Most of the stones will be shaped roughly and crudely. In this way we shall save time. The sun will pick out the facets and splinters, and will turn the glittering stone into gems. Angles and joints, when trimmed and chiselled, will become clean edges, defining the slender thread of the basic mesh, and no visible mortar will mar the subtle variety of their delicate markings.

St Beatus

The clearing of the soil has little interest for me. I readily admit ignorance of all farm work. Everyone seems to recognize the seasons by the vegetables and fruits. As for me, I should not be unduly surprised if there appeared on my table a dish of ... (the thought of making a lucky guess makes me smile), say, young marrows in the month of December.

Benoît does this work so well that he never obtrudes. Benoît is the overseer, his tasks are so numerous that to give a complete account of them would be impossible. Benoît does not question himself and is never disputed. He advises; people obey him. He knows it, and goes on his way to give further advice. His sentences begin with, 'It seems to me ...' 'Do you not think ...' 'What you are doing is perfect; however ...' Benoît never gives me trouble: my severity has never been directed towards him, for any faults he might have would be my faults too. As for his success, it goes unnoticed. That is the plainest of its proofs. To push difficulty into oblivion is to struggle continually with defect and error.

From duty and for information, I made my way slowly, step by step, to the cleared fields. I wanted to see the construction of the *bancaou*, the plantations of vines and olives, the poor soil under cereals, and the kitchen garden. So, gradually, I reached the approximate centre of the hard-won demesne. A strong odour assailed me just by the thorn and pine thicket. Well, I thought, this evening I shall be able to tell Benoît that I have seen his fields. I have no reason to encourage him or to please him specially, but nevertheless, when one does something, it is natural to speak of it. I wanted to understand Benoît's reasons for putting the manure heap just there. Still thinking about it, I drew nearer. Was it because of the animals, to keep the flies away? Because of the unpleasant smell? For our manure heap is not sweet-smelling; we mix together all the excrement of beasts and men ... Perhaps for easier spreading, at the centre of the fields? Perhaps for all three reasons equally?

Someone was there. His presence was announced by sounds of striking or scraping with a field implement, regularly spaced out in the slow, sure way of labourers. I am neither curious nor indiscreet, but to come unobserved upon the solitary work of a lay brother is always a great joy to me. Without much attempt at concealment, I drew nearer to the man. The stench in that intense heat was acrid and almost unbearable. The man was Brother Thomas. At once I was shocked; what—because Thomas never speaks, is he left in these unhealthy surroundings? This was a mistake on my part, for none of the lay brothers escaped this filthy task. However, I had that wrong impression, and for a moment I could not suppress a feeling of anger and indignation. Our sixth canonical office rang. I was too far away to get back in time. I decided to move away from that rottenness and nearer to the lavender bushes. At that moment, I saw Brother Thomas drop his tools and fall on his knees just where he was working, on his heap of crawling, rotting refuse, without making the slightest attempt to get clear of it. His arms folded, head lowered, chin almost touching his chest, Thomas recited the Creed, and I listened. Never until then had Brother Thomas's voice been heard alone. It rose, pure, young, somewhat unsure, making me forget the place, the stench. I went round the thicket to look on his face, and saw it in full sunlight, uplifted now, the eyes enormous! His expression was so astonishingly beautiful that I was afraid and felt myself an intruder; there was no room for me in that supernatural dialogue. From the thick lips, too red and soft, came the last words of the Creed, and for the first time in my life as a monk I realized the full meaning of that extraordinary prayer. I fled like a thief, for I had no right to his paradise. Now the kindly night laps me in peace.

St Blandina, second day of June

Anxiety and fear hold me in their grip; may it be granted to me to carry out my task successfully! The happiest circumstances are united here, in the countryside of my childhood. This climate is in love with architecture, defending it with weapons of light, glorifying it with a kaleidoscope of colours, and encrusting it with jewels when, after a storm, the westering sun's last rays strike across the lowering sky.

St Clotilda, third day of June

Our borings at the monastery site are completed. To the north we have found a pocket of extremely adulterated clay. We shall have to clear away this clay, get down to firm ground and repair the foundations area by laboriously filling it in; again, time will be lost because it is impossible to circumvent an unexpected obstacle. Time, money: the ever-present worries of every builder. In the raising of our abbey, any useless refinement will be harshly judged. Happily for us, beauty is still the child of necessity. It is entirely up to us to decide upon an unlimited expense of the only current coin: the luxury of our labours, the squandering of our ideas.

Each morning, we visit the quarries and get an idea of what our walls and arches will be like. I have had various sample dressings set up so that we may study and select both the internal and external faces. We approach these stones with some anxiety. It is certainly the first time that I have been confronted with such materials. These hard, brittle, irregular blocks, riddled with cavities, condition the way we build. For the first time my brothers watch me uneasily. Accustomed to regularity and good quality in stone, they examine these roughly dressed blocks with mistrust. They do not yet believe in the beauty of these boulders. One of them said to me, 'What a pity that you have not found a quarry!' Another, even more sceptical, 'For the columns and capitals, would it not be worth while to import blocks of real stone?'

I am the only one who believes that they will be effective. No one else can yet imagine that the coarseness, the difficulty of dressing, the irregularity of these stones will be both the song and the accompaniment of our abbey. Difficulty is one of the more reliable catalysts of beauty. Already I feel friendly towards this rock which resists complication and refuses to be carved. Why explain? The Abbot of Clairvaux, who has so well regulated our mission as builders, would have said nothing if confronted by these blocks, because he could not have spoken to any purpose; what we find here are stones for the Rule, stones that have the Cistercian vocation.

The man who was the inspiration for the abbey of Fontenay had clear and precise ideas about Cistercian architecture. He planned an art for the cloister, for the Rule. It was his desire that this austere form should grow by reason of its simplicity, that it should, by virtue of its utter detachment, surpass the noblest forms of architecture. He foresaw that the uniformity of our instructions would produce an art endlessly refining itself by the play of variations on a single theme, yet remaining constant. Inspired as he was, he knew that in spite of constraint the quality of a soul remains unchanged. Under the Rule, each man's personal faith is distinct and peculiar to him. Under the prescribed form, variations of size and proportion in each of our abbeys reveal its soul and its quality. The magnitude of our faith, the power of our Order, the holiness of our monks will be reflected directly in the purification or the decadence of our art.

St Norbert, sixth day of June

The cathedrals of our great masters – lacework in stone, with immense belfries – and the monasteries that have magnificent sculptures and vast bays, glowing with gems in rich designs, are clearly luxury constructions. The rich man feels the need for display, for giving. The poor man is pleased to accept and to admire. What is right for a Cistercian is not right for the world or the worldly. Our pontiff looks well in his golden tiara; the humble are proud of the windows of their church. The mother and her little child go to admire them. The father draws strength from them. The aged man prone beneath them smiles gently in his last prayers. This is the best way for people to learn the Holy Scriptures. Their faith is maintained and gladdened more often by diversions of a religious nature than by the dry commentaries of preachers. Imagination feeds better on visions than on wearisome words. A preacher who is poetic and eloquent draws the crowd like a juggler, carries it along and entertains it. Is not the same result achieved by the artist in stained glass, and the sculptor? Those strange marble figures, those bucolic or Biblical scenes, those kings with their flourishing beards have the same attractive brightness as the glass that depicts John the Baptist, the gentle Virgin and her angel, Lazarus and his shroud, the miraculous draught of fishes, the Resurrection, Father Abraham, Joseph sold by his brethren, Jacob's ladder, the flight into Egypt, the wrath of the Son of Man as He drives out the merchants, and the fall of the archangel, and gloomy purgatory, and the damned, and the angels with their music, our mystery plays, our songs – all outlined in black on backgrounds of red or blue. Where is the harm? No more there than in the gold on our altars. How many lay brothers are here because such ornaments opened to them the gates of their vocation?

Austere rule and wondering piety are two sisters, like Martha and Mary, for they are each of them separate yet similar. The first is activity, poverty, humility, the second, contemplation, adoration. One serves and washes, the other perfumes. The one requires trials, the other trust: in praising Mary before Martha, Jesus gives joy to His servants.

St Medard, eighth day of June

There is a constant conflict: the building of the abbey, and the strength to see it through. It would be wise to take one's time. Is death wise to come too soon? Is pride wise?

On a work site, any economy must increase efficiency. Thus, after observing the traffic on our roads I concluded that the poor condition of the latter was making difficulties for the animals. Their layout, determined by use and ease of access, added to the length of the standard routes.

We were well into the week when we met yesterday on the Field. As if asking advice, without first having discussed it with anyone, I spoke about improving the roads. I spoke at length of our difficulties, both present and future; these paths, now pleasantly softened by a fine brown dust, would be turned into sloughs by heavy rains. The craftsmen agreed. Paul nodded his head in affirmation and winked one eye. My brothers understood all the trouble that the mud would cause; hours wasted in dragging carts along, vain struggles under pouring rain, good material sunk, sacrificed uselessly in the ruts. I said, 'If we intend to remake these roads, we shall lose an eight-man shift for weeks.' Paul suddenly abandoned his silence to declare, 'Weeks! Weeks! If we all set to work, three days will see it through.' 'But when?' I asked.

Thus it is that since yesterday, craftsmen, lay brothers and beasts have been struggling to improve the paths, change their routes, dig drainage ditches, and by Monday, if all goes well, we shall have proper roads. Paul and Antime remained at the forge, and our brother kitchener is generous with the rations.

St Jeremy

Ever since my arrival I have kept an eye on Brother Gabriel, a lay brother, at least sixty years of age, with white hair, a short beard and an untroubled look. His face reveals much humour, and his innocent eyes look continually skywards. His body is short and slight. As with many a lay brother, no one knows him, no one knows where he comes from. After a mysterious arrival ten years ago he has pursued in silence an austere and holy life.

On Sunday, at the hour of Mass, Brother Gabriel takes the most distant corner and observes the celebrant as closely as this place allows. I singled out his voice and realized that this little man had learned the sacred songs with an exactness unusual for a lay brother. Either from curiosity or from malice, I entrusted him each day with tasks requiring great attentiveness; he submitted to them, but I had put an end to his happiness. Thenceforth I saw that he was full of care, obliged to leave his prayers in order to concentrate all his attention on counting, measuring, discussing, supervising. I never found him in error, but my decision was for him the cause of real suffering. My brothers noticed it and seemed not to approve of it. On the days when the work was distributed, after allotting to each one his tasks, I added, 'As for you, Brother Gabriel, you are to mark the trees, and after that you will go and number stones with Brother Robert, who will give you the notebooks.' I waited for a refusal which never came. Brother Gabriel lost his serenity but worked on without the least complaint. With a distracted eye, trembling hands, short rapid step, he ran everywhere without a word. I confess that I was the loser in this battle. I hoped that one day he would ask for an explanation, or reproach me. But it was I who broke the silence: 'Brother Gabriel, it is my impression that I make you suffer, that I disturb your tranquillity.' He seemed not to hear, raised his fine old eyes heavenwards in the joyful attitude he had made familiar to me. 'Brother Gabriel, why do you not say what you think? You are miserable because of me, I know; I wanted to test you, to see if you would accept my orders without complaint. I know now that you are prudent in all things. The complicated tasks that I give you, many times repeated, are carried out with intelligence. Tell me, what was your trade? I have the right to know, so that I can find the most useful role for you in the community.'

His eyes left the sky and probed me with the gentlest but most implacable of reproaches. At last he calmly replied, 'I was a priest, professor of doctrine at Toulouse. My learning raised me to the episcopate. When my true faith showed me that my soul was thereby in danger, I unobtrusively entered Notre Dame de Florielle as a lay brother. From that time I believe I have always done what God required of me, nor have I ever disobeyed the Rule. I ask your pardon, Brother, for having, by my attitude, excited your curiosity.'

My curiosity is satisfied, to be sure, but this has been a lesson to me. To be candid about it, in the case of Brother Gabriel I cannot help thinking that our Order is wrong to allow princes and bishops among the lay brothers. Let every man stick to his trade, or, if not, let us admit that under the pretext of penitence the spiritually gifted may become lay brothers and that monks may become labourers. Penitence attracts only the best. Alas, never among the lay brothers in the quarries shall I come across Frederick Barbarossa or the antipope, Victor IV.

St Jacob, twenty-third day of June

Tomorrow will mark the end of the thirtieth year from my entrance into Cîteaux as novice in the year 1131. Memories grave and gay have been coming back to me since yesterday.

'May the Lord robe you in this garment of salvation': in the year 1132 I was a Cistercian monk. As a novice I had learned my trade under a master builder; as a mediocre manual worker I was put in charge of work sites. My gifts and my zeal decided my fate; I became a master builder in my turn. I applied myself to my studies with passion; when I had acquired sufficient experience, I was entrusted with work of increasing difficulty. In 1136 I was building my first church. In one way or another I have had a hand in the building or enlargement of all the three hundred and sixty abbeys of Cîteaux so far erected. Providence has led me back to the land of my ancestors, which I had previously only passed through on my way to Italy and the Holy Land. I have a fore-boding today that my journey will end here.

St John the Baptist, twenty-fourth day of June

With a crash, a cry deep as the death rattle, a gust strong as a blast of the mistral, the oak for the chevet of the future church fell in the morning sun, raising a cloud of pollen. We had sacrificed it. For three days, two lay brothers have worked alternately, two executioners for the oak. Happily, with harsh cries, tall Philippe and little Bruno struck in turn into its flesh which reddened, a wound in the tree. As the dusky skin was torn off or cut away all round the trunk's circumference, there lay revealed muscles, nerves and arteries. The axe, swung skyward, descended with a dull thud, pulling at the hands, arms, trunk and head of the man whose legs seemed to be rooted to the ground. The action tested Philippe's long muscles—so like the stems of ivy or wistaria— and Bruno's short, knotted ones, more like briar or olive roots. The weapon forged by Antime made the conflict an unequal one. Yesterday, at last, the hundred-foot, hundred-year-old giant submitted to the rope fixed to its highest branch. The end came this morning. Like cruel judges, we all went down to watch and to help, standing, with arms folded, along the edge of the Field. When the time came, Luc harnessed the mules to the rope round the middle of the tree, and the men took hold of the other two ropes. Philippe struck at the heart; at the first creak, Luc gave the command and everyone tugged. At the third attempt, the top swayed, hesitated for as long as it takes to draw one breath, then the great movement began, at first so slowly that it seemed unending, then faster and faster, branches and leaves sweeping the sky as the tree turned on the joint of its fibres. A great silence followed. In its new disarray the oak seemed to take up endless space and create confusion on the ground. The brothers, scattered in the thorn bushes, picked themselves up. The stupid mules panted, eyes staring, ears laid back; up to their chests in the brambles, they could not understand our actions. After a moment of amazement, we were seized by remorse; we are not professional woodcutters. Someone cried, 'For the bonfires of the Feast of St John!' and the dismemberment began.

This evening we had fires everywhere; a hundred fires for the hundred feet, the hundred years of the great oak. Yesterday it rained, so the weeds, gathered into heaps weeks ago, smoked away together with the dark oak leaves. It was not until nightfall, well after Compline, that the flames managed to break through the dirty-yellow and blue smoke. Everyone was on the run from one fire to the next, fork in hand, to help the fires to draw.

The mutilated oak remained alone, laid out in the cemetery. In a month's time the planks, properly chocked up for drying, will be stored against the workshop walls. In ten years' time, this tree, felled on St John's day, will be our doors, our tables, our stalls.

Today must surely be the anniversary. *'Master, which is the greatest commandment in the law? Jesus said unto him, Thou shalt love the Lord thy God with all thy heart, and with all thy soul, and with all thy mind.'*

In 1141, ten years after I entered the Order, I was consultant to the Chapter of Clairvaux, which at that time was expanding rapidly. Meeting the Abbot Bernard was decisive for me. From the start he imparted to me his confidence and hope. Conquered by his ideas, I translated into shapes what were only recommendations. He spoke of the penury of our houses; I visualized size with simplicity. Sobriety, utility, penitence were mentioned; I translated: nobility, efficiency, harmony. His words expressed my thoughts, the abstractions he uttered became architecture. He brought about the birth of my ambition. I was like the Wandering Jew, always on the road, limping along, shoulders drooping or triumphantly erect: at times a master builder, at others a Chapter's consultant. Even now, I can still see before me that great personality who discerned what my passion and my life were to be. He seems to have accepted my shortcomings, for some profound reason; no doubt because of the usefulness of my mission. Since I was in any case lost to the service of God, he designated me for that of His troops.

All my life I was more mason than monk, more architect than Christian. If the fault was partly mine, I am bound to say also that the Order encouraged me in it. I was usually obliged to carry out my orders without any respite, travelling from Germany to Burgundy, from Brittany to Aquitaine, always conducting affairs in the service of our Order. The abbeys of Cîteaux were my abbeys. If a community was in difficulty, I had to set out to inspect, organize, alter, plan. So much activity crushed any inclination that I might have had for prayer. For me, the Apostle Peter is identified with the stone of a building.* Suffering from cold and hunger, being injured through accidents while travelling – these were tribulations calculated not to improve my soul but to enhance my career. My misfortunes were not those of a Cistercian monk but those of a man taken up with business, money and materials. I am at the end of a long existence as a pilgrim of the art of building, and I have wrecked my life. Neither through virtue, nor purity, nor an exemplary life shall I draw near to the Lord. The only thing to my credit is that I have plied my trade. The vigils, the fasts, the meagre meals, all the required mortifications – these were never trials to me. Often I forgot the time of the one daily meal during Lent. Whenever I stayed awake all night, immersed in my work, I experienced a feeling of extraordinary well-being that helped me in my meditations on stone. In my unregulated life any scruples I had arose from boredom brought on by the monotony of the daily services. Conscious as I was that they achieved nothing for me, I often thought that they were a waste of my time. If the plainsong gave me pleasure, it was because song was meant for vaulted roofs, because the naves take hold of it as a mother's hands hold the head of her child. I have no regrets: it is thus that God has willed it.

Whatever the extent of your knowledge, you would never, without a knowledge of yourself, attain to the fulness of wisdom. Would such a lacuna really be so important? It would be of cardinal importance, in my opinion. Would you know all the secrets of the universe? And the remotest regions of the earth, and the heights of the firmament, and the deeps of the sea, if, at the same time, you knew not yourself? You would put me in mind of a builder who wanted to build without foundations; he would achieve not an edifice, but a ruin. Whatever you may accumulate outside yourself, it will no more endure than a heap of dust exposed to all winds. No, he who does not know himself does not deserve to be called a scholar. The true scholar must first know what he himself is, and will be the first to drink the water of his own well.

(Bernard of Clairvaux, *On Consideration*)

* There is a play on words here in the original: *Pierre, pierre.* – *Translator's note.*

And if that water is bitter, must one go on drinking it? Must one like the water of one's own well, whatever it is like?

SS Peter and Paul, twenty-ninth day of June

It was a great day indeed when he set foot on the terrace, on the shadeless Field, and came, bustling and concerned, towards us.

From that time he has been part of our life; nothing can henceforth separate him from these stones that, with many a grumble, he tears out of the mountain. To him the abbey will owe its skin and its flesh, its bones, its muscles and its nerves.

Paul is at first a gaze: remote, arrogant, withdrawn, shunning contacts. Then his eye comes to rest, kind, mild, sympathetic, charitable. A moment of feeling: the eyelids wrinkle up, the expression becomes harsh, sceptical. A fresh thought — and all is open, the brows arch, the eyes shine with a new brilliance. They are despairing, blank, infinitely sad, there are flashes of anger, of stupefaction, of candour ... all at once he is pitiable; one is sorry for him. His head droops, his steady, deliberate, concentrated look sinks to the ground and rests vaguely on his feet as they shuffle among the pebbles. Head and hands describe the gesture that means 'impossible, hopeless'. Hopelessness? No! The struggle begins, his voice is raised, his head held high, his neck thrust forward. The gaze is there again; it is going to insist, it becomes convincing, resolute, direct. Wrath, weariness, feigned amazement, gentleness, spleen — all have their turn. It seems as though the range of possible expressions has been exhausted, but then his eyes narrow to slits, his pupils sparkle, and instead of the gaze there is laughter. The man was unable to contain the apparently uncoordinated movements of his head, his face wrinkled by an overpowering joy. He has shattered himself, by his own playacting. Earnestness, menace, candour both false and true, fear, frantic determination — all have turned into glee.

Next, he is a mouth. No possible deceit from that quarter. His mouth has humour, it reveals a great many teeth, and has just the slightest difficulty in closing. And even if it becomes bitter and twisted when he talks fast, when his teeth are clenched or when his deep voice bellows, I always feel that laughter is not far away. That mouth has laughed too much to remain serious for long. His eyes express perfectly whatever he wants to convey, but laughter has been indelibly stamped on his mouth. It does not accord with his eyes when they express disgust, anger, determination, conviction, disarming sincerity. His lips part, all his teeth show, laughter streams out—the noise is alarming. He bows his head at the first peal. His body rocks to and fro from the hips, his legs bend and he stamps on the ground, so that his whole body provides an accompaniment to his calculated miming. This man was born to think and grumble a little, to argue a lot, and to laugh most of the time. For the rest, he has a fine attractive head, abundant greying hair and a lined masculine face, always tanned. His back is arched with muscle, his gait that of an old salt keeping his balance on deck, knees always ready to counter the shocks and movements of the pitching and rolling. His hands are delicate, his feet small.

Master Paul, a hewer of stone since his childhood, fed on lime-stone dust. He looks bold, but he has the weaknesses of poets and artists. He loves sun, good food, daydreams. He is too fond of charming people not to have exercised his charm many times, and his success with women offsets his occasional failure with men. Those who are susceptible must be enchanted by this splendid creature, but he seems to have had few sentimental attachments, preferring ambition, action, his cronies and fellow jokers. He needs men who laugh; over-tense people, like me, are wearisome to him after a time. Ever since his arrival he has been obsessed by a somewhat unreasonable notion; under various pretexts he has often tackled me in terms such as these: 'Good day, Father.' A long silence, glum face, twisted mouth, grim expectant look. 'So you really do expect to make something out of this rubbish? In eight days, working like galley-slaves, we have quarried ten cubic yards, six of them chippings. There will be hardly four yards of usable stone. We have worked our guts out for nothing. Come now, use my stone! Don't be stubborn! It'll cost you nothing! I'd rather give it to you free than go on breaking my back for nothing. These cobbles of yours—they aren't worth a straw. It's stone for *bancaou*. You can tell your fellows—they're as patient as Benedictines, as good as angels—but they irritate me, their beards hide everything, and what's more, there's no fun in them. They take it all so seriously; not that I'm a great talker, but a word now and then does no harm, does it? It's you who forbid them to open their mouths: well, you're a hard lot in your monastery! So look here, I'll tell you what. I'll clear out of here, I'll go back and get some loads ready for you. With my contraptions I can cut ten cubic yards a day, finished to a "T". And by the end of the year you'll have all the stuff nicely stacked in tiers, and up you go, as easy as pie. With four men you can lay two cubic yards a day, the monastery will be finished in two years at the outside, see? You can keep the Good Mother's prayer-mill turning, and go on starving and not sleeping, working like skinflints — dear God! The lay brothers are all right for that, yes, they work hard — you've found them a job that'll get them to heaven quickly, haven't you? I'll bet you have shares in the morgues! Well, what d'you say? Are we agreed? You bring the donkeys, and the wagons, and come and load up as much as you can carry.'

All this is said without a pause for breath. He tries it on, chances his luck, though he does not expect to win. Untiringly he tells me the same story over and over again, confusing his words as he growls them out in his colourful Provençal accent. He tries to get his way by talking fast. Master Paul's only passion is for his stone, and he respects all those who love it as he does. They are his clients, his victims, his friends, his enemies, his life. He hates and reveres them by turn. Any lack of respect for his material makes him suffer like a wounded animal. If anyone takes an interest in it, his enthusiasm knows no bounds. A friend from the happy days of my youth sent him here; he did me a good turn. But I can see that I must keep Master Paul on a tight rein, talk to him every day, renew his enthusiasm which so quickly wanes. We need him. He sniffs out the stone, he can tell the good beds from the bad. Because he has been master quarryman at Fontvieille, Les Baux, Estaillade and Pont du Gard, he detests our brittle stone which is almost as hard as the marble at Cassis. Any stone that resembles marble reminds him of his youth and the gloomy tombstones of his father's workshop. His earthly happiness began with the 'crocodile', a long saw with teeth like its namesake, which cuts into the blocks as easily as if they were billets of oak. Ever since then he has laboured in caves, like huge cathedrals, dedicated to Cyclopean rites. In those white, powdery caverns each day a block of stone is torn out, and the void increased. The flat monolithic roof, held up by piers twelve feet square, is a hundred and twenty feet high. Master Paul, disgruntled, detests our broken lumps which are worked in clearings, under the open sky and at ground level. Our stone is to Fontvieille's limestone as almond nougat is to butter: brittle, variable, grainy, flawed—a dubious outcrop, damaged in a moment of divine wrath; whereas Master Paul's limestone has the calm and stability of the ocean's bed, irregular only where a seashell appears. Tirelessly he keeps up his argument through clenched jaws.

'I'd rather be hauling all over the place—Fontvieille, Les Baux, Estaillade, Pont du Gard—on the road all the time, riding or on the wagons, making deliveries, organizing the masons, negotiating with them, squeezing prices out of them, dragging my wares in baskets up to Orange and Avignon, or down to Aix. It's all the same to me! Here, I'm upsetting myself for nothing. No, Father! Come on, be reasonable! You're as stubborn as your mules! Obstinate as a monk! Well, I'm telling you, you'll have to get someone else to work this stuff. I'm off tomorrow, I'm walking out; in two days I'll be in paradise, the true paradise of stone; here it's not even purgatory, it's hell! When you touch that stuff, can't you see the devil with his horns and his tail? Doesn't he frighten you? It's a fact, he's there ... smell, sniff the odour, put your beak there, smell—it's sulphur. No, no and no again! Well, I've told you. If you agree, I'll take my tackle and tools, and away to Fontvieille!'

Calmly I hear him out, then reply, 'That's enough of your play-acting, you wretch! It's you who are the devil, tempting and threatening, you infernal, blackmailing, good-for-nothing demon! You're not competent!'

Taken by surprise, he tries to find out whether I mean it. 'Well, now, you—you're a hard one ... not competent! Not competent! I'd like to see you at it; if I leave you to it, you won't extract three bits as big as that!' Then, suddenly menacing, 'Don't you realize that if I hadn't brought my tools, you'd have been stuck, like a fool, unable to get anything out? Look, if you want to be clever, what will you dig the stone out with? With your nails or your teeth? I warn you, they'd better be good! Even my own would be left there after one go. Don't you see that if you drive the tool in under the block without knowing where to strike it gets stuck, and you'll have a job getting it out? You tell your fellows, your long-beards, to have a go at it—and give them a good breakfast!'

Then, patiently, I say once more what I know will calm him: 'Paul, my friend, you know very well that what you ask is impossible. In the first place, you don't give your stone away. Even if you make no profit, it costs money. Next, with my mules, two thousand journeys would be needed. If they kept up a good pace, that would mean one journey a week at the most with the beasts that we have. Do you understand? Fifteen hundred to two thousand weeks at least. Forty years from now I should have the stone and your grandson would be trimming the last stones for the arches.'

'Your calculation is wrong! Buy thirty mules, and you can divide all your figures by fifteen.'

'And the money? Where do I get that? Even with thirty mules, we should be at it for years. Here, with one cubic yard a day which costs me not a sou, since my long-beards are there and would be there in any case, I shall have my stone in five or six years. In three years, even, if by any chance you manage to cut two yards a day.'

After a silence, he accepts with resignation what he knows is the truth, and gives in. 'You're right, I knew it. I'm not crazy, but I haggle. What do you expect? I *have* to haggle ... Well, I'll stay, don't worry; I'll train the long-beards, Antime and I will make the tackle, I'll temper the tools, I'll organize the extraction to the last detail, the carving too, and I'll make joints for you no bigger than that.' One eye is closed, the other a slit; his hand, held up close to his unsmiling mouth, makes a gesture with thumb and forefinger pressed together. 'And then you must come and see me down there, in three or four months' time, and have a blow-out with me and my mates! What you should have done was to settle down there, at Les Baux, near your brother's house, and build a monastery as only you know how. You're a hard man, but for the job there's nobody to touch you. When I see the local loafers down there, the stone they waste ... whereas you, you'll make something of this rubbish of yours, I know—you've got stone in your blood!'

I was startled. Master Paul is ill, his days are numbered, his blood is slowly thinning, and he knows it. He realizes he is going to die, and jokes about it. 'It seems I'm going to kick the bucket within the year; it's a nuisance, I'm as happy as a pope!' he says.

It is true. This energetic creature, driven by God and the devil, is doomed to die soon. I hope to live long enough to get his name carved high in the cave of Estaillade and deep in the pits of Fontvieille. His description: a man of stone, supplier to churches, to houses, to palaces; in his time a master builder, a painter, a draughtsman; sensitive, weak, feminine, even; eager for companionship, full of flattery as a wench, spiteful as a shrew; malevolent, vengeful, devious — but the best of the best. If the tomb of this crafty giant, this peerless engineer and quarryman, were made of all the stones extracted by his efforts, his tenacity and his mechanical inventions, all the pyramids of Egypt would be nothing by comparison. He will not have been good, he will not have been worthy; geniuses are neither. The day I see him go, with his rolling sailor's gait, my distress will know no bounds. The stone will have lost its man, as a woman loses her lover. What I wish for is that the death awaiting him may be averted, that instead the huge quarry might collapse upon him; that would be a death worthy of a hero. The disease that consumes him is an injustice. Those who do not really know him cannot perceive the depths concealed in the man — the real man, whose faults, weaknesses, genius and virtues are fused together, as in all great personalities. At his last breath, whether submissive or rebellious, when a priest will probably take his hand, then the white stone will cease its trembling, and will don its everlasting mourning, mourning for purity, mourning for the dying virgin, mourning for unremitting activity — the purest of all human qualities.

St Thierry, first day of July

At last, thanks to Master Paul, the blocks are being produced steadily; the dressing proceeds slowly, but with ease. This baffling stone needed a set of special tools, particularly for the quarrying. Master Paul has designed and made them with the help of Antime the blacksmith; their long discussions have borne fruit. These two men, by nature mutually antagonistic, have come to like one another through their engineering work. Esteem is the sure sign of a special friendship. Fierce hatred gives way to admiration. Is this not preferable to those relationships based on the affinity of weakness? However that may be, the great blocks for the larger courses of masonry, for the arch-stones and even for the monolithic lintels are emerging from the chaos.

St Zoë

This sore wears me out. Treatment seems ineffective. The brother infirmarian is puzzled; my impression is that his ointments are spreading the infection. What is to be done? Try to leave the thing without treatment for a time? That seems impossible to me; my habit would rub all day long on the broken skin — the thought makes me shudder. I have no physical pain. I would rather a hundred times have the other sickness that consumes me internally without diminishing me; that tortures me without external constraints. I thought about the terrible disease, leprosy. Two days ago, I anxiously brought the flame of my lamp near and the flesh reacted sharply: my experiment resulted in intense pain. I was full of joy, and bore with this new fiery wound all through the night.

What did I fear? ... Solitude, probably. Silence is no burden to me; quite the contrary. My office has always allowed me to speak as much as I wished; I have never taken advantage of it. However, I cannot do without people. I was afraid of the complete solitude, the total isolation of lepers.

St Colomba, sixth day of July

A hundred and twenty days have passed since our arrival. During this time many changes have come about, and although I observe some signs of exhaustion or of extreme fatigue in my brothers, there reigns over the whole of our site an order, a prosperity and a security surprising to those who have not visited us for some time.

The forge, working to capacity, has contributed not a little towards establishing a basic organization for the quarries and workshops. Since the smith arrived he has either fashioned or repaired our entire stock of tools.

Provisional though our new buildings may be, they have the merit of existing and of being in use. In the centre of the lower terrace, where the first hut was built, stands the chapel. The former oratory has been converted into a kitchen, while the rest of the building is taken up by the refectory. Dorter and workshop close in the other two sides of the trapezium. A few steps from the dorters, near the stream, we have put up a stable. The animals are fat and well cared for, for we have their health and good management at heart.

In the quarries, at least thirty cubic yards of dressed stone, neatly stacked by the side of a great pile of rubble, are waiting to be transported to the site. Master Paul is getting the better beds of stone cleared and thereby preparing well in advance for future work. Joseph's task is well ahead. Slowly though the work goes, the tiles will be produced several years before they are laid. It was Joseph's age that made me decide to press on. If production is kept up we can always sell or exchange what we make to the local people, or manufacture flooring tiles, our kitchen utensils, cups and bowls. A potter's workshop and a kiln represent substantial savings, taken over the whole life of a community.

If we have reached this stage it is thanks to a little gold and to the strenuous labour of the lay brothers. These numbered eleven at our arrival. Day after day and one by one, thirteen brothers have come from Notre Dame de Florielle. In this way, I have avoided the formation of two groups, the old ones and the new. The first ones always appeared to be welcoming the later arrivals, absorbing them into their ranks. Moreover, the work-schedules were less of a surprise to the reinforcements, who, gradually assimilated, were obliged to adapt themselves without complaint to the customs of a majority already won over and quite proud of their activity. Now that is all over, my brothers have a strange nostalgia for the past – that is to say for the period that elapsed before our arrival. For them, the smooth-running methods and the exhaustion of the new era, the abundance of implements and specialized tools, the forge, the potter's workshop, the sawmill, the carts, the lime, the new ways of extraction – all that, without mentioning the work of clearing and breaking the ground, is not consistent with the idea they had formed of the building of their abbey. To have everything to hand at all times, to buy what we need for making things, seems extraordinary to them. Though they are now confident of speedy progress in our work, they no longer attach the same poetic and mystical significance to their everyday activities as they used to. Those few brothers, isolated in the forest, scraping at the ground with their hands, sleeping under shelters made of branches, praying in the open air, getting their food from scanty garden plots and from hunting every possible kind of animal, were acting out an adventure of primitive Christianity. For them, the building of the abbey was like the promise of a distant paradise. Heroic times, to be sure—and they had also the advantage of not being tiring. That way of living from day to day, with neither schedule nor fixed objective, was totally different from our new regulations, one of whose principal virtues is efficiency. For all that, they will never forget that initial period. They will always look back to it as the time of the true foundation, and despite the real suffering in body and mind entailed by strict discipline, they will none the less continue to think that now all is easy.

I have observed this state of mind in the best of the stone-dressers, whose name, significantly, is Brother Pierre.* As he was finishing his third block for the day—it was perfectly trimmed, chiselled at the edges, squared to a hair's breadth, a stone that might be laid without mortar—I said to him, 'Pierre, it must make you happy to produce such fine blocks?'

'Oh, with these tools, one can't take any credit, anyone could do it.'

'So much the better! We shall soon be able to put up good walls, and quickly.'

'Good, perhaps, but not so fine!'

'Why not?'

He rose and straightened himself, tipped over a block that had served him as a seat, and placed it with his three stones. Pointing to it, he said in fury, 'You cannot compare the work! That is one I quarried and dressed at the beginning. It's not the same thing at all, is it?' He looked at it fondly, then, stooping, began to caress it with hands so hard that they can neither open nor close completely.

The stone was irregular, every side looked different, the unchiselled edges were poorly trimmed. I thought of all the walls built of stones like this; they spelt poverty, dreariness. However,

* See footnote, p. 48.

I had some idea of what Pierre found to admire in that inadequate work; it represented effort, and challenge. So, wanting to humour and encourage him, I said, 'Yes indeed, it's very fine; what a time it must have taken you! At that rate the monastery wouldn't be finished in a hundred years.'

'A hundred years! At least that; three of us together produced only two a day.'

'Then, Pierre, you need have no regrets. Our brothers at Notre Dame de Florielle cannot be kept waiting. The Order expects other things of us; every year must see five new abbeys. It is God's will.'

'Five every year!'

I left Pierre stupefied at the thought of the work carried out by our Order. For a man who dresses from three to six stones a day, those tens of thousands of blocks were an unrealizable dream. I went a little way off and, without really intending to, kept an eye on him. I saw him talk to himself as he touched his stones, the old and the new in turn. He stood up, clutching a pebble which he threw with all his might at his work. Next he did something which surprised me; he set to work diligently to re-shape the older block in the style of the others. What did this decision signify in Pierre's mind? A larger understanding? Submission to higher considerations? Destruction of a memory once dear and now betrayed? All these, and doubtless many other things besides. I know that in time this stone, transformed and re-dressed in the new style, will be even more beautiful. In his mind's eye Pierre will see it smooth as marble; and he will be able to say, 'Ah, if you had seen the stones we dressed at the beginning, when we had nothing, that was careful work.'

This is the tendency that gives rise to legends. I have nothing against it: it vindicates and ennobles a period which I consider to have been disastrous. The brother who was punished will seem to have been a martyr struggling against a new order whose value and usefulness no one now thinks of denying. The memory of these events becomes distorted with the passage of time, but is thus preserved from oblivion. The master builder who preceded me here will be identified with tradition and the past, just as I shall one day be a different kind of ghost; who can say what tales will make me live on here?

The craftsmen, the first lay brothers and the gradually assimilated new brothers now form one whole. However, everyone chooses his own group and even asserts his own individuality within that group. The craftsmen, apart from Joseph who hopes, as we do, that he will live out his life with us, are here only temporarily. Knowing this, they are training some of the more gifted lay brothers, who show promise of becoming skilful carpenters. A fair number of the brothers will make good woodworkers; Master Étienne devotes part of his time to their apprenticeship. Paul will leave us soon. He has set himself two goals: to expose the better beds of stone, and to train a hard nucleus of quarrymen, stone-dressers and masons. Étienne, Edgar and Jean will remain until the timber framework for the arches is completed and the first arch-stones are laid. Antime has no plans; I have not heard him utter a word since the day he arrived, and I sometimes think that he would speak only if he were about to leave. These laymen, two of whom are old acquaintances, seem to feel that this abbey is my last job. It seems clear that my health is failing fast, and I sense their desire to demonstrate while they can their especially warm affection for me.

With the brothers it is very different. They live and die here. Some are pure Cistercians. At the break of day, three words are traced in their still-dark sky: chastity, poverty, obedience. For them no problem arises; we live side by side, they neither see me nor hear me. I am a human being like them; they owe me their obedience, I owe them my authority. Prayer dominates their whole lives. They attach not the slightest importance to any material progress which they might achieve; for them, obedience does not imply attention. Although I love them dearly, I am not sorry that they represent no more than a small minority, for they are unfit for any other work than that of subordinate, helper or labourer. If this attitude spread, it would prevent me from leaving them in peace; I should find myself obliged to tear them away, willing nor not, from their piety, as I did with Brother Gabriel. They make up the corps of labourers, and their willingness knows no bounds. Old or new, they reflect no more on today's work than on that of the past, for conceptions of time and contingency are completely beyond them.

A second group of brothers, who, though firm in their faith, are not altogether dominated by it, have shown a marked liking for one trade or another. These men, the sons of serfs or villeins, having but lately decided that God's discipline was preferable to a life of servitude, joined the Order more out of a desire for tranquillity than because they had a vocation. They are lay brothers because they could not become monks, and are happy in our equality and brotherhood under a common discipline, which to them is perhaps hard, but in no way humiliating. Since they have come to understand and accept my ways, they have acquired a new desire: the ambition to perfect themselves in a trade they find interesting. They represent yet another minority which, little by little, is subordinating itself to the work in hand and also, in my view, gaining spiritual benefit. They are aware that something is coming into being, and they dream of it. In wood, iron or earth they are finding happiness where, before, there was merely employment. They hold me in the esteem due to one whose mind is quicker and whose knowledge is greater than theirs. It is in the mystery of the trade that we are united: as apprentices, they feel fear, respect and envy towards the master. I am counting on them for the future; laymen in spirit, one day they will take the place of the craftsmen, and they know it.

The most numerous are those who are attached to me as brave and loyal soldiers are attached to their leader. For them, there is the master, his two lieutenants Bernard and Benoît, or, according to their duties, one or other of the craftsmen. By their characters they are drawn towards each of us in diverse ways. They are enthusiasts with an undiscriminating devotion to everything — to peace, to prayer, to the abbey, to the chiefs, to the Order. They are not the most outstanding, but they are loving, and I confess that I like them best. I prefer them for their simplicity and their inexhaustible good will. Middling craftsmen, they form the majority, doing as others do; what trade they follow is immaterial to them. When an extraordinary effort is required, when strength must come before skill, when work becomes a wager, it is to them that Benoît turns, and they are proud and pleased with themselves after the effort, and grateful if rewarded by a word or a look. It is from the expression on their master's face and the gleam in his eye that they know how well they have worked.

With an air of authority, Paul came to fetch me. At first I demurred; then, when I noticed that I inspired a kind of pity in him, I changed my mind and asked him to wait for a moment until I was ready. My sore could not bear bandaging and I was unable to walk with my habit chafing it at each step; I shielded it, more or less, without pressing on it too hard.

Paul had gone; he came back later to say that he had twisted his ankle at the quarry. 'But it's not far,' he went on, 'I've told them to get the little cart ready. Luc will come with us.' Walking down, I saw that he was limping. We sat in the back, legs dangling, feet trailing at times on the road, and set off gaily. On that fine sunny morning, before the heat of the day, the outing gave us intense, if short-lived, pleasure. Together we were going towards an adventure, a discovery. 'It's not that there's any hurry,' he said, 'but I think I've got my hands on a small quarry of building stone. It's a little lighter than ours, but you can get large blocks out for making your capitals and your bases. It can be sawn with the little "crocodile" and finely sculpted.'

A mile or so out, on the Pont d'Argens road, we went up by the path that climbs to the Villard; Luc waited for us below. Like a real conjurer, Paul gave me a demonstration of hewing, dressing and carving with a series of tools which proved to be quite adequate to the hardness of the block. I had indeed to admit that this stone was more manageable; the cutting edge and the chisel, without working wonders, made fine work possible; the grain was sound, without fissure. At that moment I was grateful, and I expressed my pleasure enthusiastically and at some length. Paul likes that. 'You could never have carved in that hard cheese of yours up there: you think you're taking a finger's breadth off, but when you strike it's a lump as big as your fist that's gone.'

Afterwards, on the way back, I cursed his discovery, and the trouble he had taken in ferreting out this carving stone. I had been hoping until then that the capitals would be hewn out of our rough material, with no palm-leaf moulding, without even the simplest volutes: shapes torn from, and decorated with, coarse rock. This is not going to happen. 'Master Paul's quarry,' as we shall call it, will doubtless be known to all, and no one would attempt to understand why I am against it.

When we got back again, Paul ran to his work. He had forgotten to limp.

St Henry, fifteenth day of July

Bernard, Benoît and I live together in a hut made of stone, earth and branches. To simplify things, we have divided our dorter-workshop into two parts, one in which I can work with Bernard, and another in which my brothers sleep. The whole has a surface area of two hundred square feet. In order not to be in the way of my brothers, I have my living quarters in the workshop. My sick body constrains me to a life apart.

The lay brothers live under our surveillance, for we can observe them from our workshop. The chapel, which stands near the workshops and the refectory, will easily hold fifty religious. I made it big enough to take all the monks and lay brothers of Notre Dame de Florielle when they come to Le Thoronet. Built of resinous pine, our poorest wood, it will be icy in winter; there are chinks in the carpentry, but it keeps the rain out. The lay brothers are supervised by Benoît, who often sleeps among them.

The craftsmen have a settlement five hundred yards from the site, to the west. I have forbidden visits from their families to ensure that discipline is observed. They take their meals with us; occasionally, at various times, they forgather for feasts of meat and wine. They have their own table in our refectory. It is our custom to invite each of the craftsmen in turn to our table, three times a week, with the exception of Joseph, who leads an isolated life, and of Master Paul, with whom our food does not agree. Joseph keeps himself apart. He has made a retreat for himself, a quarter of a mile from the kilns; his old woman cooks his meals and puts him to bed when he has had too much to drink.

The three quarries are situated on the southern slope. The forge is lower down, on the east side of the abbey, near the abandoned quarry. Master Étienne is the craftsmen's delegate when any problems between the laymen and us are being settled. This arrangement has apparently given good results. There can be no grounds for offence, and all seems to portend a perfect harmony in our relations. Master Paul is a lord, and rich; he has rented a house, about three miles away, where his wife—daughter and granddaughter of quarrymasters—watches anxiously over him. Master Paul needs constant care and a lavish diet. She brings two meals over to the site for him, and warms them up in a little wooden cabin near the quarries. I did not express my views at the time the arrangement was made, otherwise I should have asked Paul to set up house farther away, because of the way he lives. We are not a genuine community, it is true, but the Order forbids the presence of women. Paul lives like a master in our midst; he has his horse to take him home in the evening, a fine, fast-moving, well-fed beast, and his wife comes on foot, then waits for evening to ride back behind him. I know such things are absolutely prohibited, but these habits were formed long ago. To me, Paul's health and food are overriding considerations; stone, for the moment, is more necessary to us than water.

When Benoît divides the labour force every day, the tasks allotted are usually about the same. The majority are specialist quarrymen, and it is in this direction that we must push ahead. Even under the most favourable conditions six years will be taken up with quarrying and dressing.

One lay brother is always claimed by Paul, Joseph and Étienne—Brother Philippe! Six feet tall, he weighs fourteen stone, and has a fine head set rather low between his shoulders, close-cropped hair, a short curled beard and a dreamy, sad, gentle, rather open expression. Relaxed and well bred, he wears the scapular and the girdle with singular ease. Brother Philippe is dedicated, obliging, unobtrusive, silent as any monk. He lets fall a few words which delight Joseph, enchant Paul and win him the approval of Étienne and even Antime. When he swings his way into the forge to get a tool sharpened, he whistles in greeting, and the grave Antime smiles, welcomes him and bustles about to oblige and help him. For my part, I admire Philippe, as does everyone else here. He is a lay brother out of the ordinary, but one cannot say anything against his conduct. He is passionately fond of nature, contemplates in his singular way all created things and pauses very often to muse. Though his behaviour sometimes seems strange, he is as silent and discreet as Brother Gabriel. Brother

Philippe's favourite daily task is undoubtedly the potter's work. I have great hopes that he will one day rid us of Joseph. Quite often, I watch Brother Philippe at his meals; he eats with good appetite, and takes particular care with his food, cutting his bread into thin slices and soaking it in our local oil in a way that does not go unnoticed. I make no comment; still, it seems to me that on this method, common to all of us, of eating his bread, he bestows a degree of care which must improve the taste. With Bernard we say, 'Look at Brother Philippe, he savours while we feed.' At times, the brother gardener provides fresh vegetables: broad beans, celery, lettuce, *cébettes*, pimentos, beetroot roasted in the embers. On these days Brother Philippe behaves outrageously. He prepares the vegetables long and meticulously, slices, cleans and seasons them carefully, and at last savours them as if they were the rarest game or the choicest dish. Brother Philippe is over-happy in his situation, but if I had to reprove him for anything I should feel shame at the first word. I have no comment to make; to draw attention to his attitude would be very bad. A lay brother or a monk should do penance; for Philippe nothing is a penance, everything seems pleasure and amusement. It is not his fault if he is refined and relishes the fare of the Rule. He likes his life, and is deeply happy at the kiln, the wheel or the quarry.

St Alexius, seventeenth day of July

'Now, let's go to the quarry!' So saying, we remind ourselves every day that stone for the walls is our first preoccupation. The entire abbey depends on it. Although each day we faithfully go there, I must admit that we do no work. We know that there are no miracles. Time and the work drag along, each keeping pace with the other. After a moment spent watching Paul, Philippe and the others struggling to get the stone out in the easiest possible way and shortest possible time, we feel unwanted and distracting. However, if we are absent for a single day from the rite it is noticed, and Paul says to us next day, 'Well, what about the stone? Nobody cares a damn about it! It's quite a time since we saw you.' So that's how it is. One must come often, not stay too long, notice their efforts, without making them think that we can afford to waste our time. After the quarrying, we pass on to the stone-dressing; no lengthy halt there, either. For all that, it is intensely interesting. I prefer to do my thinking here rather than at my table. We must deny ourselves that; the men labour and suffer too much. A stroller, even one occupied in thought, must go on his way.

It sometimes happens, however, that after a long halt during which we watch how the brothers move about and expend their efforts, we are able to give an intelligent direction which improves the routine, so that hundreds of hours' work is saved as a result of a brief period of reflection. This has actually occurred, but for all that it does not give us the right to stroll about idly the next day. Our job is to be inventive. Similarly, if the stone-dresser strikes a thousand times in the right place, that does not entitle him to miss with an equal number of strokes.

Today was no ordinary day; important and mysterious work awaited us. We were to choose, from wall sections, pillars and various specimens, those finishes most suitable to the design or to the required technique. Up till now I have had courses of various heights dressed without deciding on anything, thinking that later we should be able to assemble items already sorted into categories and put up our walls without wasting time. Now the day has come; Paul is demanding directives and asking for decisions. I made my choice long ago, and though I have sometimes spoken of it to Bernard and Benoît, I have never clearly expressed my wishes to Paul and the lay brothers. I dared not tell them, already coping with many difficulties as they are, that what I require is the most difficult and the most precise work of all, and will therefore take the longest time.

My decision concerns mainly the exterior facing of the walls and of the cloister. Everyone thought, when I asked for rough dressing, that the stones would be laid roughly too, and that all the careful work would be carried out in the church interior and the principal rooms. I wanted to try to get everything settled today, without mentioning the exterior walls. So we began with a study of the interior facings, which caused no constraint since we are all in agreement and Paul has prescribed the stone-laying methods.

In the interior the facings will be smooth, as regular as possible. The blocks, laid in horizontal courses, aligned with the help of one-tenth-inch wooden wedges, will be soaked with wet, almost liquid lime, poured from a bowl into the vertical and horizontal joints. Clay will be used to stanch the joints during pouring. Gaps will be judiciously distributed to allow the lime to flow along and spread, so far as is possible, over the whole contact surface. These gaps will be closely watched to prevent overflows, and stains will be cleaned off and brushed as they occur. Finishing off the joints will be carried out after removal of the clay, with a strongly adhesive lime paste, forced in with the spatula and then scraped smooth with the wooden knife. No wizardry here; it is conventional stone-laying, and Paul is training lay brothers for this meticulous work. There is no risk that it will be spoilt. This method is intended for the interior, which is sheltered from the frosts and from the burning of the sun. The joints will not crumble in the centuries to come, for lime goes on hardening until it becomes as hard as stone. Discipline will be used to ensure that the facings are ceaselessly brushed and washed from top to bottom. The density of the stone does not allow anything to soak in. Only a few re-shapings of detail should be necessary, to make some ill-dressed stones uniform.

Next, we examined the fillings between the two wall facings, and agreed that all were satisfactory and might be carried out. This method makes it possible to use up all the chippings and spoilt stone, and takes about as long as others. Filling with ordinary masonry is quicker, but requires numerous bond stones to traverse the entire breadth of the walls. Filling with roughly dressed masonry does away with two-thirds of those long stones, difficult in quarrying and long in dressing. Unfortunately, we shall lack a supply of those squared stones that the dresser rejects when, in the course of working them, he judges them unfit to serve as facing stones.

The trial pieces of masonry submitted, three in number, differed in the thickness of the joints and the regularity of the stones. We decided that the finish of the work should be varied according to the functions of the abbey's rooms, and that the finest stones should be kept for the church interior. To give pleasure to everyone, and to gratify the lay brothers' pride, we admired their best pieces: a column hewn from a single block, arch-stones and springers put carefully together.

Then we began our discussions about the exterior facings. The specimen I had timidly requested was tucked away in a small space in a corner, so naturally no one took it seriously. It was laid with dry joints, that is, without mortar. This method, rarely used now, was standard practice in the days of antiquity; in our day it remains the exception even for fine-grained stone. It demands so much care: perfectly dressed faces on all horizontal surfaces, joints no thicker than a line, and difficult placement, entailing re-cutting on the spot of any roughness that impedes the matching. A stone that rocks will cause other stones to crack. The orders I previously gave to make the facing stones rough and crude will not result in much time-saving, for the stones will have to be re-dressed and the joints made precisely. Trimming and laying will certainly take twice as long as they would if we used mortar. To these difficulties must be added the need to use numerous deep long-tailed stones to provide anchorage and firm cohesion in the walls. Nor is that all; for though it is true that our material is one of the hardest and most resistant of all, none the less to lay it with dry joints will be dangerous because of the heavy loads imposed by binding joists and roof vaults. The stresses are exerted principally on the exterior facing, and the fitting together of the courses at certain places will have to be effected by filling and re-trimming, until the course is adequate; it will never be perfect.

Paul, who already knows all this, has never taken my suggestions seriously. My arguments are weak: infinite conservation of the joints, neat work, an elegant method of laying for a crude material. Our stones, despite Paul's efforts, will never be other than what we can produce from shapeless lumps, and therefore will be lacking in steadiness and rigidity at the joints. Arch-stones and special blocks will nearly always be dressed with an eye to economy. I am even thinking of arch-stones in the shape of irregular polygons, to allow of maximum utilization.

This method of laying, *my* method, will give a touch of richness to what is otherwise austere: it will weave a design on every wall, a net of variously shaped mesh or an open lacework of dark threads. My decision, matured over a long period, would not be called in question today. So, after long, useless, inconclusive discussions in which I expressed my various preferences and objections, I chose to postpone the decision about exterior facings till later, in order to gain time to convince Paul in private. Resistance to my views would have been too strong today, and, most of the questions about the project having been settled, I succeeded in avoiding battle without disheartening anyone or interrupting the work. Tomorrow then, as they say in the East for everything that is put off indefinitely. But tomorrow cannot wait for long.

I shall not, I hope, need to use my authority. Although filled-up joints and smooth surfaces will add softness to the half-light in the interiors and the church, in the full light of the sun such joints, soaked, filled and rammed with mortar, would destroy all the subtlety of the fabric, dressed as it is in facets, like precious stones in their settings. The façades of our monasteries being solid and straight, they call insistently for the fairest of coverings.

The nights have turned chilly since last Friday. Our overheated little valley is being visited by a wind, an offshoot of the mistral, against which we are ill protected. The dry air makes the light harsh, tires the eyes and makes the trees metallic. The silvery green of upturned leaves appears as they wave in the summer gusts. Where we are, a cloud of dust wanders from one corner of the site to another and does no good to the lay brothers' eyes, which are already sore. This cold wind, which does not usually blow until the fifteenth day of August, gave us an excuse to have a fire lit for the first time in the hearth built by Benoît with his own hands — a little egg-shaped corner fireplace, constructed with our first bricks. The fire has to be a small one, for we fear a conflagration; not a drop of rain has fallen on forest or scrub for two months, and it would all blaze at the least spark. Our fire is a luxury.

Every time that Bernard can keep watch with me, it is like a holiday. We savour the occasion, having plenty to talk about. This morning's choice of walls — or rather the choice that we failed to make — still worries him, and he would like to understand my views, as is only natural.

We sit on my straw mattress, the door opened wide to a night of stars; this wind brings them in thousands, more brilliant than one could believe possible. The squalls are dying down — getting their breath back, as they say here when the wind drops at nightfall — the gusts of the mistral come less frequently, more gently, scarcely sighing.

The fire keeps watch with us; under two short logs, hollowed by the embers, it flickers and burns away, ashy or glowing. Tiny blue flames try to merge to keep it going; they fuse, then vanish, but our gaze gives them courage. This is the moment when one says to oneself, One more log and we should have a real fire. It is pleasant like this; the whitened ground reflects a strange light which picks out the pale folds of Bernard's habit and leaves his red, sunburnt face in shadow. We muse on what we are going to say, we prepare this ritual combat between the young cock and the old. Not a sound in the intervals of the breeze—the summer insects have no liking for this wind and are keeping an uneasy silence on this unusual July night. It is Bernard who breaks the silence.

'Well? Are we ready, Brother?'

'Yes, of course, we are ready!'

'Are you satisfied with everything?'

'Yes, we have worked well.'

'Is it just as you wanted it? Just as you thought it out? Benoît, you know, doesn't quite understand, he's always puzzling over the why and the how of your decisions. He says to me in a worried way, "The chief has planned this or that, here or there, and he doesn't tell us why." This business of dry-jointed stone bothers him; he knows that you are not acting without reason. He would, I think, have liked you to explain it all to him.'

'How can one explain what is of the earth?'

'What do you mean?'

'You know, Bernard, in the beginning the Creator gave men a liking for fire—originally the only difference between us and the animals, I mean outwardly. Then wisdom, or folly, led us to hunt, till, breed animals, weave, speak, fight, cook and build. Everything that is instinct I call "of the earth", and although building comes after fire, construction is still connected with the instinct. As the piratical wasp or the virtuous bee constructs its cells, so we build our hearths, our cities, our communities.'

'So, you claim that in so far as the construction of our abbey is concerned, we here are like ants before they dig out their galleries and set up their underground homes? ... You mean you organized everything solely by your instinct?'

'Not altogether, but by using some elementary knowledge which, in its deliberate systemization, is akin to instinct.'

'How then do you explain the working of that knowledge — which I would rather call invention or experience?'

'Just suppose, imagine, that the magician of the world has turned me into a number of insects, and has endowed me with the gift of ubiquity; made me partly into a spider, partly into a lot of larvae. On my long legs I move and stride and walk about. Curious about everything, from brooklet to spring, from rich soil to scrub-land, from forest to cliffs, I study the sun's path, the prevailing winds, and, as a predator, the prospects for hunting, the haunts of the insects: that is to say, I pick my territory. At the same time, in my larval guise, I idle away my pre-existence between two kinds of water: the meandering stream and the depths of the dark pool filled by the spring. You have noticed, I expect, the wonderful construction of a web: how the filaments are cast into the air, and descend; how the cross-threads are spun, stout shrouds woven, ingenious stays contrived. From ground to branch, from rock to stalk, the primary supports are stretched and strengthened, crossed and counterbalanced. I am making my web: first the framework, then the radiants, after the radiants the weft, after the weft, life. Meanwhile, the larvae — that is, my ideas — are maturing and emerging from the depths; and already the first strange-looking ones are escaping from their sheaths, hatching out on the surface and floating for a moment in the first cradle of their infancy. They forsake the water for the azure sky and for love. Gnats, may-flies, dragonflies and butterflies in many-coloured flight, new-born or guileless, are blinded by the western light, and drop like acrobats into the elaborate snare, where the eager, industrious spider seizes and stores them against a future that may be either uncertain or bountiful. First the hunt, then the harvest. Velvety, gossamer or enamelled, the wanton insects rise, streaking the still, golden twilight as they soar and flutter. Every one of them hurls itself on to that yielding, unseen wall that is destined to engulf and hoard it. The spider, you understand, acts and selects; it does not invent, it learns; it is experience, materialism. The larvae — underwater ideas, to begin with — are essentially bearers of inspiration. By circulating, they bring about their own destruction. Accepting their destiny, and perhaps jealous of the second life that has terminated the first, they anticipate their natural end. I needed to be both at the same time; I had to inspire and to act, to sacrifice in order to devour. It is all merged into intention and action, experience and instinct. When I was changed back to a man again, that was how I knew where the quarries, forge, sawmill, kilns and workshops should be placed; they are the rock, the branch, the stalk on which the web is stayed.'

'So the web of our abbey,' observed Bernard, 'is ready to accept ideas, to choose. That is how you define this conception. Where everyone else sees only a trade, a mere organization stemming from knowledge of the techniques, you put forward a system based on instinct. In choosing the wall this morning, and consequently the way the basic stone was to be dressed, you claim that feelings, instinct and experience were so intimately linked that you can't manage to single out the part that was played by craftsmanship, imagination, the heart and the sensible desire to avoid waste. So much so that, to illustrate your point, you spoke of the most complex works of nature: aquatic embryos, and multiple meta-morphoses. I understand you, but I don't believe you. I don't claim that I have different ideas, but I think you overestimate instinct. I don't agree that, in the whole of our enterprise here, the major task is to be performed by a sleep-walker. I don't mean to discredit your inspiration, but your trade (which you know very well) and your experience have certainly been of more use to you than your inspired notions.'

'Aren't we always having to make a new approach? Remember, Bernard, that circumstances or facts never turn up twice in the same guise. To come back to the stone: believe me, I have never used anything like it; I had no thought before coming here that I should one day have to build with this material. Yet I knew in my heart, shortly after I arrived, that these stones had to be roughly finished and delicately assembled. How can I explain to you that the beauty of the walls will depend on that feeling, if I don't refer to this subconscious and complex emotion? You see me as wise and experienced; you refuse to approve of anything that seems to you not to come from the essence of those qualities. You have known for a long time that I wish to have these stones laid with dry joints. The explanations I have given do not satisfy you. Where can I get the will-power to oppose you, for a time, if I don't bring my feeling into it? So, on every occasion when I am in agreement with you all, you claim that it's all due to knowledge or experience!

Could it be that you would rather rely on learning? That you are afraid to be found wanting in instinct? Excluded from the world of imagination?'

'You are unfair to yourself and to us! I don't yet understand why you want the stone like that, but that's not a contradiction of what I was saying. These stones that you are in favour of are no more than makeshift materials for me, for Paul and for everyone, as you well know.'

'Why?'

'Because there are no others! We have to be content with them. Admit it—it isn't stone at all!'

My eyes opened wide. I had never thought that all of them—and especially Bernard—were stone-dressing for fifteen hours a day without believing that the stuff was stone, without hoping that the beauty it was to inspire would compel admiration. Recovering from my astonishment, I continued, 'All right. You like the fine-grained stones of your region; do you consider them to be superior material?'

'The noblest! Its nobility surely proves that it is first-class material.'

'What do you think of marble?'

'I have never seen it used in quantity.'

'And of bronze?'

'There would never be enough of it in the whole world to construct a palace or a church in bronze.'

'Suppose that limitation were overcome, and imagine a church made of brass, like the great bell of a cathedral. Do you know the granite of Brittany, the marble of Tuscany or of the Athenian Acropolis? Have you seen in imagination the domes of Persia? Three hundred feet high, a hundred and fifty feet across, with a facing of gold and mosaic. And Ravenna? Enamel everywhere. Does it trouble you to roof our abbey, not with stone, but with tiles? Our art sees no medium as either more or less noble, it employs the substance given by God and creates forms that are dictated by its nature. In our own region, fine-grained stone is often abundant and near at hand. In many other places, there is none to be had for fifty leagues around. Such was the case with Saracen or Persian art. Will you let that circumstance diminish your talent or your imagination? Will you be handicapped?

Would you weep if you were obliged to use the marble of the Acropolis? Would you regret it if one by one the tiles, the architraves, the plinths, the friezes, the cornices, the flutings, the columns' tambours were carved and polished out of pink marble, soft as the skin of new-born babes? Or if fine gold were smoothed over the domes?'

Bernard listened to me attentively. Bernard is under the influence of Paul, the carver of soft, beautiful and easily worked stone; and also of Benoît, the young supervisor of works who fails to distinguish the theory of building from the material, subordinating them both to the conformity of an unimaginative ideal. The embers, almost burnt out, give no more light. Bernard's silhouette in the frame of the door stands out darkly from the background of dazzling stars in the wind-swept sky.

'You have opened for me,' he replied, 'the door to a world I know little of. You have spoken of various materials, but you have said nothing of any substance which it would be impossible to use because of its defects. You see, perhaps I should understand better if you said to me, "We are going to build strong, thick walls; afterwards we shall look for a pleasant coating or fine casing to hide these stones that are unworthy to show themselves in our church." I can grasp that our stone is useful, and that therein lies its beauty; but to try to treat it like northern limestones, to ennoble this poor stuff by laboriously working it, seems to me impractical, as it does to Paul and Benoît.'

Bernard went on for some time with his memorized lecture and criticisms. As he was talking, I saw a glimpse of hope, because the more he said the more bitter he became. I interrupted him.

'Bernard, kindle the fire again and make a drink for us. I think I am wasting my time trying to convince you. I am going to be compelled to overrule your wishes, and Benoît's and Paul's; I shall have to counter your scepticism by my authority. Later on, when I am gone, you will love me the more for it. I am defending more than just a material, I am defending my faith in matter itself. There is no beauty without faith. I can allow a master builder his preferences when, freely and without subservience towards his client, he may choose his own shape, technique and material. Rigorous systematism is a sign of weakness in an architect. Fashion is one of the forms taken by decadence and mediocrity.

It is a commonplace that the artist who follows its detestable dictates realizes in his own lifetime the foolishness of all his work. To cure himself of it, he takes once more the trodden path. Disappointed by a fashion that is out of date, he still believes in that of the present. One ought to tell him, "Friend, never turn back, always live like the donkey with his carrot." Fashion is good only for those who launch it. Thus, with genius, it may become a true art and, without talent, an amusing joke for him who can take advantage of it. Continual freedom, being without prejudice in the choice of materials, leads the master builder to study all the techniques: wood, being fibrous, will allow of great spans, bold projections, an architecture of cornices and fore-parts. Stone will constrain him to the rigours of calculating in statics. Brick will make him direct his researches towards curved shapes or vaults, attainable through the lightness and the module of the basic unit. By adapting himself like this, the artist does not endanger his own personality. If he always sticks to his favourite shape, everyone will recognize his work even under the most varied guises. The strength of his soul will, like a philosophy, guide his hand and his eye.

'Sensibility is not at the mercy of techniques, it always remains the same. Whether the painter uses three colours, or fifteen, or a hundred, his style will not change. As for the sculptor, all his modelling, whether he works in marble or in wood, will belong to the same family. It's the same with the master builder: stone, as the sole material of a piece of work, would correspond to black and white in a painter's work. If he adds wood, then enamel and bronze, the architect augments the richness of his palette without thereby improving or ennobling the quality of his sensibility. To return to our subject, you may be sure also that the naive client who says, "These horrible dreary bricks, these disheartening walls of common grey stone, these wretched wooden buildings, these pebbly mortars that soak up all the light," should really declare, "I have had the misfortune to choose an architect who did not know how to use materials made by God." Ever since we came, we have been concerned to select our materials and to produce them in sufficient quantity to keep pace with the progress of the site. I never had any doubt that in this valley we must devote our first efforts to the stone—quarrying and preparing it. Don't you remember what I said? Next, the wood and tiles. A roof of stone would have taken too much time and money. My choice was guided both by tradition and by economy, even taking into account the remoteness of the clay-pit, the building of a kiln and the organization of production. As to wood, its scarcity made it necessary to use it sparingly. So, proceeding from my deep-rooted convictions and my feelings about architectural projects, I established both what was possible with, and what was aesthetic in, each element used in the construction. This analysis of the materials settled the rules of the game we were to play, and they in turn determined precisely where we were to play it. I did not say, "I want," without looking. I examined and weighed the difficulties of everything, and upon reflection I could say, "It will be possible." '

We were in darkness, and I had said my say. The night, now still, was waiting for the wind to stir again with the dawn; the trees were hushed. Bernard had revived the fire and prepared some mint tea.

'All right,' he said, 'will you give a truthful answer to this question: if, about three miles from here, we were to find a fine quarry of real stone, easy to extract and to dress, what would you do?'

'We should immediately begin to work it, we should buy three more mules, and I should feel no regret at abandoning our quarries.'

'So I am right?'

'No! For life is stronger than love, and life is building faster, is trying to produce the effect of an easier, less tortured material —'

' — and a better one.'

'I did not say that, or think it.'

'Then you love this stone?'

'Yes, and I believe the feeling is reciprocated. Since the very first day, I have had a respect for it that I did not even dream of questioning. I should never have been able to speak of it to you as I have without love. Now it is a part of myself, of our task; it is the abbey. I caress it in my dreams, the sun sets on it, returns to it in the morning in that awakening that stone has, endows it with its colours; the rain darkens it and makes it glisten. And I love it the more for its defects, for savagely defending itself, for its tricks

75

in attempting to evade us. To me it is like a male wolf, noble and courageous, lean-flanked, covered with wounds, bites and bruises. It will always remain so, even when it is well and truly laid in level courses and tamed to bear the stress of the arches. Although I have given the abbey its proportions and harmony, it is the stone alone that will preserve the independent soul of the place; when it is reduced to order, it will remain as beautiful as a rough-pelted wild beast. That is why I do not want to use mortar or daub it with lime; I want to leave it a little freedom still, or it will not live. Will you feel indifferent towards this stone when I can no longer be there to love it?'

'Brother, I shall perhaps forget many things said this evening, but I believe that now, suddenly, I understand. Why didn't you begin as you have just ended? ... I shall always feel the warmest friendship for you.'

'Do everything in the same way.'

'You mean that?'

'For me, yes.'

'I accept everything, in order to be like you.'

'Little Brother, arrange things so that all will end well. We may be taken by surprise on the way; the road will be rough.'

Before parting, we drank our mint tea in silence.

St Camilla, eighteenth day of July

It is always a pleasure to meet Joseph the potter. Old and bent, with a small round head, he is baked in the sun, like a brick, and then stewed in five quarts of wine every day. Thin, wrinkled and white-haired, he looks at me keenly, maliciously, even malevolently. His huge hands, beautiful in the precision of their movements, are given to caressing his pots. His feet are bare, and contracted from perpetually working the wheel, so that his arms and legs look out of proportion; and his body is lumpy and bent, like a great knot. This morning he greeted me thus:

'See, Father, the work is getting on. Have a look at this clay in the pit; it's always right, pliable, well moistened, not too much nor too little—a couple of pints from time to time, it needs just as much as I do, no more, no less.' I looked round the workshop; I had not been there for some time. I had heard that Joseph's wheel had arrived and, what was more important, that the first tiles were ready for firing. 'What are they like?' I asked.

Thereupon he sat down at the head of a low, raw-looking table, settling himself there as if for a ceremony. It was a massive, squat bench, its great close-set legs bound, pegged, and braced by crossed diagonals: a table so heavy that it took four men to move it, one at each corner. On his right he set a stool, on the stool an earthenware pot, and into the pot he poured water. On his left there was another stool, on which he settled a tray of fine, bright-yellow sand. While this was going on, I noted his quick glances seeking my approval, and his tight-lipped mouth curved in a half-smile. Then he went to his earth pit, lifted up the damp cloths and brought back a lump of clay weighing at least sixty pounds. His movements were slow and unhurried. Joseph was showing me that he was going through the complete operation, but not more quickly than usual. Three implements were hanging at the bench: the first, a trapezium-shaped iron frame, half an inch thick; the second a flat ruler; the third a thick, rounded form, a massive wooden tile hafted at its broadest side, like a convex scoop turned over. After placing the iron frame with the trapezium's long base towards him, he grasped the table corners with his two hands, lowered his head, closed his eyes, then with a gesture directed me to stand clear, no doubt to protect me from splashing. This pantomime, as I realized, signified, 'There, I am settled, now I can begin.' Precise ritual movements followed in rapid succession: he plunged his hands into the tray and sprinkled a thin layer of sand on frame and table; then he dug his fingers into the lump of clay, his thumbs met, his fingers closed, and he extracted a piece of clay that was exactly right. In the same movement he dropped it into the centre of the frame, where it spread out to fill three-quarters of the trapezium. Continuing his smooth movements, he dipped his hands in the pot of water, then spread the clay and pushed it into the corners, wet and shining as it was squashed and moulded. With the flat ruler, the beater, he smoothed it over and over, pressing lightly on each edge of the frame in turn.

At this point he stopped, asked me to watch carefully, and repeated his movements, slightly tilting the beater now one way, now another. He murmured, 'It has to be worked towards the middle, that's where it takes the stress.' Swiftly he lifted the frame, slid the slab to the edge of the table, and caught it on the rounded form. The slab moulded itself to the implement's shape: it had become a tile. Then he turned round, took a few steps and set it on the ground next to some hundreds of others protected by straw matting. With one sharp, precise movement he slipped it off, and it kept its shape like a supported arch, delicately balanced —a marvellously enduring compromise between clay's plasticity and the law of stresses. Too stiff a mixture would have made the shaping long and difficult; too soft, the tile would have collapsed or warped. The ceremony was over. Joseph looked at all his children under their mats. Turning his head without altering his stance, head to one side and hands on hips, he looked at me with a smile. The attitude expressed the craftsman's vanity. I was full of admiration, and Joseph realized it; he changed then, and looked over his rows of tiles, simulating my own very real feeling. I guessed that he was going to apologize. 'Ah, Father, the magic, you see, it's not in me, it's in the sand. This devilish stuff rolls and slips and gets tricky, but the sand tenses it. You saw just now, it didn't stick, the frame didn't pull any away, it slid over the table and then, whoops!' He grasped the handle and with a jerk imitated the movement he had first made when stooping over the bench. 'Oh,' he said, 'when I go past one of my roofs, I know that I have caressed it thousands of times, and that's a grand feeling.'

It is true: all these things are the work of his hands, from the moment when he plucks out the clay with his great fingers until the day when he empties the kiln; a hundred times over he will have caressed that ever-beautiful surface, with the smoothing gesture that brings out the quality of the material. Long did I gaze on those shapes that are to lie side by side for centuries; I wish they may love each other and live happily together. I would really like Joseph to know all the things I am thinking, to believe in all the things I can appreciate, to understand that what I have seen is one of the joys of my life.

St Margaret, twentieth day of July

The productive buildings planned by the abbot consist of a farm in the valley bottom to the west, a cellar with a winepress, an oilpress and a sheepfold. These buildings will be separate from the abbey. To the north of the Field I have marked out the great quadrilateral that encloses the monastery and its invariable arrangement. The present site of the chapel and dorter is where the permanent workshops, guest-house and infirmary will be built. If the abbey should grow instead of remaining a 'little prayer-mill', as Paul would say, the terrace between the workshops and the abbey will take buildings intended for the novices, with a separate cloister. I have likewise provided for doubling the area of the monks' dorter and the consequent enlargement of the monks' hall and the warming house, situated beneath.

This definite overall plan is the only drawing I have managed to make up to now. Those for the abbey are still in limbo. The production of materials is overtaking me; there must be no more delay. My evasions are unjustified. My brothers, the abbot and the craftsmen must wonder what I am waiting for. Every morning I feel their questioning gaze on the back of my head; soon they will be looking me sternly in the face. There must be no more delay. The days are long, and the weather will be favourable for many months; this will allow us to lay foundations for the main walls, which may then be built higher next winter.

St Victor, twenty-first day of July

I heard, as it were the noise of thunder, one of the four beasts saying, Come and see. And I saw, and behold a white horse and he that sat on him had a bow: and a crown was given unto him, and he went forth conquering, and to conquer. (Rev. vi 1–2)

I am angry with myself, I am not doing what I should. Time is pressing, each day means delay. I cannot make a decision; I do not make a start. Am I afraid? ... No, I think not. My hesitation arises from an unwillingness to grapple with reality. I know only too well that enthusiasm will create finality at one stroke. I shall be swept along towards the end—the end which is sadness and regret for what is in being, while the unknown, in which I delight, is hope for what is impossible; and what is impossible is beautiful as are only those forms imagined by men. My delay prolongs the feeling that the impossible is possible. Imagination dies as soon as it comes down to earth. I delight in buildings in the air. Reality is commonplace, apart from the pleasure of bringing it into being. As to closing the work site—the place is like a book one has read a hundred times: what was absorbing and novel has become routine, the plot is tiresomely repeated and rehashed. Stale kitchen smells linger when a meal has lasted too long. As things are, I rise from table with hunger unappeased, like a monk. The aroma of humble fare will remind me in passing that my stomach is still empty, and I shall feel a sudden hunger for my unfinished activity.

There is laziness, too, in my present inaction, and lack of courage. Creation happens when boldness is released at the very moment that something brilliant is done. Timidity produces nothing of value, and the timid are legion. They think of themselves, of other people, and of what people might say. They wonder if they are sufficiently original or sufficiently with the trend. They do not do what they like. The pusillanimous creator with a critical eye says, 'No, that's not enough,' or 'No, that's too much.' That 'too much', that 'not enough' have to satisfy and flatter and *be* the soul of the work; it is a great deal to ask of it. Drawing with the right hand and holding back with the left, keeping an eye on one's own eye—that's too many eyes. Courage lies in being oneself, in showing complete independence, in loving what one loves, in discovering the deep roots of one's feelings. A work must not be a copy, one of a group, but unique, sound and untainted, springing from the heart, the intelligence, the sensibility. A real work is truth, direct and honest. It is simply a declaration of one's knowledge to the whole world. In architecture, the only guides are craftsmanship and experience; all the rest is instinct, spontaneity, decision, the release of all one's accumulated energy. Never is one's courage courageous enough, never is one's sincerity sincere enough nor one's frankness frank enough. You have to take the greatest possible risks; even recklessness seems a bit half-hearted. The best works are those that are at the limits of real life; they stand out among a thousand others when they prompt the remark, 'What courage that must have taken!' Enduring work follows from a leap into the void, into unknown territory, icy water or murderous rock. If today I am in the grip of fear, as I am for every enterprise, the reason lies in that unknown: I have no faith that I shall be able to create even a mediocre thing.

I no longer believe that the impetus to start a new work springs from the spirit of those already accomplished; the past is dead.

St Anne, twenty-sixth day of July

Go to the ant, thou sluggard; consider her ways, and be wise ...
How long wilt thou sleep, O sluggard? (Prov.vi. 6–9)

I have not slept; I feel listless; my days are spent in idleness. I take pleasure in gossiping. Fearing and avoiding all looks, I keep up an air of self-assurance. Yesterday Joseph left his workshop, and was walking about the site in search of someone to talk to. On the path that leads to the sawmill he met Étienne, and I too was near by. Joseph was saying, 'Don't you see, he's finished ... he has no strength left ... he's a mental drunkard ... thin as a rake. He wanders about at night like a ghost in the moonlight, raving, talking to himself, and sighing like those old women that reek of urine and stale church candles. No! I tell you, he's hankering after paradise, he is no more use on earth! Well, let the devil take him. This walking corpse, pale, thin as a skeleton — we ought to give him the final knock ... or let the abbot get rid of him; otherwise, he'll end by building this monastery, and what will it be like? I know, I do, I am not just saying it, I know it ...' Greatly angered, and to keep him from saying more, I came forward. 'Well, Father Joseph? You are cheerful today, no doubt the clay was thirsty?'

'Yes ...' he said uneasily; then, after taking a look at me, he was reassured, and added, choosing his words carefully, 'I was saying just now that you, looking ill as you do, you're a strange man. When I think that soon we shall have all we need here — in this little valley nobody thought that life would rise out of the earth; now we are equipped to build a town! That's courage, that's energy.'

'Yes, but let me tell you something: to build a town, one needs plans and sound men to make them. The materials are not everything. Just now I feel a little weary, I am thinking of asking the abbot to replace me; I no longer have much courage. Frankly, Father Joseph, what's your sincere opinion?'

'Well, it's for you to decide, Father; when a man doesn't feel well, he must think about retiring, and you, obviously, you need to rest; experience isn't everything. Oh, I know, I'm getting old too; if only I had some savings!'

'No, Joseph, don't say that. You know that you're an expert in your own line. No one, not even a man in his prime, does work like yours nowadays; you're both an artist and a craftsman, and I envy and respect you.'

I knew as I said it that Joseph would be both pleased and remorseful. The potter's confusion grew.

'And I, Father, I have not told you everything. Sometimes I joke about you; I say you can't stand on your feet, but at heart I know that you have the biggest brain of us all, and ...'

'Joseph, enough! You know I don't like flattery, or lies, or malice. We are all brothers, and your charity must be as great as mine, the more that ...'

'Stop, Father, stop! I understand! I see now that you have manoeuvred me like an old horse, you have fooled me; if I was drunk, if I lost my head, believe me, I'm no more stupid than the next man. I call Étienne to witness; if he wants to, he can tell all, I give him my permission. I'll be damned and double-damned for it, do you hear? Yes, I know, I'm spiteful; cruel, even. Do you want to know everything? You ought to know what's in the potter's little head! Let me speak now! I've made a start! If you won't listen to me, I shall shout so loud that everyone will know what the potter has inside his skull: I love you, monk of our dear God! More than you love anyone alive. Oh no, by the dear Mother, you're not done for—and even if life seems to have broken you, your body is like an iron bar. Only ... you have over-done things. When you should be asleep, you stay up later than others and you're already up and about at an hour when people are still enjoying the evening. If you want me to say it in front of Étienne: you're crazy, but nobody else could have achieved in three years what you have done in three months! Only afterwards one says to oneself, Why doesn't he make his plans in three days? Build in two years? You understand me? The more one gives, the more they want. You're like a cow that gives twenty measures, or a hen that lays three eggs; people say, "If we push her a bit, she'll do the half-dozen." '

Joseph had unburdened himself; he wiped his streaming brow, his tipsiness had melted away. His anger had been salutary. Thank you, Joseph, I was calmed too; I liked your way of speaking, you made me both wretched and happy for a moment, like a child. This scene has influenced and moved me; tomorrow I will speak to the Chapter, and the abbot. Joseph spoke about both the good and the ill; sometimes drunkards speak the truth.

St Natalia, twenty-seventh day of July

> *But what is all this business about you, then? Whence came the slanders that have been spread concerning you? You claim that you do nothing more extraordinary than other men; but you would not be the object of so much rumour and gossip if you did only what other men do. Tell us the truth of it, that we may not lightly judge of your case.* (Plato, *Apology*)

'Struggling with guilt, admitting my weakness, confessing that my conscience is disturbed—I leave it to you, Father, and Brothers, to judge and decide!' The Chapter of Notre Dame de Florielle seemed to be dismayed. My brothers, simple folk, did not understand. With bowed head, the abbot reflected. I had told them everything, and I awaited their decision. After meditating for some time in that pained atmosphere, he first straightened his broad back, then his heavy hands, which had been resting on his knees, interlocked in a gesture of strength and decision. He raised his shaven head, and his burly, powerful, slumped body straightened. His lofty brow and terrifying gaze confronted me pitilessly, with an i.·difference that was no doubt intentional, and his voice was firm, resolute, deep and hard. 'As a monk,' he said, 'you are an instrument of Providence. So far we have not been disappointed in our expectations. We feel for you in your sufferings and shall pray for your health. What does the shameful doubt of your soul's predicaments matter to us? It has nothing to do with that Providence which directed you here. You have demonstrated your ability many times: we do not wish to know its origin. We think your will must control your weaknesses. They are, if I understand rightly, useful in your task. So far as we are concerned, you are solely responsible for our house. We command you to rid your conscience of these trifles and to act as best you may. And,' he added, like a prophet, quoting Bernard of Clairvaux, '"To the task, then, know that the moment has come for you to go to the heart of the matter, since the time of meditation has prepared for it. If, so far, you have stirred only your mind, now must you bestir your tongue, now must you bestir your hand. Gird on your sword, that sword of the spirit which is the Word of God. Amen!"' So spoke the abbot, and I was happy.

Matins. My fervent desire to offer my best prayer must be understood: nothing is yet lost. O Lord, *there* is my meditation, in three dimensions—my prayer in stone, my way of proving my deep faith! This abbey is both a prayer and a means of redemption. I thought I could withdraw from it, but look at the result! Listen to the echo in these vaults: it is myself! The steeple rising straight and honest before Thee is myself! This stout cloister, these walls, these roofs, these proportions—once more myself! Behold, O Lord, this is my soul; my aberrations are before Thee. Carelessness, neglect, inattention and impatience in prayer are embodied here in shapes and masses for hundreds of years to come. I know that Thou hast no need to build, Thou who hast made all, yet deign to look upon what our minds and our hands have wrested from Thy creation. Look upon this valley; tomorrow a house will stand there; is it better now? Dost Thou not desire that morrow? If I have existed, it has been to mark out the world with the memorials of Thy rule, to prove that we are warring for Thy kingdom of earth, sky and stars. We, men of the valley, conquering knights of the adoration of earth's peoples, cry to Thee, 'Here are Thy bastions of the true faith, Thy fortresses of contemplation.' To whom dost Thou owe those walls and that conquest, if not to Thy builders—to those who from east to west have been building Thy churches for centuries? Thy rule is now established. What mortal ruler will be able to assert that the strongholds and castles in his lands—even if they were of the most enduring granite—will ever rival the number, the excellence and the durability of Thine own?

May my courage rise and make me immerse myself in my proud task! By the exercise of my will, evidence of my powers will soon be standing. I am that divine spark that re-creates matter, transforms nature and, for all time to come, sows fervour in the pilgrim's breast.

St Germanus, thirtieth day of July

Misfortune has come to us: Brother Thomas has breathed his last. His death throes, which began after Vespers, were brought about in this way: the quarrymen stop work at five in the evening; for some time past they have suffered from a disease of the eyes carried by minute splinters lodging in the delicate tissue. Brother Gabriel, as unofficial infirmarian, applies compresses, with some success; he makes a hobby of herbs and knows numerous remedies that are effective in the care of wounds and infections. This treatment takes a long time; for a period of several hours it is essential to apply compresses soaked in a thick boiling infusion. We are alarmed by the way the disease develops. The men's eyes become no more than red, swollen, lashless slits, tainted by a yellowish fluid.

Brother Thomas had stayed behind in his quarry, the highest one, to get the dressed stones in order—his everyday task. When it was time for our meal, he did not appear. Being anxious, Bernard went some way down the road and called him, but without result. We rang the bell again: no Brother Thomas. Brother Eugène, sent off to look for him, made the round of the workshops and the forge, and finally went up to the quarry, but saw nothing that seemed to him unusual. He came back and reported that Thomas was not to be found. It was then that I decided to order a general search. Thomas *was* at the quarry, his skull crushed by a stone of the size of a large gourd. The hand of Fate had struck our holy brother. Thomas's breath was coming in a low rattle. At three in the morning all the monks assembled. The abbot was in Avignon; the prior recited the prayers for the dying and administered extreme unction. Towards five o'clock, Thomas, surrounded by us all, rendered up his spirit. Thy will be done, O Lord.

St Brévin

This last sleepless night was peopled by hallucinations. To escape from these frightful visions I went with Bernard to watch over Thomas, who died for the abbey, the first victim of the site. Serenity and happiness illuminated the beauty of his face.

The day had been a hard one for everybody. After the burial, no one wanted to admit his weariness. The craftsmen, with our permission, paid homage to their loyal and industrious labouring brother. The first cross will be the work of Master Étienne.

'On the site,' I said, 'death has picked out the simplest one and the holiest: the labourer — he whom no task offends, who makes no complaint, who never receives congratulations or praise; who is taken for granted on all the sites in the world. Bend your heads, bow down, men, before the humble one who serves you without hope of recognition. Learn to love the labourer, acquire a respect for his ant-like work. In the construction of a building, the labourer contributes three great virtues: patience, perseverance and humility. Who could claim more? The skilled craftsman, proud of his work, paid every day with admiration and high wages? The proud master builder? No one in our group is more deserving than the labourer, for the stone that he contributes has no name, and his reward will not be on this earth. Amen.'

St Geoffrey, third day of August

Life goes on. Already two days have gone by, and there is nothing on this vast site to show that one of us has fallen — only the first little cross, lost among the brambles of the future cemetery, and the evening prayer for our little brother's soul. What was he? Whence came he? No one will know. He was eighteen when he entered Mazan; from that moment he never ceased to be a model of purity in silence. The saintliest of all will never be made a saint, except, O Lord, by Thee.

St Justin

I inspected the installations by myself. The quarries would produce ten cubic yards a day if we had eighty lay brothers: unfortunately, I have only between five and seven, and I really fear that they are going blind. Antime is evolving a device, a sort of helmet, pierced with holes; they will never be able to work armoured like that.

St Laurence, tenth day of August

To our great satisfaction, the first helmet has been tried out by a stone-dresser and he can see perfectly. The men's eyes would not have been able to hold out. Master Paul, although not tender-hearted, asked me to suspend stone-dressing long enough for them to heal and for helmets to be made.

St Clare, twelfth day of August

I have just left the chapel. It is all my fault. Yesterday, Thomas … today it was Philippe's turn. I cannot bear to think about it. At nine o'clock this morning, Philippe lit the fire in the lime kiln — a rough structure of masonry lined with piled-up bricks. This kiln has been in use for only a short time. As he was engaged in repairing the hearth, he imprudently crept beneath to prop up, with some bricks, the insecure slab of the trap-door. Everything collapsed; his body was covered with red-hot stones and fire. As I think of it I feel a shudder that runs along my spine and stiffens my neck. We got him clear at once and carried him out in a blanket tied to a pole. I had him placed at the foot of the altar in the chapel. It was necessary to undress him: atrocious was not the word for it. Wooden half-hoops were rigged up, and over them we stretched a large canvas; only the head shows beyond it, almost unharmed. Philippe is suffering agonies. Tonight the infirmarian will be coming, and the abbot as well. Now we can only wait. Philippe is watched over by Bernard and Gabriel. Master Paul sits by his side and cools his face with mint-scented water. Antime has wrought a bowl for him to drink from. He speaks. It is horrible; he speaks calmly through clenched teeth, as if he were not concerned. Gabriel says that tomorrow the pain will be worse. Everything on this site is too dangerous; because of me, the work goes forward too hastily. The kiln called out for repair, but I had said, 'So much the worse; this kiln needs rebuilding, keep it going until it falls down.'

St Gall, fourteenth day of August

Philippe slept for a few moments. As soon as he is asleep, he moans in a heart-rending way, so that we are relieved when he recovers consciousness. He clenches his teeth and makes no further sound, but fixes his eyes on Paul, the abbot or myself. To the abbot he said, 'Forgive me, Father, I have troubled you;' to Paul, 'Go to your quarry, it will be all right, don't worry about it;' to me, 'Go and rest, or we shall have you ill.' The infirmarian can do nothing. He is not in favour of applying oil. We await some sort of decision from him, a miraculous remedy, but he remains seated by the door, thinking. The heat is stifling. There is nothing we can do, nothing.

At noon Philippe became delirious; the infirmarian attempted to treat one of his legs with a protective ointment made of oil and plants. We tried to change his clothes, but he howled like a wild beast. The abbot said Mass; the friars of Florielle will be here this evening to assist him. The site is at a standstill.

After Compline, the abbot gave Philippe communion, and the brothers chanted. Philippe, though his eyes were closed, had regained consciousness; he wept. Paul has not left his side; he says nothing. Unwearyingly he wipes his face, gives him drinks. This awful torture puts us all to shame. Such courage is unbearable.

The Virgin Mary, fifteenth day of August

The poor man is still alive; in our hearts we hope for a speedy end, today. But his huge body is strong—too much so now. What use is it? The smell is frightful. Flies in their thousands have invaded the chapel; we have to be on the watch the whole time to protect his grey, sweat-bathed face. We have stopped up all the gaps in his covering. No one has slept in the last two days. Philippe has taken the sacraments. The abbot and all the brothers are kneeling and chanting. I have twice vomited blood—but what does my suffering mean to me? Nothing! I wish for pain, pain that would take away my life, and I feel nothing. The infirmarian and the prior put me to bed by force: as soon as they left I got up again. Tonight I shall not be allowed to keep watch.

I should like to write down what I feel. I am alone, I have slept for hours. Why forbid me to help Brother Philippe? Hear me, O Lord, put a stop to all that, I implore Thee.

In the chapel, my brothers were asleep on the ground, and a few lay brothers sitting by the door seemed to await Philippe's deliverance with resignation. Paul, still calm, never leaves his place. The smell, mingling with that of the incense that burns constantly at the foot of the bed, is suffocating. Tomorrow we shall have to change him again, and the thought of it haunts me: what shall we find underneath? The prior brought me back because the abbot will not allow me to keep watch. He himself will not leave the chapel between Matins and Compline. Philippe neither sleeps nor eats. A frightful, searing idea occurs to me; I must banish it—and anyway, how could I set about it? Even if I wanted to, there are too many people about him. I long to sleep; that blood exhausted me, and if I am to influence all these people, I dare not be too ill. But it is madness, there must be something we can do. Because Brother Philippe is a man, must he undergo this torture? No!

Sixteenth day of August

He is still alive. Paul collapsed from weariness and was carried to the dorter; the infirmarian and Brother Gabriel are taking turns to keep flies away from Philippe's head and to moisten his face. He is no longer able to drink; we have to force his teeth apart with a wooden knife and pour water into his mouth. After Tierce I stayed at his side and, speaking close to his ear, I told him the story of his life. I told him all the good he had done; I spoke of his quarry, his tiles, his stones. I thought that he could not hear me, but when I fell silent, he opened his eyes and smiled at me; I smiled too and then, together, we wept. I stroked his brow and kissed him. Then I continued my story until Paul's return. I told him what the abbey would be like in all its details. Whenever I paused, he opened his eyes as though to tell me to go on. It was the cloister that chiefly interested him—the cloister with its great square of sky, the passing clouds, the stars, the dawn light and the bright sunlight, the wind and the rain. I described the pavilion over the spring, too, and the garden plants. I spoke to him of coolness: he listened for that coolness, longed for it so much in his burning, withered body. When he spoke, Paul and I were beside ourselves with pity. He unclenched his teeth a little, and his burnt, bleeding lips murmured, 'Look, I want to see it when it's being built. Put me in a place where I'll be able to see it.' Then he threw back his head, he could not go on, he could no longer hear, he was suffering too much, too much.

Paul questioned me with a look, and I could not help staring hard and long at Philippe. It was too much: an unavailing struggle.

Later, I set myself against a proposal to change his clothes, and I was right. What good would it do to disturb that immense wound, rotting from feet to shoulders? There are other things to be done.

One service follows another in Philippe's presence. Never in my experience has the intensity of prayer and chant been greater. The brothers stand in two ranks, one on either side of this open hearse. For them, Philippe embodies the suffering of our redemption, and I have the impression that they are making use of him. This throbbing horror, this insane courage, seem to excite them; they are living with the superhuman. No, I am unfair; they are doing what they can. Their faces are closed like iron-barred doors: they are trying not to give way to pity. They think of Christ, certainly; that is why they remain impassive. Philippe sacrificed himself to bake the abbey's lime! The abbey is well worth humanity! What is Philippe to die of—suffering, hunger, thirst, sleep? All that takes time; he will hang on for days and rot alive. I thought of worms. No, it's not possible. Take him quickly, O Lord, make haste, I implore Thee; prevent another tragedy—we have had enough already.

The day has passed, another night begins; it is the third. I have told the abbot of Philippe's wish and it has been granted. Philippe will be laid to rest above the quarries where there is a view down over the abbey.

I shall not be able to sleep; I have left Paul with him. In the evening the flies settle; they sleep, as do the brothers. Philippe has passed beyond the possible limits of torment. He no longer fights, he just moans softly, drinks and rocks his head like a bear on its back. I pressed Paul's hand as I left him; I think we shall still have to wait until day.

St Elmo, seventeenth day of August

Philippe is calm, still, almost serene, at last. Paul sent word to me first of all. The brothers chanted and then went out. I detailed two lay brothers to prepare the body. I forbade them to touch the trunk — there was no point in it; they seemed relieved, and so was I. We washed his hands and arms, trimmed his beard, cleansed his face. Then we bound up the wounds; one hand being un-touched, we left it bare. Next we took away the hoops and wound his body in the canvas; there was blood, a great deal of blood. Simon said, 'Lucky that he burst, otherwise he would have lived on for days.' I agreed. After copiously washing everything, we laid the body on planed planks and wrapped legs and trunk with tight bands. We were bathed in sweat. Finally we robed him in a new tunic and scapular and put the cross into his hand. I was content. We called the brothers when all was finished. Philippe's fine looks had returned to him, smooth and calm. The faces of the dead are smaller, and this alters them a little. The dreadful smell had vanished, along with the flies. Paul did not return either.

I went out, dazzled by the light, to rest beneath the great oak, near the spring, while waiting for the service. Suddenly I saw again the brothers, the craftsmen and the lay brothers. For many days past I had forgotten them; for me they no longer had names or faces. I had had the impression of a crowd with three presences: Paul, the abbot and the prior. Yet everything had come to a standstill, apart from the grasshoppers, but I could not have heard them either. Never had there been so many people at Le Thoronet — forty, perhaps fifty brothers. The prior was busy digging the grave, together with Master Jean and Pierre. It seems it was a hard task, for they struck rock two feet down.

After the service, four brothers carried the body. Philippe was with us: from now on he will always be with us. The abbot led the procession, the prior on his right, the master of novices on his left. The monks climbed in two columns, one on each side of the bier. I followed behind them with Bernard and Benoît; then came the lay brothers, and lastly the craftsmen – the whole family from the site. I looked back twice; Paul was not there. Before lowering Philippe's body, the prior drew the cowl down over his face. The ceremony ended. Philippe slept; from up there he will see the abbey. We went down for Vespers. Afterwards my brothers went home to Florielle.

St Mederic, eighteenth day of August

The site has started up again. The fever never leaves me; I have vomited too much blood. There is talk of taking me to Florielle.

I got up despite the prior's ban, for I had things to do. I went to the quarries; Paul was there. I went up to him and he followed me without a word. It was by the slight bulge of the grave that we spoke. After Philippe's death, he had sent to tell me that he was going home. He had drunk a great deal and slept a great deal.

'What do you intend to do?' I asked.

'Go away!'

'Why?'

'Well, you see, I can't stay, I am accursed, am I not?'

'Philippe spoke to you?'

'Yes, of course.'

'Was it he who asked?'

'Yes and no. He didn't want to harm me, nor you either ... Oh, I don't know ... perhaps I didn't understand.'

'I don't see what you mean.'

'Well then, goodbye!'

'No, Paul ... later on you will go home; for the time being, stay; is it agreed?'

'Yes, of course!'

'How long could Philippe have ...'

'A few days, a week. Apart from the fever that he'd contracted, he held on too well, he held on too well.'

'Did he see, did he realize?'

'No, it was dark.'

'Thank you, Paul; later you shall recount this story just as it happened. You may tell all; I believe you will find someone who will understand ... like me, and then it will be finished.'

'You know, I looked ... beforehand ... well, it had to be, there was no other way!'

I clasped his shoulder for a moment and I left him near his friend.

I have begun my studies but, alas, I cannot see my hands any more. My sweat stains everything — it drops from my forehead and flows from my fingers. Crowds of people get into my workshop; they walk behind me and look over my shoulder. Some laugh, others breathe long and heavily, so that I dare not look at them. Many times today I wanted to tell them what I thought of them. I turned round quickly, but no one was there, and my door was shut. How do these strange people get in? I am very much afraid of them; I don't know them. Perhaps they will come back. At night they watch me through cracks in the roof. I hear them climbing up and down — they make the branches creak.

St Enimia

Today I have not got up; I am working lying down on my straw mattress. There is someone talking under my pillow. I have had enough of their wrangling. I listen, it stops; as soon as I stop listening it starts again. There are two tones, or two voices: one that berates and argues, and another that speaks in a monotone, trying to calm — or perhaps, on the contrary, to annoy or weary — the other. Oh, to forget, to forget everything! The abbot brought my parents to visit me: I could say nothing to them. They were annoyed and scornful. My mother, whom I had not seen for thirty years, is still very beautiful. Still she cannot be young now — perhaps forty; yes, she must be about ten years younger than me. They thought my room was dirty. It is no castle, I know, I know very well.

I want to live, I am cold, with this water flowing over my body.

From St Bartholomew to St Lazarus
from the twenty-fourth day of August to the second day of September

Her filthiness is in her skirts; she remembereth not her last end; therefore she came down wonderfully: she had no comforter. O Lord, behold my affliction; for the enemy hath magnified himself. (Lam. i 9)

I was tied down to my bed in a large room that I had never seen before. A woman forbade me to speak. I wanted to write, so I asked for materials, and then she untied me. Where is my habit? I am naked without a habit. This house is clean: how is it that the rats make that noise? I shall have to see Bernard to get rid of them. This lavender smells sweet. How long will this idiotic life last? I must escape.

I dragged myself over to the window; it is very high, I cannot climb down. Well then, I shall fly, and I shall be happy. That woman forced me to eat. Tonight I shall fly away. I have had enough, I shall go under the cemetery – there must be doors from one grave to another. I shall slip away, no one will see me. I shall get out, I shall go and rouse the abbot. After all, I must speak, mustn't I? Am I to be forbidden everything then?

How comfortable I am really; I enjoy sleeping. Last night I slept well. It is dark, the floor is polished parquet. Come, now is the time; I am going. I have been travelling during these last weeks. I want to write, I am cured, don't say anything more to me, do you hear! 'I have had enough of this. You know yourself that you are mad.' She is coming, she is here, I can hear her; listen. I can hear noise that she cannot hear. I shall pay her back – I am treated like a child. I see so many strange things. I felt that I absolutely must tell them what is happening to me; I went to Le Thoronet, I went in through the parlour, nobody saw me. This blood that is flowing down my arm. They have bled me. I attract the slimy rats with this blood; they will come back into my room, under my bed. I have a lot of visitors at present, sly people. It is really over; I am completely cured; I shall go back to Le Thoronet, the monastery is being completed.

The Lord hath done that which He had devised: He hath fulfilled His word that He had commanded in the days of old ... (Lam. ii 17)

94

The steeple's pyramid lit from within, soaring into the night, phosphorescent, ringed with light: what a marvel in that dark, lowering sky; luckily, the sun. My eyes hurt, looking, I can't hide myself any more, or walk along this bare finished wall, or go to earth. Only the pyramid between sky and earth. Weight of all these stones. The nettles come up to my knees. I can't see anything; luckily my brothers are helping me ... the door silently shuts again in the night. I am much better so, I knew it, these columns are too heavy; slip between them, the weight of the stones. I am shivering.

They are there, my good brothers, bowed towards the Lord, and holding a service. I feel out of place before the circular altar, completely empty. To see it! Never should I have thought it; a beautiful, magnificent, green and tawny beetle, big as a horse's head. A slimy liquid comes from its mouth, a yellowish liquid, bright as sulphur, a liquid that burns. My hand touches it, everything collapses. The beetle struggles clumsily; it melts. I knew I should not have touched it. No, it is night; only the pyramid above me, translucent, held up by the light of the altar, which shines brilliantly in the hollow space. My brothers are vanishing into the night: 'Don't leave me, don't leave me, it's not fair.' The liquid no longer lights up the white backs, tiny in the distance. Catch up with my brothers; my running steps echo, echo under this immense vault, my head strikes a column, my foot stumbles against the body stretched on the flagstones. Abbot Gerard holding his belly in pain, he vanishes in the far distance. I was going quickly, he falls and my head hurts. The vaults are above, very high; thank you for coming to me, thank you, it is over; I was weak. The woman binds up my arm that was bled, and smiles gently: 'Mother Clare, it's you! Protect me! Fear, you know, fear has put me here, this hole is deep and the water is rising, a sort of mud.' The door closes again, she has gone – she too. I can't see anything, and that closed door, I see myself in the depths, it is pitiful. I am frightened, I want to go away, leave myself behind, the mud is rising.

> ... *whosoever toucheth the carcase of them shall be unclean until the even: And whosoever beareth aught of the carcase of them shall wash his clothes, and be unclean until the even.* (Lev. xi 24–5)

Dreary desolation of the trees. Lichens and briars are growing over the walls of earth and mud, swollen facings ready to crumble on to my head. To get out of here. I want to get close and see why these walls are crumbling, falling with muffled noises around me. No, not worms—those black, ringed caterpillars that move about in columns in the summer. This decay is their work, I see them clearly now, the walls are made of worms. Bunches of them gnaw and fall, I crush them in thousands. They slide, fall, climb, bore, their numbers making them into one monstrous animal; the eggs were in the mortar. They are in my walls, everywhere, they are dropping from me all around. I can't stir from the walls, I'm wedged, I can't go either forward or back. The infirmarian lets me go, the door closes. He won't be able to come in any more, or hold me. To be able to sleep, to sleep, for pity's sake.

The door among the briars in full sunlight, the darkness shut up behind the door. To walk freely in the sun: calm, warmth, my tunic soaked, my enormous hand gives me no pain at all, none. I am walking over the rough, warm flagstones. To be allowed at last to breathe fresh air, icy air, snow, cold wind, fill my lungs. On the other side of this thick, warm steam. I can't see any more —what does it matter! Heavens! The cloister steps, they are pushing me: 'No, not so fast! Don't be foolish, I can't go down so fast, not so fast.' Below, the face, the hole—no, they're eyes, everywhere, oh stop! And in that calm I tell them everything, they look at me amused, they don't believe me, they think I am mad, I have to shout, 'A monster: you must go through a wall of loathsome, black, ringed worms, and then throw yourselves upon it, chain it up.' No, they say nothing, the shut faces remain silent.

> *I charge you ... that ye stir not up, nor awake my love, till he please ... eat, O friends: drink, and be drunken with loves.*
> (S. of S. ii 7, v 1)

The lanterns light up all that I have done. From my bed I can see the candles swaying in the icy night wind; it will soon be the feast of night. The cloister gay, the columns heavy, massive. The night blacker than ink. A supernatural effect, the fountain shines with all its fires, each jet has its taper. The candles burn in hundreds; the heat they throw out, like a brazier—it's lovely. I am going to die, why have I waited for this day, why do they leave me? I am alone, forsaken in this great dark room, a room in which a meagre fire is burning itself out. The cold strikes through me. Over there it is light, warm, the air comes through the door; the open window ought to warm me, so many tapers, but no, the chill of death. I am not thinking now of that adventure, it is a question of my soul. Impossible that they should not know, one goes through the rotten wall, penetrates to the monster's den. The monster? I must live, I must grasp the sword of my youth; ah, slowly to cut its throat or to drown it like a rat!

A head passes by the corner of the half-lighted wall: the abbot! ... he hides himself, watches, secretive as a small boy. I try to cry out, to speak; finger on lips, a sign to me for silence: he is to be taken by surprise. True, there are a number of them, they whisper. At last, I hear them playing a ball game, they are happy! They are in good health. Another head goes by, then another, each casts a glance, says to me, 'We are here, friend, but we cannot come near you, it is forbidden.' Thomas, Edgar, Paul, the abbot again, even Bernard and Étienne. There is one I was not expecting: Joseph, though not brave, has thrown something to me. I grope about for it, anxiously, he shows me by signs: more to the right, lower, lower. Ruddy-faced, they come one by one, they hide from one another, but they come. All utter the same word: 'Well?' and each goes away when the next arrives. They have all filed past, it is kind of them; why do they hide? The room is dark, I cannot see the vault now, only the walls; the cold has completely numbed me. Did they all come? Almost, yes, almost: hiding from one another. The light, the heat of the candles make me uneasy. Brothers, stay with me, I am afraid to look out of the window just behind me. Throw back your head, stretch your neck, your vertebrae are grating! Strength! support your forehead, crush yourself against the wall! My head drops noisily with one movement, no one heard the noise as you did; your neck is broken. You see the columns, the lights, the fountain, the church, the pillars, the columns. You see everything. Your brothers are chanting in the distance. The white habits appear to you in the perspectives, the cascades, the incense! All those people upside down. Upside down, my head on my swollen, dislocated neck, again arches, arches, a fantastic night ... admire it all! ... all is beauty ... perspective of thick alabaster, translucent matter ... see the plan, the sections, all the rooms ... the lanterns pass through the walls, paler now. The black strokes of the drawings are superposed on indistinct forms, then detach themselves, recede again. White! Everything is white: grotto, Estaillade, heavy columns, light columns, capitals, vaults superposed, superposed to infinity. The lights illuminate the night: the walls' whiteness, marble; no, it really is my stone, scaled by repeated strokes. The black lines reappear on the milk-white parchment, while my hand draws on that moving whiteness; I begin at one side and a moment later the stuff of the habits erases everything.

> *Thy breasts are like two young roes that are twins, which feed among the lilies. Thy neck is as a tower of ivory ... I have put off my coat; how shall I put it on? ... A garden enclosed is my sister, my spouse: a spring shut up, a fountain sealed. Your shoots are an orchard of pomegranates ... My beloved is white and ruddy ... (S. of S. iv 12ff)*

The Kyrie Eleison fills the vaults, swells, dies away, again increases your joy, the true joy; gold, gold streams everywhere in innumerable flames. A brother runs – Bernard! It is Bernard! 'Come, Bernard, light those thousands of candles. They are all singing for me, Bernard, you are fading, superposing, melting away, a pale silhouette, you are passing through the thick walls. Come back! come close by me.' He runs joyously: 'Light up! light up again! There will never be enough light.' Wax flows in the bowl, an icy fluorescence, crystal-black, stalactites of wax, fountain cascades: 'Light up again! Sing! Sing for me, again, always!' Your hands, hold out your hands, look at this long thin body, my neck broken, my fevered eyes throwing back the light – there is too much beauty. Body of charity, warm me! Help you to live, why? Do you not know my death? A passion bent on the infinity of white perspectives, lights! Song! Vaults! Transparencies! ... A calm repose in me ... peace.

> *Hearken to me, ye that follow after righteousness ... look unto the rock whence ye are hewn ... (Is. li 1)*

Temptation has fled. Pleasure is shattered, no movement is possible, everything is dying away. The songs have vanished, a sombre echo gives back the last long monotone: peace, silence, night, happiness, simplicity, one, three, seven lanterns.

> *Look unto ... the hole of the pit whence ye are digged. (Is. li 1)*

The door opened, and Sister Clare appeared. Taking my hand, she put her own on my brow; I shall sleep. The brother infirmarian came back, he smiled. The abbot entered, took my sheets of paper, and read them. Softly, on tiptoe, he withdrew to a corner near the window, settled himself and went on reading. Three times he turned towards me and gave me a long look. He seemed to make a decision, walked over to the fireplace and, when he was near it, bent down and threw the papers on to the hearth. I was uneasy, but no word came from my mouth. At last he saw me! Stooping, he picked up the pages of my notebook one by one. I managed to utter softly, 'Father'; but he seemed not to understand, and rolling them all up he pushed them under my blankets. I saw his thoughtful, astonished face melt into the mist: then I fell asleep. On waking, I touched my notebook. My dream, my nightmares, my hallucinations are there, I know. I shall try to transcribe them, to fill in the details of that world in which I have lived. I remember that I was haggard, emaciated; I fought like a devil in my bed. The little sister came in, I hid myself. She came over to me, raised my head and bathed my forehead, temples and mouth with vinegar and water. I observed this pitiable scene. When that accursed door closed again, I was afraid of the solitude; I drew near to myself and looked at myself very closely. It was at this moment that I regained consciousness, and saw myself hunting for my notebook. I drew in it, not letters, but curious signs, then I lost consciousness again. And, shivering with cold, I huddled once more under the blankets.

Sometimes I feel so comfortable, hovering between being a dying man and a dreary, barren return to life. At least I am alive and thinking, whereas my self is prey to the horrible and the supernatural. I envy myself, I detest myself. That sunken, pale face, that feverish gaze is painful to me. I do not want to stay with myself any more. I go out on tiptoe, for if I wake myself I shall be obliged to remain, to keep awake, always to see my poor body stretched out, drenched, unshaven, smelling of fever and death. Enough of that: I am going to breathe the fresh air, smell the plants, take advantage of the fine weather. I was dedicated to myself, but now the self disgusts me. Look out! noises ... they will find me in this dark passage, tie me up, lay me down with him once more. It is just what I had expected. I took myself in my arms, disgusting though I was, and held myself hard — poor me!

In the semi-darkness the walls are grey, then blue — that blue of the very early morning, of the heralding of day. The walls grow light, but everything else remains dark; the curtains about my bed seem to stir against that luminous wall. A pungent perfume, memory of early joys ... I think I am dreaming: only my pain reminds me of my real life; the walls go on receding. A soft, light, perfumed air — the air of a cool, sunny morning after a stormy night. I touch my eyes and pull down my eyelids with my hand; when I reopen them, I know I am alive.

St Lazarus, second day of September

It has been given to me to live through moments in which supernatural things seem familiar and logically connected. I do not claim to discern a sign from God in the descriptions of my delirium, nor do I attribute symbolic significance to the effects of fever. No, these dreams are usual and bring with them visions which we must accept. All my life I have meditated on the power of dreams, on the undeniable aid they provide in our lives as builders. I have never tried to start a controversy with anyone. In the deep secret places of invention, the dream holds a predominant place. Inspiration may be conscious or unconscious: the work is without prejudice and can profit from anything.

This morning I awoke clear-headed and refreshed. I got up and walked about. Later I ate with a good appetite. I feel light-headed. I want to get back to my site, my hut, and start on my drawings.

St Sabina, third day of September

Tomorrow I shall return to Le Thoronet. The abbot was torn between the need to assert his authority by making me stay here and the desire to see the plan completed and work begun. He chose the deadly sin and identified it with higher considerations. In the discussions between him and the infirmarian, 'Will he have enough strength to work?' was really the only question to which he wanted an answer. I won without speaking a single word.

Bernard came to see me. I told him how much progress had been made. 'But', he remarked, 'you have decided nothing so far.' That is quite true. I do very little drawing when I am making a study — at most a few tiny sketches on the corner of my drawing-board, erased at once. I prefer the shape to rise within me in succeeding visions which become fixed, imprinted, and accumulate behind my eyes. While this slow, difficult work is proceeding, I speak, walk, sleep, dream, carrying over into my daily life the state of hypnosis induced by obsessive preoccupation with the task in hand. When the time is ripe I bend over my drawing-board and draw the basic features of the world I have imagined. I feel certain that musicians proceed in this way; they must surely wait for the composition to sing within them before writing it down.

This account of my method troubled Bernard. 'I did not think', he said, 'that a master builder could keep everything in his head, that he could dispense with preliminary drawings and with the important part played by the many questions that arise out of technical problems and static calculation.' In making this observation, Bernard was committing the error of separating visible form from internal calculation. All roads lead to Rome, and each of us approaches form in his own individual way. For my part, I have frequently admired the method of the Oriental masters; it appears to have been handed down from the earliest times. Common to numerous Byzantine, Arab and Persian architects, it is expressed in the form of a dream:

Cloaked in mystery, the master builder comes at dawn to the site, assembles the craftsmen on an area of smooth, prepared, fine sand, traces out the day's work with the tip of his gold-pommelled staff, and, mysteriously, carries away to his cool house the conceptions and shapes he will define at the next day's dawning. In the evening, as he contemplates his white marble, many-spouted fountain, he dreams about his plans, which are as perishable as his own life, as clear as his firm gaze, as poetic as his own nostalgic land. If the fancy moves him, he claps his hands, and his round-armed slave appears. In the curving shapes of her body he will visualize the domes, the piercing of fabulous vaults, and astounding pendentives. In the beloved voice, he will hear an echo of galleries of slim columns carved with abstract shapes, the course of a small cascade, the planting out of a garden with orange trees, jasmine and stramony. In his dream he will prepare for another dawn to be enchanted by his gold-pommelled staff.

To the nobility of the method is allied a deep humanity: the craftsmen are more the fabricators of the building than simple, careful workmen carrying out orders. These master builders allow all the men on the site to participate in the project, thus leaving them the right to interpret their part, without, however, damaging the architectural proportions. We in the West consider that exact plans are indispensable, but they — they replace them with rhythmic songs, suggest them by lines in the sand. An imperative module governs the whole edifice and lays down the basic dimension; after that, word of mouth suffices. Thus each one can live his share of the dream in divining and adapting the original thought. I am not inventing this — things really are done in that way. It is enough to follow the lines of a Greek fret carved on complicated pendentives to be assured for ever of the initiative and the liberty accorded to the eastern artisan.

Lying on my bed with my eyes half closed, I amused myself with lecturing Bernard. Whenever I speak to him of my distant travels, his mind becomes less curious, he accepts ideas without questioning them. He asked me, 'How do these masters know in advance that a building designed in that way won't collapse?' This was what led us to consider the idea of unity of conception, the cornerstone of our art. In his previous remark, technical problems had already seemed to be isolated from formal design. When did it happen, this separation — if only in spirit — of the plastic arts and technique, of form and materials? 'Architect' and 'master builder' are no mere titles; they really are definite and independent functions. Forms, volumes, weights, resistances, thrusts, the rise of arches, equilibrium, movement, lines, loads and overloads, damp, dryness, heat and cold, sounds, light, shadow and half-shadow, directions, earth, water and air — in short, all materials, each and every one, are contained within the supreme function, within the single brain of the ordinary man who builds. That man will be everything: clay and sand, stone and wood, iron and bronze. He will integrate, identify himself with every material, every element, every external and internal stress. Thus he will carry them, estimate them, sound them, see them with his very soul as though he held them in his hands. These presumptions are not metaphors; I deny any poetic intention. I am asserting material facts which for me are indisputable. I think of them prosaically. If I am a wooden beam placed between two supports twenty feet apart, I estimate the resistance of my fibrous loins, and I thicken to attain the sectional dimension that will enable me to resist the flexion entailed by my own weight and that which I am to carry. At the same time I think of my outward appearance, my trajectory's visual effect and my colour: in this way I decide what I am to be made of, oak or spruce. All this process is going on during the time when I am thinking creatively in plastic terms: it is a parallel activity. The elementary example I have just described applies to all contingencies; the beam is a simplified image for the flying buttress and its light structure, for the solid buttress and for the arch. I can and must divide myself into the stones of an arch, feel myself to be keystone, breast, summer or simple arch-stone, know the stone in my flesh, look on it as my own skin, make it follow the chosen line and the nascent volume. The form will be justified by the choices made. Structure is everything, form is everything, matter is everything. How can this mystery be explained if one does not admit that man contains these 'everythings' under his own roof? Why speak of calculations that are nothing, that create nothing—all the technical problems being summed up in the form? Is it necessary to check the volumes once they are achieved? Probably for the satisfaction and pleasure of telling oneself, 'Yes.' And if the reply is 'No,' what is one to conclude? Must one start again, go back over the task? My own views are that nothing owes its existence to the brain of a sick man, and that no man practises a single craft any more—perhaps they never did. Calculations are a proof, they will never be a means. Could the first builder count? No. On the other hand, he had an aim, an intention: to shelter himself. The necessity became beautiful, because that man had before his eyes Nature and her sky, light and its colours, mountains and their shapes, stones and their substance. In the collapse of the first edifice there was the first failure and, no doubt, the first anxiety, the first calculation. To make calculation sacred would amount to recognizing failure as original work. Is that admissible? Every theory can be defended, but I leave the task to men of good faith. In conclusion, I believe that duality or plurality in the work's conceiving is worse than a weakness — it is a vice. That is to say, beauty cannot exist without balance, technique without material, nor, finally, balance without beauty. My only anxiety tonight is that Bernard may not have understood.

> If, strictly speaking, I prefer a twofold god to a manifold god, I am no longer interested in him at all once I find a single one; for, to express myself like a good Catholic, this single god alone is truly God. He no more has in Him this or that thing, than these things or those things; He is that which is and not the things that are. (Bernard of Clairvaux)

St Giles, fifth day of September

Yesterday I came back to Le Thoronet. How many journeys to Florielle have I made since my first arrival? I think I must know all the roads; the shortest paths, the fords over the Argens, on foot or on mule-back, and the cart tracks. Now I know the reasons which lead us to abandon Florielle: the poor soil cannot feed the community. Despite the advantage of the stream which never runs dry and thus enables us to water the cultivated land in hot weather, the monks are too numerous to be able to go on living there without help. There was, obviously, another solution: to remain at Florielle and build a farm at Le Thoronet; but it was too far away. It is not right to leave the lay brothers on their own, or to make the monks travel continually; it is a long way, all ups and downs. In Champagne, with its less frequent changes of level, six leagues are nothing; here one seems to be going from one province to another. We have to cross the Argens; and then again, the walk to the north involves hours of travelling in an easterly or a southerly direction; the contours of this country make one despair. For heavy loads the easiest way is to make the crossing at Pont d'Argens, go by way of Lorgues, then climb up to Tourtour.

A quarter of a league from there a rough road connects with the valley of the Florielle and with the abbey. From Le Thoronet one must therefore go down to the bridge, and then up an interminable hill to Tourtour. When loaded, the carts take six full hours — if there is no wind and if it is not too hot. The return journey is quicker — four hours — and pleasanter. For a long time one is walking towards the sun through the forest, and the light and shade are beautiful, especially in the early morning.

The rabbits and the smaller carnivores play as they run away. The partridges startle us with the sudden flapping and then the whirr of their wings as they take flight. The blind wild things rush for their own paths through the briars, and the anxious wild sow shepherds her young away at the trot. I love the forest and its wild life; I also love to get back to Le Thoronet. Florielle is too enclosed; in winter the sun must appear late and disappear almost at once. It is very cold there, apparently, because of the mountain air. The wind from the north-west sweeps through its little valley, which lies as if that were intended. The abbey was unskilfully founded, set down anyhow. The plan must have been cramped by the temporary buildings, level ground being scarce. It was written that we should not remain there.

I set out at dawn, under a clear sky and in the kind of cool September weather one wishes for all year round on the sites. The abbot and infirmarian came with me and helped to settle me in the litter. On the way, cradled by the motion, I fell asleep, and woke again in the forest when the grasshoppers were loud. Enviously I noted the handsome trees — many more than we had, and quite straight. Then, in the slanting rays of the first warm sunlight, I watched the wildlife. I looked for the arrogant fox, as curious as he is timid; before disappearing he cannot resist pointing his muzzle at the intruder while presenting his hindquarters and deplorable summer brush. I did not catch sight of a single one. In this blessed month the animals, freed from love's cares and from dangerous venturings into frequented paths, are taking advantage of the last fine days. One sees fewer of them, one senses their presence on their perches or crouching in remote clearings, near a spring or stream. I was happy despite my weakness. I was expecting to find great changes. It was a fortnight since I had left Le Thoronet, and nearly a month since I had looked at anything. Returning to a site after an absence, one has the pleasure of noting what is new, whereas progress made while one is there is hardly realized. Will they have levelled the ground next to the Field, dug out the boulder on the cloister site, faced the northern excavation that threatened to fall in? Will the stack of dressed blocks be impressive? And what of the kilns, the felling, the fields soon to be sown?

Life goes on. For a few days no doubt the shades of Thomas and of Philippe were everywhere, and then other events must have gently effaced them. So it is with all things. Perhaps, I thought, the gap up there is already filled. In any case, sites are stronger than feelings and men; they carry memories away as a torrent bears off the tree torn from the bank. The leafy branches grow heavy and disappear, the trunk sways, the roots break surface, showing their hooked, hairy, witches' fingers. On the dark-green bed the distant foam shrouds what had seemed fixed in its place for centuries to come. After a few days, one would be surprised to see the great tree once more bending over the torrent. On sites, the walls that rise and enclose the countryside are still more impressive: they abolish what seemed to man to be made to last for ever. No builder can imagine the ruin and annihilation of his work. Not only does the site occupy a space: it also claims to become the main feature of the landscape, of which Nature is to be merely the complement. I was at this stage in my thoughts when, from Sainte Foy Wood, I caught sight of Lorgues, and I murmured, 'The steeple of Lorgues rises on the plain, against the blue background of the hills.'

An hour later we had crossed the Argens, swollen by the first storms. Once over the bridge, the mules, despite the rising ground, hastened their pace. For us, the remainder of the journey is already covered; we have arrived. No, I shall not catch sight, in Joseph's den, of Philippe at the wheel or taking tiles from the kiln. No more shall I see the slight head movement that said, better than any words, 'Good morning, elder Brother.'

This last ascent made me think of the monks pushing and dragging the wagons that are to come all together from Florielle some time in the distant future. They will be singing as they take the slope, then they will arrange the straw mattresses in the chilly dorter where the smell of lime still clings. In the church with its honey-coloured stalls they will sing yet again, wear the passage flagstones to a smooth polish and round off the sharp corners of the oak, so that it becomes like old grey bone.

At the last turn in the road I heard familiar sounds: a distant clanking accompanied by heavy thuds and screechings from the sawmill.

The Field, in full sunlight, was more dried up and dusty than ever, without a single patch of the grass that had given it its name. My brothers had left everything to welcome me. After the recent dramatic events they were eager to see me again. Benoît and Bernard helped me to alight. The intense glare of the site forced me to shut my eyes as if in a dazzling dream. It was at that moment that I was seized by an incomprehensible anger. With bitter irony I asked, 'Is it time for the break?' With a gesture, Benoît sent everyone away; only the craftsmen came to greet me. I was weary from the journey but I insisted on going everywhere; and everywhere I was disappointed. I gave voice to my displeasure. Sickness had put me in a position of inferiority; that was why I criticized everything—the orders that had been given, the initiatives taken, the relaxation in the schedule—even though this last was justified by an appreciable shortening of daylight hours. I reproached them with wastefulness in the work of consolidation. Benoît, irritated, then said to me, 'If we had had your plans we should have known, and these mistakes would not have been made.' His ill humour soothed me, for I felt myself less alone in my ungraciousness—I had a companion with a guilty conscience. Since dawn that day I had been determined to take over control of the site once more, and I had thought to assert myself by abuse of authority and by injustice. The hour of our meal brought me release. I had asked the craftsmen to our table to discuss the work. That finished, I asked Bernard to read out the regulations, then I rose to announce that the common repast at Sext would be abolished: the brother kitchener would take soup to the places of work. By this means, I concluded, we should gain one hour's work. The period on Saturday set aside for upkeep of clothes and shoes would henceforth be spent on the site; such petty tasks could easily be done by lamplight. Instead of causing dissatisfaction, these orders were well received; it was thought, no doubt, that this frail brother still had a strong hand to keep discipline; and then again, I think I may ask for life itself now.

A new brother has joined us since my arrival. He listened with attention. At table I sat on his right. He now occupies the central place in our assemblies, directs prayers, celebrates canonical offices in the chapel, inspects everything each day, briefly asks for advice and explanations; then he offers his opinion when all are silent. He never breaks in. In the attitude I took yesterday, his presence incited me to be outrageous and challenging — so much so that I feared at every moment to be interrupted, contradicted or called to order. I meant to assert before him that the site and the schedule were my business, to define my rights over the physical life of the craftsmen and lay brothers. On this monk depends the spiritual and temporal discipline of the Rule. He arranges for the assemblies, strikes the hours, attends to the steward's work, organizes the menus and directs the farming. He has installed himself in a shelter we call the sacristy, placed under the bell, against the chapel. Brother Pierre, Prior of Florielle, represents the abbot at Le Thoronet; thanks to him we are a true community.

From Sext to Vespers we went on with the tour: the quarries, the forge, the kilns and Joseph's cave. We returned to the workshops. I inspected the store room and stables, then we walked for some time in the fields. The clearing in the flat land to the west is encouraging, it will be good soil for vines, heavy and rich.

I could no longer manage to lift my bad leg, and I felt queasy. My brothers told me that I looked ghastly but did not dare to stop me. After a brief turn round the upper quarry, we ended up at the sawmill. It was there that it happened; just as I was hoping to get to the workshop in time to lie down, I suddenly saw the pile of chips spin and become huge. I had fallen. Bells were ringing, hastily, gaily. Among the clean, fragrant shavings a bright red froth was spreading. Little by little the gurgling in my throat ceased. Because of that blood, everyone today is showing me affection. Uppermost in my men's hearts was not my deplorable behaviour but the pluck of the sick man, rousing mixed feelings of pity and admiration. I hope this relapse will not hinder me from working.

Nativity of the Blessed Virgin, eighth day of September

Is it due to all the reflection of these last months, or to the mediocrity of my initial sketches? I do not know yet, but I am designing and locating with ease, first the church and the apse, together with the four round-ended apsidal chapels, then the sacristy and, round the cloister, in the usual order, the library, the chapter house, the dorter staircase, the passage to the parlour, the monks' hall and the warming room, the refectory, the kitchen, and finally the store room and the lay brothers' dorter, which complete the cloister on the west, on the obtuse-angled side. These conformations, which used to frighten and overawe me, now emerge effortlessly as I use my four instruments. Maybe this is how our venture will end — without worries or suffering, but in the joy of controlled activity. If I did not know that there are pitfalls ahead, it would seem that I should be finished in a few hours, a few days. Why this dimension rather than another? Why this proportion rather than another? I do not know, I have never known.

When I first set eyes on the site and the position, I visualized the abbey we were to build as one of those elaborate Tuscan constructions of smooth marble: a thing of infinite, complicated luxury. What I am drawing now is heavy and clumsy. I am immersed in the pleasure to be had from simple volumes and rectilineal walls ... a simple Cistercian abbey, like hundreds of others, composed of the set of buildings to which I have given a unity and which embodies a part of me. The difficulty in this unique piece of work will therefore be, as before, to retain simplicity and humility. The complexity of my earlier thoughts has vanished. I walk about calmly, without anxiety, in this plan and these sections. I walk beside the façades as if I had always lived here. Where are my abstract ideas, my world of dreams and hallucinations? It is so easy to plan as mere master builder of a strict Order that will allow neither weakness, nor falsehood, nor variation in its scheme: church, chapter house, warming room, refectory, all enclosing the cloister. My day was spent in drawing like a good monk, mason and master builder.

St Pulcheria, tenth day of September

You wish to see, listen then: hearing is a step in the direction of vision. (Bernard of Clairvaux)

Bent over the drawings, we follow the sketches on the overall plan, which shows the buildings in relation to each other. Our eyes move about rapidly, surveying, following, then pursuing and briefly capturing some fugitive vision. The outline recedes from our minds, swallowed up in a temporary obscurity, for everything that is no longer clearly seen, vanishes, leaving in the memory only an impression that blurs and then disappears. In this gallery of the cloister, the eye falls on a new object; there it is, above, to the right ... let us walk along, don't let us slow down ... Let us establish the fact that as we turn our heads the large masses hold still, or turn more slowly, as though they were on a sculptor's stand. In this way we check or moderate the displacement entailed by our walking. Let us now adopt the pace of an observant stroller, let us select, let us halt. One's eyes rest, the shapes tilt or succeed each other, pass by and return, according to the movements of one's head, so that three-quarters of the interior surface of a sphere can be seen. Let us go forward; now the volumes disposed about the great space we have already passed through are about to disappear. Our gaze fixes on the door of the chapter house; it and the wall come towards us, growing, taking up the entire angle of vision; the arch is level with our shoulders and above us. Swift though it is, the effect of our movement is striking: before, during, after — there is a complete change lasting for a time that can be limited at will. Henceforth the range of our perceptions will be extended in this place. Our gaze, curious at the threshold, grows used to the half light, falters in the confined space enclosed by these low vaults, is caught at last and falls into contemplation. The eye will be aware that, without straining, it is the centre of the sphere. Through half-turns and slight inclinations of the head it can retain an impression of the whole, for everything is near; it has no need to search because it registers without moving. Small enclosed areas bring restless people to a halt and cause them to look, to think and to seek in their hearts for another way.

Would it be fairer to say that the movement of the eye inside the plan was only one way of imagining? Drawings, being small-scale, abstract representations, show only two dimensions. It would be better to consider the eye as not moving and to put before it an endless number of three-dimensional drawings, making them turn and tilt within the angle of vision. Or again, starting from the drawn plan, one could build the verticals with stiff filaments; each filament would represent the straight or curved edges of all the volumes, thus reproducing the lines of the drawings in plan, section and elevation. Such a skeleton of shapes would be to the eye what the cage is to the bird. On reflection, this solution to the problem of vision would be only one more way of describing a system. The power remains in the imagination; is the ability to visualize a special gift?

Volumes are full and at the same time empty. Sometimes they are like milestones along a road, sometimes enclosed spaces, covered in or open to the sky. In the cloister, for example, we are conscious of a volume of air and light set into the stones: arcades, columns, walls—a double awareness existing side by side with their three dimensions and their movements. The mould is of stone, its product will be air and light; they cannot do without one another, and we owe it to ourselves to imagine them together. As we walk in the garden, we shall see that air and light flow like liquid crystal; we shall see them penetrate into and fill the galleries up to the summit of the vaults, embracing every shape up to the rooftops and finally merging into the sky. After this, both stones and atmosphere will seem to be volumes, the one impenetrable, the other fluid and transparent. United under one 'skin', their movements will coincide.

It is this constant visual evocation that decides the nature of architectural structures. If a master builder, a pure aesthete, could visualize with perfect accuracy, he would be able to avoid the adventure of construction and keep his imaginary edifices to himself. It never is so; every builder gets his share of surprises in the realization of the project. This is quite usual. No artist does exactly what he wishes; the brush either helps the painter or plays him false. Sometimes it can startle with an unexpected effect; sometimes it counteracts the trembling of his hand; the bristles may be too dry or the colour too liquid. We must frankly admit that the site always holds surprises for us, whether good or bad.

Architecture keeps back a part of its mystery, revealing it only piecemeal, and not surrendering it completely until all the volumes are in position. The work in progress is a discussion, whether disappointing or full of promises. We search for arguments. We listen to reverberations without yet knowing what they will be like in the end. All these excitements cannot be entirely foreseen and understood in advance. That is good; a site without worry would be like a life without suffering.

After the cloister, the halls and the galleries, let us examine the plans of the church. In the interior of the cloister we were considering volumes sculpted in the round; they were important elements in our imaginary battle. Here our care will be for the surface of a volume hollowed out of the mass. The notion of density has vanished, it no longer concerns us. The arches merge into the walls, and everything is in low relief. We must imagine that we are under a mountain of stones; so this void will be planned with greater depth. The light will come from above. Sheltered from the world by infinite thicknesses, we shall communicate only with heaven. Below, slits, low doors; above, round windows whence our songs will escape like a great flight of doves; those circular apertures are the doors of the spirit.

St Raphael, twelfth day of September

The plan is making rapid progress; the volumes merge, separate, then re-form. Everything is scrapped; then, the problems having been solved, the shape becomes simpler and purer. I no longer go out, for I cannot move about easily. I am completing my convalescence at my table. Bernard stays with me, curious about what I say and draw; he completes my sketches. He is now more skilful in drawing than I.

Not that everything is simple; the fever of anxiety rises. The abbey will be essentially of Le Thoronet, not just any abbey. But the further I proceed with marking pillars and walls on the smooth, ivory parchment, the more conscious I become of the difficulties. The ink flowing from the sharp point fills in or encloses the stone volumes, traces the edges, outlines the halls, indicates where strength is needed and where passages must be kept open for air, light or monks. Sometimes I am guided by reason, sometimes by sentiment or the need to straighten a line. In some places geometry and symbols come together, and their synthesis determines shapes. Every moment is serious but light-hearted. I feel sure of myself — too sure. Frequently I find that further scrutiny of a problem leads to something preferable, better, or quite simply to the best solution. It is at times when a master builder allows his mastery of technical skill to guide him, or when he is bent on working out the details of a complicated form, that the serenity of a building is in danger. Fortunately one's second self knows this, lets one go on, and waits — then suddenly makes one aware that at last the truth is about to emerge. One hears a warning click, as it were. As long as scruple and conscience do not set down the line as surely as would destiny, we must be on our guard against imagination. It also happens, in the course of drawing up the plan, that some parts of the building look better to us than others. To think this natural seems unavoidable, yet we should take it as a warning. Go over it again, strive towards perfect unity of the elements one with another, seek the Whole. In an abbey there should be nothing that is 'best', nothing that is 'not so good'. Our acts as monks and our gestures, even those made unconsciously in our sleep, are under the eye of the Lord; they are the gauge by which the unity of the house is measured. If the conception of the apse makes particular demands on our skills so as to mark the place of the Real Presence of the Body and Blood, this merely confirms to us that the whole monastery is everywhere a place of prayer and contemplation, a unity of action and intention.

It is an exciting thing to bring an abbey to life, in company with the monks, before its inauguration. For me, the moments when I really perceive how my brothers will live are perhaps the only times when I express my faith. I see them rising, kneeling, walking towards the church, round the cloister, making their ablutions at the fountains, dreaming in front of the warming-room fire: a slow, precise, measured rhythm. I see them really going by, I follow them with my eyes. They are no phantoms; I hear them breathing, murmuring, walking, I catch their smell. With cowls pulled forward, heads slightly bent and hands in sleeves, they go by. I efface myself, my back to the wall, to give them room. They go about, performing their orderly movements without unseemly haste. The Rule requires their lives to be devoid of needless bustle; they must not waste their time, nor attempt to catch up with it. Our architecture is moulded around their actions. Each day, each night, the passing of the monks is like a thread being wound up, smoothly, with slight, regular sounds. The canonical offices, accompanied by subdued chants, measure out the day from one dawn to the next. Feast days mark out the year from one Christmas to another. The architecture supplies the setting: we have to follow that thread of white wool in the form and the spirit of our volumes. To create without unity would be to run counter to the way we express our existence. Nothing is unexpected, not even a monk's death, for each day we think of our own and our brothers' end. When a monk begins his death throes, strokes are sounded on stone slabs in the cloister to remind the community that the whole of that day is to be dedicated to one of us. From that moment, nothing else influences what we do. The death of a brother is like the end of a chapter in our books. Tomorrow another will be begun. His place in the dorter and the refectory, his stall in the church, will be taken by another monk. Some days later a man knocks at the door: 'What do you want?' asks the porter ...

Once more I have evoked the monastic life that I have imagined a hundred times, but never experienced myself. Even if such thoughts have the power of purifying and exalting my creation, I must nevertheless admit that I am deeply disturbed, full of anxiety and material cares, of remorse, anger and temptations. How could it be otherwise? To set the scene for a life of serenity one must surely lead a different kind of existence, in contrast. Suffering begets joy, disequilibrium aspires to stability. Human creation is vanity in the eyes of a saint, yet in the work itself lies the redemption of him who carries it out. The happy man is dull in company; but jugglers and inventors of tricks are said to be always melancholy folk, and for my part I believe it. We are building the abbey, not in the midst of harmony, but with struggles, doubts, accidents and strife.

Since my return I have not been going to the quarries and the workshops; I venture only to the site. There the need for plans is felt every day, and this obliges me to improvise on the spot, to sketch out almost at random the work to be undertaken. Benoît has complete responsibility for the preparation of materials; he reports on daily production to me. Like a miser, he amasses notes and figures about stones, wood and tiles. I receive few visits; they don't want to disturb me. The sense of waiting is stronger among the others than it is here in our workshop. For me, the birds are on the spit, the fire glows red, the guests are about to go to table; I must attend to the roasting.

St Edith, sixteenth day of September

The abbot paid me a visit in company with the prior. For a long time he looked at the steeple on the overall drawings of the exterior.

'Too high,' he said, 'forbidden by the Rule. I require that you reduce the height, or do away with the steeple altogether. A plain wooden tower would do for us.'

Yet, ever since I came here, I have been obsessed by this design. It is going to be difficult to win the abbot over.

The slope of the ground both necessitates and suggests a most unusual arrangement of the cloister galleries: the southern one will be higher than the rest, and two sets of steps at the south ends of the east and west galleries will bridge the difference in level. The abbot was not satisfied. 'We shall not be able to meditate without needing to watch our steps; always going up and down—this strikes me as impossible.'

'It is not necessary to walk round the cloister,' I replied. 'This arrangment is imposed upon us, in this situation it is a necessity.'

'Let us go and look at it,' he said.

My faltering steps showed the abbot the way. The best thing in these cases is to let the other talk and find out. The hard rock settled the matter; he was convinced. However, as we were returning he said to me, 'If you were King of the Persians with a thousand slaves, what would you have done?'

'I should have added ten steps.'

He halted, looked at me for some time, his shoulders thrown back. 'Know that I have not been deceived, but the ground became the first accomplice of the falsehood; I myself am the second.'

'The third is more certain: we shall save time.'

'Oh, time! Do you believe in that?'

He was right; time is either an ally or an enemy. But the steeple is indispensable; I have made many drawings showing it from every angle. This simple, sturdy pyramid is needed to justify the monotonous blind façades. As one approaches from the east it will rise, appearing suddenly in one dimension; from the west, it will reign over the valley like a statue.

St Sophia, eighteenth day of September

One day announces this truth to another day and one night gives knowledge of it to another night. (Ps. xix 1)

It was on the day after Brother Philippe's death that the abbot sent us Brother Pierre, Prior of Notre Dame de Florielle, a monk of my own age and in robust health. I had wanted an abbot, I have found a friend. I was hoping for a restraining influence, I have got a tactful, clear-sighted helper. This man with his contemplative mind did not pronounce his views immediately, he is quiet and deliberate.

'Brother,' he said yesterday, 'I have looked at everything, I believe I have seen everything. The chief problem here is your failing health; you wanted to give your life to this task, but you have given your soul. Without you, the world that you have created will be no more than a body without a mind. The Lord has preserved my strength; when you are obliged to rest, I want to be the keeper of your flame and to guard your memory until the end. I shall learn here, for as long as possible, what you intend. If I survive you, I want to carry on, to become your heir and dispose of your goods. Meanwhile I shall share with you the burden of your affairs.'

'Thank you, Brother. I do not deserve what you say, but the support and affection that you give me are a great comfort to me. I was not expecting you, yet you have come, bringing me the fruits of your whole lifetime. You know me well; for that very reason your help will be all the more valuable. This site is in my view more important than the previous ones, so forgive whatever may be surprising in my behaviour — certain instances of rash haste, for example.'

Pierre the prior was looking at the distant mountains, and I felt that he was troubled, undecided and worried. We were near the banks of the stream; it was the day's end, and after Vespers, and a calm night was in prospect. I suggested that we should rest beneath a young willow.

The silence was broken only by the noise of the stones that Pierre the prior threw into the stream. The sun, a glowing disc, cast pale rays like golden dust, in which the gnats played out their one evening of life.

The prior was the first to rise. Facing the light, he went on, 'I, a monk who has known the life of an ordinary man, have become attached to you as a friend. I am sure that God will forgive this feeling in me and will understand it. We can no longer treat your disease; the good Sister Clare has expressly charged me to give you soothing drugs to ease your sufferings, and help you to bear the sickness that consumes you.'

Impulsively I managed to bring out these words, 'Pierre, one day you will be the Abbot of Le Thoronet. For your sake, and thanks to you, I know that I shall find in my heart that fire that shapes a soul. Never forget, whenever you come across it, that it was you who gave it to me, that I owe it to you, that it watches over you and wraps you about like a light, warm garment, exhaling an everlasting perfume of love. May God pardon me these transports and this joy!'

His large, sinewy hands gently took me by the shoulders, and his look was penetrating. 'It is true', he said, 'that the Cistercian Order was founded for supreme penitence. It is true that long ago we gave up freedom, wealth, pleasure; I realized that in those good things was hidden, like the worm within the fruit, bitterness for every day, rottenness at the last. Then let us not be hypocrites! Let us relish the serene joys of penitence, let us live our enthusiasm, reflect on our struggles, and measure their importance by victories won over our internal foes! Let us accept our joyful life without pulling the long face of the false penitent! The steady intensity of that life will lift us up even to exaltation — even to the dangerous point beyond which it becomes pride!'

St Eustace, twentieth day of September

That ye ... may be able to comprehend with all saints what is the breadth, and length, and depth, and height; and to know the love of Christ, which surpasseth knowledge. (Eph. iii 17–19)

What charm those buildings have that are added to by numerous master builders at various times! This one will not have that quality. The difficulties of the site's unevenness govern the whole plan; the architecture must follow the gentle turbulence of the slopes. Out of a large block of soft clay, the ingenious and skilful Brother Alfonse is moulding and carving a model in relief, cutting walls, pillars and columns up to a height of two inches. The entire chapter is much interested in this work. Today our abbot gravely escorted them here. In this house of silence news travels quickly, so no one was unaware of the scheme in hand. Conversation and criticism were authorized for the space of one hour. 'This is a chapter meeting,' said the abbot. The excitement aroused by the plans for the new residence, which is now sure to be built, is very understandable. Determined to speak out, I described the steeple as a merchant vaunts his wares, ignoring the abbot's views.

'Brothers, this steeple is a direct inspiration. Though most of the elements of the composition have aroused many doubts, the steeple has obtruded itself upon me like a vision. Let me explain, Brothers, that it represents the mantle of the Virgin, who watches over the monastery. For me, it is certainly not an unfinished statue, it is the expression, the general shape of that stiff mantle, so heavy, embroidered and gem-covered is the cloth. When in place, it will cover the apse and dominate the transept. The sacred cape will envelop your monks' stalls in the imagined extension of its folds. An abstract shape, if you will, but to us, to me as master builder, it is clear that we are thus intimately blending poetry and reality, plastic form and preconception. You remember, no doubt, that worried monk who looked for his Cistercian brothers in paradise. Not finding any, he threw himself weeping at the Virgin's feet. The Lady of Heaven leaned towards him, helped him to rise, unclasped her cloak a little, and showed him all the Cistercians grouped about the Abbot Bernard. That sacred legend inspired our abbey's steeple.'

They could already see themselves beneath this imaginary mantle which encloses their stalls in its folds. Benoît and the prior escorted the brothers to the site, while the abbot and I sat down on my mattress.

'My son,' he said, 'you have surprised and shattered me; why did you not speak to me like that when I visited you? Do you think I have no feeling? Now tell me, is this story really true? This mantle?'

'Father, forgive me, my convictions caused me to dramatize. In fact, everything is both reality and falsehood; we never know what is sincerity and what is deceit in what we think and speak. Was it so at the beginning? I do not think so. Only recently the steeple was to me an indefinite and abstract shape; but when the moment came for drawing, I seem to recall seeing that slender pyramid as a saint, a monk. Then the triangle of the Trinity suggested to me the representation of a fourth: the mother — a form without shoulders, slim, delicate; it appeared to me everywhere predominant in the valley. Now, Father, I believe that I believe what I have related. And for you, Father, is the legend of the mantle true? What do you think? Is it an image or a future reality?'

'The one as much as the other, my son. I believe that this blessedness is real in paradise: to be close to Her whom we love with all our souls, who on earth took the place of the wives we have voluntarily forgone. I can see myself, without seeing myself. Reality and legend come face to face. Paradise is as much an image as it is an immaterial place created for the happiness of souls. Body and habit are with us no more, but the holy, uplifting presence is there in a form which admits of contemplation by our unmasked senses. So that for us poor humans the actual representation, as shown by our artists, is true; it must suffice us. Children, villeins, monks, bishops and kings can believe in the same forms and holy visions. I tell you, my son, I was moved when you spoke; I saw myself really under that mantle, just as you described it. I handled the thick cloth and, grown chilly with age, I thought of a fur lining. As you went on, I was filling in your suggestions in the most material of ways, do you understand? I know that it is impossible that it should not be so, and it shall be. The power of God's paradise is as far removed in size and feeling from our powers of perception as we are different from the universe; then why should there not be images, skilful or naive, and artists' visions? Henceforth, my son, I shall be in truth the best champion of that symbol which it so moved me to glimpse. He will be strong indeed who shall hinder you from building our abbey's steeple. I believe now in your vision; you have deserved it; I envy and bless you.'

Why am I hesitant and evasive, reticent and bashful over questions relating to my work? In everything else I feel at ease; but this subject causes a strange modesty, a mysterious timid feeling to seep into my consciousness. I feel that in speaking about it I reveal something intimate, precious and embarrassing. I have to make a real effort each time I show something that matters so much to me. On reflection, I imagined myself a merchant or an actor when I spoke of the steeple; by so doing I felt protected enough to reveal my deep and sincere feelings. The abbot has helped me to understand.

St Matthew

Hear Him speak to men: 'By as much as the heavens are raised above the earth, by so much are My ways raised above your ways, and My thoughts above your thoughts.' (Bernard of Clairvaux)

My brothers are sleeping; I have just come home from Florielle. Leaving very early, I arrived for Tierce and was present at the chapter meeting. The abbot gave us good news of France: Henri, the king's brother, will shortly be Archbishop of Rheims. This prince is our pope's best friend, his greatest supporter next to Louis VII. His influence is necessary to us, for the king has a changeable character: he often hesitates, favouring now Plantagenet, now Barbarossa. Peace between France and England must be maintained until the schism is ended by the victory of Alexander III over the antipope Victor IV. The Abbot of Clairvaux is no longer among us, alas! He would speedily have set this sad affair to rights. The kings of our time make use of the Church for their personal ends, either to disguise their demands or to justify their appetite for domination; the whole trouble comes from that.

Temporal and spiritual are on opposite sides in struggles between sordid factions, while good Christians wonder where the truth lies.

At Florielle it is already cold; despite the fine weather the chapter house was chilly. After the meeting the abbot detained me to speak of my project. Our father is always serious; though his words are often affectionate, from his former life he has preserved a resolute manner, decisive speech, a soldier's gestures: a fighting monk. On him, the loose habit looks like a robe for leisure; one always has the impression that he has just thrown off a heavy suit of armour. Everything about him is heavy and powerful. In our discussions I feel like a locust grappling with an ox. This situation would be disagreeable if I had not superiority over him in my trade. We manage to have respect for one another—I for his gifts as an organizer, he for my technical ability and my feeling for form.

After complimenting me on my plans, in which he said he discerned, as in the past, original forms, a sound technique and a concern for humanity, he reproached me with doing too much alone, with working solely for an enclosed world and with resisting change. The abbot was too positive for me to dream of defending myself—I had to let the storm pass; he continued in these terms:

'You seem impatient—you want to speak, to protest, to say that Le Thoronet will remain a monastery for sixty brothers. How do you know that? What are our communities, if not toiling cities? Cîteaux, Clairvaux, Molesme, Fontenay, now have thousands of monks. Under the holy Abbot Robert they each had ten. Do you not believe that we shall one day see immense cities of holy priests? Do you not fear that your buildings, enclosed as they are in a restrictive plan, could cause lamentable confusion if everyone followed your example? Our houses will perhaps become towns; it is essential to foresee this, and to construct them upon a plan that is laid down from the beginning. It is the duty of the first establishment to anticipate rapid development. Clearly, ours are cities of a special kind: their centre is the cloister, a small forum for meditation, and around it the chambers of the first community appear; the refectories multiply; then the oblates arrive in crowds, the hostel is built—one day it will be doubled, tripled. The church with its two hundred places will be inadequate, so our Chapter will decide to build another sanctuary. The infirmary for ten lay brothers and four monks will suffice for a time, then, when we concern ourselves with the body's infirmities as we did in the great epidemics, charity will direct us, and the infirmary will reach fantastic dimensions. Believe me, with a farm, a mill and a workshop, we form a hamlet. With sheepfolds, cattle sheds and extensive cultivation, we are sleeping in a market town. With workshops, forges, infirmaries, hospital centres, hostels and churches, one morning we wake up in a city. You must agree that this nascent world needs advice and examples. Militant Christianity is everywhere organizing itself, building its towns. To us, among the first, has fallen the mission of beginning, of initiating. The evolution of our prayer-hamlets into immense cities makes it our first duty to sketch out on the plan, and especially in the valleys or on complicated, uneven high ground, the basic lines of a development the extent of which we cannot know in advance. I do not want balanced horizons or the realities of the present: I don't deplore them, either. My part is to choose, to organize and calculate everything from the output of the springs to the line of the sewer, from the choice of site for the first bell-tower to that for the last, which in a hundred years' time will peal in answer to those already raised. We owe it to ourselves to lay out exemplary cities; we call ourselves an Order and we have a Rule. Though this determination may be determinism, creating the future form is no small matter, for it is also indeterminism. The monastic, cultural, agricultural, hospital and hostel arrangements, and the workshops, all develop differently, by modification of schedules or the more speedy evolution of certain activities. Our vocations are still unknown. But we wish to inspire order in every case; the master builder will create the rule of the regard for volumes, plan for them in their most distant embodiment, trace out the ways, keep clear the spaces — all this so that the monk may remain a monk and the invalid be cared for, far from the workshops and the wheels that the river turns round. This rule must, like our own, precede settlement. We live in an extraordinary century, in certain respects similar to imperial Rome's most fruitful period, when whole cities built, so to speak, in a day, arose in the desert. To the compact network of the place's chief necessities must be added a general sketch of the ultimate shape, like the first rough outline of a sculpture.'

The abbot had risen; he walked up and down, halting a moment to punctuate, with a chopping gesture of his broad hands or sometimes with clenched fists, the theory he was expounding. His deep, soft voice would suddenly rise as in a sermon, then change in tone according to the importance of his subject—principles, ideas or poetic comparisons. When he is speaking, he cannot bear to be interrupted. The end of his harangue revived vivid memories of the past. I knew him when he was prior at Clairvaux, and abbot at La Bussière; an emblematic figure of our Order, he always seemed to me like the eternal Cistercian. He is a solidly built monk of middle height, with impressive shoulders and a thick neck. His face is full, his features heavy and unlined, and his shaven skull, marked only by a deep scar in front, might have been drawn with a compass. His expression, always impenetrable, seems to be deadened by the absence of human feelings. His views on me are often full of scepticism, mixed with sudden amusement at my unorthodox utterances or my neurotic anxieties. More often than not, he looks inspired yet controlled, and this gives him an almost cruel expression, so devoid are his eyes of pity and weakness. The main reason why I observe this great Cistercian, this embodiment of our Order, so closely, is that such men have done a great deal for me. They have done good by their example and their advice, and wrong by their indulgence towards me as a bad monk and by the demands they have made on me as a useful, even indispensable master builder.

When he paused to judge the effect of his words, I waited for a moment—just as long as it might take to think of a rejoinder—although mine had been burning my tongue all through his speech.

'Father,' I replied, 'your perspicacity amazes me. I confess that in so far as it concerns me, I have doubts: not about the evolution of our monasteries, for I have collaborated in the setting up of over fifty communities, nor about the necessity for a plan and an outline of development, but that a generalized discipline might be to the detriment of sensibility and art, of humanity and originality of design.'

'Do you mean that you would rather have a harmonious disorder than uninspired order?'

'I haven't thought about it, but—yes.'

'Why? Don't you think that the two might exist happily side by side, like feelings that are under control?'

'The unexpected often helps and plays a part in achieving pleasanter results.'

'You forget to mention the essential condition in which the unexpected can happen: that the quality of the architecture should be sustained or exceptional.'

'Yes, why not?'

'Our monasteries,' he went on, 'in their basic plan, like that of Le Thoronet, are subject to the strict Rule which from the beginning determines the shape of the church and cloisters, as well as the sequence of the rooms surrounding it. You have had to work to that scheme all your life; have you ever felt it was a limitation? Does it prevent you from expressing yourself?'

'No, Father, on the contrary, I have welcomed the constraint imposed by our plans—one still has much freedom as regards form. But I agree, the first and only requirement is a perfectly definite scheme. I fear that I should revolt against an indeterminate plan, definite only in its forms and details. Though I am averse to the hideous and disorderly sprawl of certain suburbs, I confess that I love cities that have evolved by a slow, harmonious process from elements of both order and disorder. Public buildings and houses heaped up by the centuries within a circle of ramparts are much more to my liking than those that are built in straight lines and regulated in size.'

'What you wish for is, as you well know, impossible: once decisions are taken, communities grow as fast as any tree, and the forms they take spread and stretch out in an amazing fashion, like boughs. In good soil an oak will thrive, its predictable shape evolving out of the infinite and unpredictable variety of its branches. You see, we have to decide on the species and select the seed or seedling, whether it is to be a romantic fig tree or a walnut, an olive tree that kneels on the earth or a poplar that stands upright. Our monks' towns are built in a few years and are thriving in less than half a century; without choices, without decisions, without set forms, what would become of them? We cannot yield to the whims of master builders who one after the other bring us their stone and their skill; who, each in turn, and all too often, impose their own basic plans; who disregard, misjudge and are jealous of each other.'

'Father, I beg of you, think of order without soul: the whole concept rendered austere and sterile by being too rigidly defined at the outset.'

'My son, *you* think of *dis*order without soul: crude and depressing.'

'There you are right, but I cannot, I will not, admit such a possibility; thousands of master builders have proved their worth!'

'Who says that will always be so?'

Sext was over an hour ago. The sun in early autumn gives a pleasant light; it is less harsh, less glaring and is already taking on a colour which later it will bestow on the vines. A patch of this sunlight which had lingered for some time under the cloister climbed over the sill of the lay brothers' bay and suddenly the rays came spilling into the room, over the flags of pink Salernes stone, making the white walls look gay. This happy incident interrupted our talk, diverting us from our thoughts and our irreconcilable ideas. I looked at the abbot; he had sat down, drawn the folds of his habit round his knees and was lost in thought. An abbot's habit, though not different from ours, has more distinction; not that it is cleaner or less patched, but it is more uniformly worn and soiled, and this indicates higher duties and general responsibilities, the work of a father: abbas.

I looked at the abbot, who was far away, meditating, or in some remote dream, perhaps. His life is like a legend. The Abbot of Clairvaux, had he lived, would now be as old as he. They were childhood friends, and long ago Bernard de Fontaines tried to persuade him to come to Cîteaux and bring his thirty initiates with him. He could see no point in the venture and chose to undertake another. He set off alone for Palestine to return with a group of men, their heads shaven, clothed in shirts blazoned with the cross, heavy coats of chain mail and the wide cloak which has since become renowned. In the year 1128, this company, under the command of the Count of Champagne, Hugues de Payne, a *magister templi*, went to the Council of Troyes to meet Bernard, now Abbot of Clairvaux. During the course of the Council, the young Cistercian, already an extremely powerful figure, gave a definitive form to the Temple. The Order of the Knights of Christ was founded. In those days no one had yet seen on the roads those strange horsemen who, tanned and dusty, wore no glittering gold and silver to distinguish the man from his steed. Their noble, distinguished bearing impressed us. At that time we found it hard to accept that a knight should take vows of poverty, chastity and humility and then go galloping off into battle. It seemed an obvious contradiction of the Scriptures: 'He that lives by the sword shall die by the sword.'

Soon afterwards, the Abbot of Clairvaux demanded that the new Templar should return. The abbot was already thinking about his crusade and wanted an able organizer with him. He came to the Order and stayed there until the holy abbot's death. All during this period, which lasted more than twenty years, he arranged for the establishment at Clairvaux of nearly a hundred copyists, monks or novices, had a proper monastery built for them and translated a great number of manuscripts into the vernacular. In addition, he supervised most of the master builders of the Order, this task being his principal responsibility. Lastly, he organized the unsuccessful crusade, accompanied Bernard on that venture and realized, bitterly, that it had failed. He returned long after the abbot and had the joy of giving him comfort on his deathbed. In 1154 he left La Bussière for Florielle, where he was to supervise the construction of the abbey of Le Thoronet.

What tranquillity after so many adventures and so much suffering, how many memories he must have. In this simple, vaulted room, with its whitewashed walls, bright and peaceful, dreams of distant and unfulfilled undertakings had come to a standstill. What could my abbot be thinking about? He had forgotten me, seemed startled to notice me again, sitting beside him. Wearied by my presence, perhaps ashamed of his melancholy, he hastily picked up my drawings again. He was severely critical of the disposition of the annexes, which clearly stand in the way of any extension of the abbey to the west. He directed me to keep a considerable space clear on that spot and to push the hostel and the farmhouse farther out. I was about to withdraw when he stopped me with a gesture. With sadness in his eyes, he said to me in a harsh, wheezing voice, 'He who looks ahead must not allow himself to be intoxicated by words and fables. May secular disorders serve as a warning to the men of our Order.'

Going out, I felt free again. The abbot, like me, had been aware of the futility of our argument. Yesterday, both of us had let ourselves slip into an exchange of sentimental secrets; today we again spoke of a profession close to our hearts, until he became lost in daydreams. He wanted to have the last word and thereby re-establish our relationship, bring us back to essentials. We Cistercians are like that; it is considered proper that we should punish ourselves for our weaknesses. If others can control their thoughts, well and good, for my part I do not wish to try to do so. The building stands too much in need of my feelings, my affection.

St Victoria, twenty-third day of September, eleven hundred and sixty-one

In all honesty, Athenians, I do not believe there is any need to continue my argument in order to convince you that I am not guilty of the misdeeds with which Meletes charges me, what I have said is enough; but as I have already told you, I have many violent enemies ... (Plato, Apology)

The cart, loaded with a cubic yard of stone blocks, was being led by Brother Luc, who also controlled the brake. It is not a difficult operation, but the slope is steep. The brake is primitive but reliable enough. Benoît had said, 'I do not want the cart to go down the slope without a man there to work the emergency brake.' On work sites, habit means danger. Benoît's order had not been respected for a long time, and everyone knew it. So many working hours were being gained each month and, thus, a number of extra blocks. Halfway down there is a boulder with a rut each side of it. On each descent one is obliged first to release the brake so as to pick up momentum and then to pull hard on the bar so as to avoid running away on the slope. Today the wheel stuck fast on the upper side of the boulder. While the mule was getting its breath back, Luc made some calculations. Thinking that by slewing the cart round he would get it free, he undertook the task on his own. He went round to the front of the cart, started it moving and quickly grabbed the brake again. At a slap across Poulide's back, she reared up, pulled forward and got over the boulder. The impetus was too great for the animal to stand firm between the shafts. Luc strained down on the brake but the lever, though solid, snapped in two. For a moment Poulide tried to push against the unbalanced load alone. By now an accident was inevitable. The animal stumbled and fell, breaking a foreleg. The cart came down on top of her with the left wheel wedged on her belly. Poor Poulide was bewildered and round-eyed with terror. Every movement she made worsened the wound which was being torn open. It was a dreadful and pitiful sight.

We came running at Luc's shouts, but there were not enough of us. Someone dashed off to sound the alarm. We pulled in vain at the cart, while the animal was tearing herself to pieces in her attempts to get free. It was a nightmare!

By the time adequate reinforcements had arrived, Poulide's blood was gushing out like a great spring. Her entrails had burst open in several places and had spilled out to mingle with the earth and sand. Brother Luc, responsible for all this suffering, was on his knees, trying to cram the animal's entrails back into the wheel-torn skin. For a while the rest of us thought that this was what needed doing and left him to his task; we were dazed and shattered. Finally, though, I came to my senses. I took Brother Luc under the arms and drew him to his feet; he turned his tear-stained face to me. 'Little Poulide, I loved her so much. She was such a plucky little thing.'

'Come along,' I said, 'we have other things to do.' He allowed himself to be led away. Edgar and Étienne had just arrived. 'Quickly,' said Master Edgar, 'go and get a sharp knife, and hurry.' It was Antoine who ran off and returned almost immediately. Meanwhile Master Edgar continued, 'We shall have to cut her throat; she'll suffer least that way.'

Luc had come back and he bent over to take the great head on his knees. He put his arms round it and kissed it through his tears. Poulide seemed to find some relief and comfort in this. At least in her exhaustion she was no longer trying to stand up. The heap of smoking intestines had quivered with terrible spasms at each pitiful attempt. Now she grew calm, and as the shivers ran along her spine like the after-effects of a drawn-out sob she looked as though she was crying.

Everyone was reluctant to do anything. The lay brothers turned away and the craftsmen looked furtively at one another. Who was going to act? I was ashamed for our men. We were like a lot of women. The craftsmen were behaving like men. If I had had the skill and the strength, *I* should have been the one to cut the animal's throat, but I was afraid of making a butchery of the business and did not know the best place to make the incision. The craftsmen deliberated, purposely excluding us from the deed, and finally the task fell to Antime as the most efficient of them. The whole thing was over in a moment. There were just a few rough words and those movements of the chin which silently indicate what has happened. With clenched teeth, Antime went up to the animal, felt under her neck for the jugular, caressed her affectionately and took a new grip on the knife. But Benoît was there. I think he was hoping up to the last moment that one of the lay brothers would come forward. He intervened, taking Antime's left arm above the elbow, and drew the man towards him to look him full in the face, deep in the eyes. Antime simply held out the knife. In a flash, Benoît drove it deep into the correct place. Luc, who was watching the business, leaned forward and hid Poulide's eye in the folds of his tunic with his hands spread out to make an extra blindfold. Poulide gave no further signs but died peacefully, her great good-natured head in the arms of her companion and friend who, during her last moments, gently kissed her nostrils and forehead, delicately as one would a small child about to fall asleep. Her legs jerked out; her eyes grew dull. Poulide's days of work and pain were over. We were completely stunned, and deeply affected; the craftsmen, aware of our feelings, withdrew. Benoît came up to me and tried to speak, to explain himself.

Luc wanted her to be buried like a human being. I was on the point of agreeing with him, then had second thoughts. The mule, plucky animal that she was, could still be useful to us. She had to pay her way in death as she had done in life. Brother Benoît led Luc away. He looked as if he had been swimming in blood; he was covered with it from his stockings to his neck; his hands and arms were dripping with it. Even his beard and his forehead were sprayed with the jet of liquid that had brought Poulide's death. Benoît said to him, 'Come, Luc, it is over. Let us go and wash now, it will take us some time.'

Back in my quarters, saddened that I had not granted Luc his wish, I wrote, 'On the twenty-fifth day of September, at the first hour, the animal is to be skinned, and the hide prepared for tanning. The best meat will be salted and packed in casks for the winter, in a cool place where it is safe from vermin. This will enable us to feed our labour force in the off season. A share of it will be given to the craftsmen, part salted and part fresh. Any inferior pieces, unsuitable for the salting tub, will be distributed among the poor. The largest of the bones will be broken up and divided into the same number of shares. All this work is to be finished before Tierce. Little Brother Bruno will go and spread the news in the neighbourhood, setting out immediately after Lauds. He will tell everyone that distribution is to take place in the second hour after noon. Before nightfall, all the offal and scrapings will be taken to Florielle for the swine. The bones will be burned to ashes to make the black dye for our writing and drawing ink. Brother Gabriel has had experience of this kind of work, so he is to supervise it. A piece of the trunk of an oak, a yard long, must be hollowed out to store the fine powder. The container will be stopped by a tight-fitting lid, in which an opening has been left wide enough for a large spoon.'

If all my orders are followed correctly, the community will recover half the price we paid for Poulide. Everything can be turned to advantage. An animal, slaughtered in the right way, will leave its skin, its salted flesh and the precious black of its bones: a pitiful advantage, perhaps.

St Michael, twenty-ninth day of September

> *Let those whose care for the interior leads them to despise and neglect all that is without, raise for their own use buildings shaped to the form of poverty, imitating the model of holy simplicity, on the lines drawn by the prudence of their Father.*
> (William of Saint Thierry)

I have planned the church in the most minute detail. As it stands, I am in a position to say that my drawings will admit of no further additions. I have given the vaulting of the nave and the transept a slightly pointed shape which is hardly perceptible. I have done this for reasons of economy and because I wished to obviate the necessity for buttresses on the façades. The shape of the aisle vaults is entirely determined by the abutment of the vault of the great nave. This architectural layout is completely sound, and I have no reason to regret it. The transepts are continued flying buttresses, while the arches, which I have designed in the shape of quarter circles, leave me no feelings of doubt and not the least suspicion that I have been false to the overall design. I have no anxieties about my decision. Economy is beautiful in itself, since it is not a question of sadness or sacrifice but of a worthwhile decision. Taking all my experiments into account, it will be of my plans for the proportions of the apse and apsidal chapels, of the east wall of the transept and of the bays and oculi, that I shall say, This particular view is the most inspiring to be found in any abbey church. The slope in the ground has forced me to plan for a drop towards the cloisters. I do not think it will be very noticeable.

St Jerome, thirtieth day of September

Tomorrow will be the two-hundredth day since we arrived here, feverish after our exhausting journey. I have promised to complete an apse for the Feast of the Virgin next year; it will be there, of that I have no doubt. There is one misfortune common to construction sites, and that is that they are always set under way at the wrong time of year. In the north, where there is snow and frost, all work is interrupted during the first days of cold. In Aquitaine and Provence we can build all year round, but work starts on the sites at times of storm and wind. Some accident always seems to delay the start and it has to be postponed until the threshold of winter. In our case, the progress we had made had the same consequences. We should have been ready by next summer without feeling that we had been lagging. Unfortunately, I had been so anxious to press on that I had stolen all the lay brothers from Florielle and melted the fat off them till they were just skin and bones, with muscles as hard as wood. I do not mean that monks are lazy and fat, on the contrary, but despite their privations they have a certain plumpness which is the result of their well regulated way of life, the quality of their food and, some even say, of celibacy. I must admit that we are not strictly observing the Rule. We add fat, meat, eggs or milk to our soup at every meal. I have kept back enough from the construction funds to send Master Étienne secretly to Carcès or Lorgues to go to the market and bring back what we need. Of course, the prior realized this within a few days and I thought he had forgotten about it until, last Saturday, he mumbled, 'I am thinking of laying in wine for the winter. Now is the time to do it.'

'There is no winter here.'

'Last year it was very cold, you know.'

'At Florielle?' I inquired, innocently.

He smiled and went on, 'That's true, Florielle is up in the mountains and the air is warmer here, don't you think? Supposing we were to put bacon in the soup instead of laying in the wine, starting on Monday?'

'I commend your idea, Prior, for wine sustains but it does not strengthen.'

That is how it is with Brother Pierre; he knows what is going on but finds deceit painful.

We have been working so hard that the fear of wasting time is becoming an obsession. Even on Sundays, when we usually go for walks in the forest, we are off to inspect the different sites. The carpenters go to the quarries, the quarrymen to the kilns or the forge; they no longer feel detached from them. We seem to be welded together, engrossed with one another as if we had made a pact with the devil. In this connection I think I am justified in saying that Tiburce, the latest arrival, who came to replace Brother Philippe, told me of a dream he had. At first I refused to listen to him and advised him to recount it at confession.

'No,' he replied, 'it is not the dream of a sinner, rather a warning with regard to the site. Well, you and the site are practically the same thing, aren't you?'

My curiosity was roused. I shut the door and listened to him as he went on.

'As I believe you know, I do a bit of everything here, but I am really a mason by trade, a stone-layer. Well, the walls were quite high and I was working at the top of a pillar fifty feet from the ground. Every day I would climb up my ladder which was so long it bent under my weight. One of the brothers was helping me from below, but I carried the stones up on my own and set them in place. As soon as I reached the top I would find myself in a wind blowing like a hundred devils. Every day I added three courses of stone to the pillar and three rungs to the ladder. I could look down over the whole site. One morning I said to myself, Well, I never! The ladder was five rungs higher than the stones. You can imagine, it was quite a problem, eh? I didn't say anything but just worked harder than usual. When I climbed down in the evening I counted very carefully and there were fifty-one rungs. Then the next day, the ladder was higher than the stones again. I ask you! So I counted them: fifty-one. During the next few days I still couldn't manage to catch up during the day with what was melting away during the night. I began to watch my brothers at work on the walls and I realized that they were bothered about something, too. We would look at one another furtively, just worried at first, and then really terrified as the more stones we were laying the more the walls were subsiding. We were all thinking, If the chief comes along and sees the way the stones are getting eaten up without the walls growing any higher, there's going to be a massacre! Well, you know what I mean. One evening we marked the stones and counted the rungs; and the next day we had eyes like saucers because the stones were there, as we'd laid them the day before, and the ladder was three rungs above them. The following night I went by myself; I hid and took two forked branches as guide marks and kept my eyes fixed on them; it was a new moon so I could hardly see anything, just my pillar looming in the dark. I peered and peered but still couldn't see anything. Then suddenly I heard someone going up my ladder, slowly and surely; it was creaking. To think that I wasn't even afraid! Well, anyway, I said to myself, No one's going to tell me that's the wind. I couldn't see him, he was round the other side. Then two arms and two hands appeared, and a monk's cowl. I held my breath. As far as I could see he was putting something on top, going down again and up again all without leaving the ladder, and over and over again. I peered out again but nothing had changed. I told myself, If I catch the monk, it's bound to be the chief or Benoît or Bernard or the prior and I'll be in the soup again. "What are you doing there, Tiburce?" he'll say, and I'll be punished for it. So I stayed where I was without moving. Then the bastard went off, laughing. I said to myself, It's not possible — or maybe he's been drinking. At that moment the moon disappeared behind a huge cloud and I heard what sounded like a thousand night birds flying overhead. There were screeches and the noise of fighting, as though they were quarrelling over a corpse, the sounds of beaks and gullets. I took a quick glimpse and saw things as tall as steeples, stuck up everywhere, even on my pillar, struggling with one another to eat whatever had been left on the walls. I'm ashamed to tell you how I was feeling. When they had finished they stood quite still, and, without peering out, I saw everything slowly sinking, inch by inch. The moon was hidden still, and I heard the noise of them flying away, and then nothing. I went up to the pillar and realized what had happened; we had been counting everything but the courses, and now three of them had disappeared into the ground. I was rooted to the spot. I wanted to run and tell you about it when an armed man, all in white, came up to me and said, "My poor Tiburce, you've finally realized. You knew that they were demons and that no one had told us. However, you know that that is what we are there for. Tomorrow, take your crosses, all of you, and hide them at the top of the ladders; I'll take care of the rest." '

Tiburce is a young man and works well, without pause. He is small, with powerful shoulders, and continues to look healthy. His face is round, full and beardless. He is said to be the child of a man of Barbary, expelled from Malta, and a Christian woman from the coast. All day long he hums our canticles, stopping work to listen to himself when there are any subtleties or changes of key in the melody. 'When I was a child,' he says, 'our village priest had everything set to music, and I enjoyed all that so much that I came to be with you.'

'Is that how your dream ended?'

At first I had found him amusing with his shrill voice, but afterwards I began to shiver a little. His dream was very improbable, it was too well rounded; even so, there were drops of sweat beaded on the down above his lips and on his forehead. The pink of his cheeks had become purple, then grey, and his shoulders were drooping. He seemed dejected. His Oriental sensitivity made him guess that I did not believe him. Insulted, he said:

'It all happened like that, I swear! Obviously I haven't told you about the distortions in the images; the stones were laid in a dream-like way, you understand, not as they would be in real life. But everything I've told you was as clear as you are standing there in front of me. My fear woke me and I could remember everything. I was bathed in sweat, perhaps even feverish. It is from that point on, you see, that I am less sure. It was dark, and I was holding my cross clasped tightly in my hands. I got up, went out and groped my way up my ladder, shivering with fear and cold. At the top I pushed the cross into a hole left by a broken rung, level with the pillar. I was still on the ladder when I woke up. And I really thought it was true! Well, at that point, I couldn't be in doubt any longer because the bell was ringing and my brothers were getting up. I had forgotten everything. They were tidying their mattresses, all the usual things in fact. Then we had prayers, chapel, and, just like any other day, I went off to make tiles. I was supposed to be going along the lower path with Antoine, who was going to the forge. We were to wait and leave together. I couldn't see him, and said to myself, He's gone on ahead. So I took the path by the stream. As I walked past the building site I began to laugh at my dream. I looked up to the right and there was my pillar, standing on its own, right in the middle, fifty feet high, lit by a ray of sunlight down to the last course! Its feet looked like rags, its legs like pieces of shredded linen. I went up to have a good look. The walls had gone. The ladders and scaffolding had been knocked down and lay at sixes and sevens — only my pillar was standing in one piece, with the ground around it quite clear. But at the bottom of the ladder, in full daylight, lay the monk. Can you imagine! I shook him; his habit came away in my hand, so I picked it up and something fell out — it set my teeth on edge — a bundle of bones dropped out like bits of old, dead wood. I screamed, I was lost … and I woke up again. Oh, goodness! The bell was still ringing and my brothers were filing out of the dorter. A moment later Benoît the monk came along, felt my forehead and said, "You are hot, Tiburce, stay in bed. I'll come back and see you later."

' "No, no," I said, "I'm coming. Wait for me." I was ready in a moment. Then I went to prayers again, chapel again—but I didn't let Antoine out of my sight. "Let's go," I said to him. As he saw I wasn't well, we went across the Field with the others, it's easier that way. Luckily the building site was clear this time. Antoine asked me what day it was and I replied, "Friday, the Feast of the Archangel Michael." That was the limit, I thought it was all going to start again.'

Tiburce paused, anxiously. He had told his story as much with his hands, head and eyes as with his voice. I was thoughtful. The first part had seemed imaginary, I knew that the end could not be.

'I do not disbelieve you, Tiburce. Tell me, though, are you quite certain about your story up to the apparition of the man in white?'

'I'm telling you, more certain than I am of the rest! It was natural, continuous, like a real building site. By the end I was going mad; you ask Benoît how he found me, you'll see. I don't dare.'

'Don't worry about it any more, Tiburce, you'd been working too hard the day before. It was tiredness and your anxiety to get the stones up, fever too. As for myself, you know, I only believe in concrete things.'

I continued in this vein. Then the conversation turned to the best way of cementing stones. Tiburce was off on his favourite tack. He laughed and slapped his thighs. His eyes were clear and his conscience at peace. To carry my part through, I put my arm round his shoulders as I saw him out. This dream of his is strange, but true, of that I am now convinced. Tiburce is gifted with imagination and the ability to tell a story. It is a beautiful one, frightening and full of symbols. I can see the story now, painted in black and white on a long fresco.

Work has begun now. In the places where the east wing and the apse are to be, pickaxes bite into the rock. I have said many times that a start has been made on the site. It was true. First of all we were busy making part of the foundations under the west wing. Then there was the scrub to be cleared and the ground to be levelled. Finally there were temporary jobs to keep surplus labour occupied on certain days, when the men removed any rocks which would have stood up above intended levels. In fact, the only part of the work which could be thought of as a true building operation was the packing down of the clayey soil beneath the north wing. For some time there had been compelling reasons for this, and besides we were able, in this way, to clear the quarries of all the waste stone taking up ground space there. So the building site was started on long ago. But the real start comes when the supervisor, after studying the plans, banks up to the correct height each of the platforms which are to represent at differing or uniform levels the boundaries of the rooms and of the church. That is what I consider to be the real beginning, and yet I know from experience that the very first day will be the day when the materials arrive and the first courses are laid. Today I was able to produce the definitive drawing of levels and layout, and to get the first cords stretched out with markers in place. Antime has made a water level. Étienne has constructed a tripod for us, a heavy but first-rate piece of equipment. Jean eagerly seized the plans and withdrew to try and make them out on his own. Tomorrow he will ask me various questions, wanting to know why I have planned things this way. He will try to obtain modifications so that the work is easier, to economize. I shall have to say no to it all.

Between the Field and the refectory platform there is a drop of twelve feet. I have provided for a sinkage of the church floor and a slight raise in the north wing. In this way the differences in the breadth of the north-south transversals will be less noticeable. They will be reduced to ten feet at the most. I shall tell the abbot in all good conscience that this is the maximum possible. The church will be sunk six feet and it is there that the most work will have to be done; there are five hundred cubic yards of rock to be torn out — flawed I have no doubt, but hard just the same — once one gets under the top three feet. There is more to be taken away than to add to this part. Once the holes in the east wing are filled, the surplus can doubtless be used as filling material and sand. The longitudinal axes present no such irregularities; there is only a dip in the east wing, and that is very small. Generally speaking, we shall have no trenches to dig. Over the whole area, or almost the whole area, the rocky ground will take the walls as it is; there we shall make up for work in other parts of the terrain. When we come really to tackle the work in elevation, I hope that we shall be able to see, over half the area, a great flight of steps going down towards the stream with every room carved out like Brother Alfonse's block of clay, enlarged a hundred times.

Since the full moon the sky has not been so clear. The clouds look threatening. This September has been too fine; the mist glides up here from the Argens as soon as night falls. This evening the prior assembled us at the sacristy. He was pleased to learn that the plan is completed, at least in its broad outlines, and, for him, this commencement of the building is an important event. The abbot has asked us to be prepared for the laying of the first stone. On the fourth day of October, church and abbey will be consecrated by the Bishop of Fréjus, Raymond Bérenger and Hugues Balz. The arrangement of the festivities will begin to-morrow. As far as the stone is concerned, it has already been dressed and hollowed, though we still have to decide exactly where it will be laid and prepare the place. Everything is ready.

My leg has been very painful and I have been forced to remain seated. Benoît and Bernard have had to carry me. Brother Pierre decided to take supper with us. The kitchener and two lay brothers set up trestles, and the prior came with flowers and a jug of some excellent wine. The party continued after Compline. We were happy, perhaps a little drunk. I often think about living here for a long time, watching over this site like a patriarch for several years. Benoît told us stories, spoke of some of the men, then others and incidentally of Tiburce. 'Speaking of Tiburce,' I said; 'if some day, after I have left, anything strange or inexplicable should happen on the site, ask Tiburce's advice. Don't forget, he has a few ideas.' Although I spoke casually, my brothers scented some mystery.

St Constant, fourth day of October

The stone which the builders refused is become the head-stone of the corner. This is the Lord's doing; it is marvellous in our eyes. This is the day which the Lord hath made; we will rejoice and be glad in it. (Ps. cxviii 22, 23)

From the first glimmer of dawn each day since Monday, we have been preparing the site for the laying of the first stone. I have had to be everywhere at once. Bernard's willingness and Benoît's activity have not been enough. It was with Master Paul and Master

Edgar that the continuous work had to be done. We had not taken full stock of what the many necessities of the ceremony implied: from clearing the site, which was cluttered with all sorts of rubble, to equipping the kitchen to feed twenty monks and the train of noblemen, flowers to decorate the site and torches and lamps for lighting.

While all of us, lay brothers and monks alike, washed and mended our garments there was a succession of tasks to be done, both large and small, without much regard for order and in a feverish atmosphere.

Yesterday, at nightfall, came the pleasant moment when, with everything ready, we were able to look calmly at our finished work. I was satisfied; everything was clean and tidy, the necessary installations had been made, the pulley and crab were in place, and finally there was the stone, ready beside its foundation with the material for laying it. It was all perfect. More for our own pleasure than out of conscientiousness, I wanted to test the working of the pulley. The ropes tightened, the claws bit into the side of the stone and it slowly rose ... Gradually I became aware of the blood beating in my head. With growing intensity I realized the mistake without believing it. The foundation we had prepared was only four feet from the axis of the apse. I knew that in the proportion three to one this measurement was wrong. I was so despondent I had to sit down and close my eyes. From a great distance, imprisoned in my despair, I listened to Paul and Benoît quarrelling. The argument was violent, unfair and harsh on my younger brother who could not do good work at speed, as I knew. It was impossible in the few hours of the morning already earmarked for final preparations to change the position of the foundations we had already been struggling over for two long days. The quarrel was pointless, ugly and would lead nowhere. Sadly I looked for a moment at the twisted mouths and the gestures of pity directed towards me. It had to stop. I stood up to interrupt the argument.

'Master Paul, Brother Benoît, all of you, Brothers, I am responsible; all your insults are therefore addressed to me. But I assure you that the stone will be laid in the right place tomorrow. We have two hours of twilight, eleven hours of darkness, three hours after dawn and a great deal of determination; we will make it. Get the torches and the lamps ready; ten brothers will work with Benoît, three with Master Paul, four with Master Jean and the others will rest until midnight. Then a new shift will take over. If necessary Étienne, Antime and Bernard will replace the leaders. At the sixth hour the first shift will get up to finish off the work. And I said, to finish ...' Only the prior was not convinced; in his opinion we would never get through it. Contrary to his usual manner, he spoke out, urging me to abandon my wild resolution. 'If we leave everything as it is now,' he said to me, 'no one will be any the wiser; after the ceremony we'll move the stone.'

'Man of little faith,' I murmured.

'That is true. Then, for my penitence, make me work.'

'I was intending to, Prior!'

'And you, what are you going to do?'

'I? The same as you and everyone else! Before nightfall I am going to go over the layout again with Benoît. I would like you to attend to the meals, to organize the shifts, send the night shift off to bed and to have soup ready for them when they are relieved; they'll need it. For the time being I'll keep Tiburce and Edgar with me to put up the lights. Warn the kitchener to keep their meal for them.'

I cannot possibly tell you what that night was like. I continued to do all I could to prevent wasted effort or misdirected skill. The east wind blew out the lamps, fanned the resin torches so that the blue flames no longer gave any light. Then the lay brothers began to use their tools from memory, the only light being the sparks made by sledge hammers and pickaxes. About the third hour, tiredness overcame us. None of the second shift had been able to sleep, out of worry no doubt. As blow followed blow, Victor's hand and Marcel's arm were crushed by the sledge hammers, then burned by Brother Gabriel's treating them, a painful offering of blood and bruised flesh. It hurt me to see them, to see Benoît who was weeping, as if from the wind, at his mistake. So as not to waste time while I was in charge, I collected the splinters into little heaps and carried them off in a basket to a place, twenty paces away, leaning on my stick as I went. The prior, who was a strong and competent man, worked along with the best of them. Finally our torches paled before the mist-white sky. The work was slowed down by a feeling of discouragement. The team were a sorry sight, with their ashen faces, red eyes and uncoordinated movements. When the first shift returned, the six hours of wavering exertion had produced very little result.

Soon afterwards we lifted out four cubic yards of rock with the crowbars and rolled them to the end of the east wing. Paul and Jean had moved the pulley, the crab and the tools. The brothers who formed the last shift were rested and serious. When the sun was clear of the mist and began to burn our skin, Paul, Jean and Brother Pierre, the lay brother, were the only ones working on the foundation, now perfectly smooth and chiselled as though in a quarry. As the prior watched us thoughtfully, we stretched the two cords and traced with an iron set square the angle at which the stone was to be laid. One by one the lay brothers came to look, newly tonsured, washed and looking very fine in their scapulars drawn in by leather belts. We were not sorry to leave the site, and though there were none of the satisfied looks of the day before, we were proud, if a little sad, as one is after a victory over oneself which leaves the taste of temptation in its wake. Obviously one might ask why we had done it at all. Yet without this frantic night's work we would never have been able to see the consecrated stone as 'the first', the cornerstone ...

And so it was that I was unable to be present at the ceremony. Shivering with fever, I fell on to my mattress and have not stirred since. I should have liked to sleep, to stop thinking, to be unable to hear anything any more. Bernard did not leave me once, but sat in the embrasure of a window and enabled me to follow the ceremony through him. My enforced absence did not trouble me; on the contrary. In my opinion, a master builder should be an imposing figure; to see me as I was would have been a sad disappointment to many of the spectators. Men trained to wear heavy armour easily imagine a master of stone very differently from the shattered invalid that I am.

Some time ago I wondered whether the abbey would be affected by my weakness and general state of ill health; after I had finished the first drawings I completely changed my mind, and now I am convinced that the contrary is true, for my plan conveys a sense of power and confidence. It is the most forceful I have ever made in my life. I suppose that everything inside me is being drained away through the flowing of my blood and the wasting of my body so that the soul of the building may live. How could these visitors, however generous and anxious about me, comprehend this paradox? To them this basic truth would seem contradictory. It was better to remain hidden despite the sorrow of my own people.

Bernard was describing the scene like an auctioneer. 'There are the white habits, the black scapulars, the red of the bishop's garments, the gold of the crosiers. Our abbot looks very impressive ... Here come the noblemen. The valley is beginning to look like a stained-glass window. The silvery coats of mail are like scales on live fish ...' I could hear the horsemen riding up towards the Field.

'They're wearing great cloaks fastened at the neck with heavy chains. Their shields are magnificent, and tall enough to cover their bodies from shoulder to foot.'

I was feeling ill and stopped listening. I thought about Raymond Bérenger and Hugues. Later, Bernard went on:

'They have opened their travelling chests and lit their fires. The barons are settling in. They're rolling out carpets and putting up tents on the Field ...'

'Bernard, have you noticed my brother?'

'How could I pick him out in that crowd?'

'By his shield. A silver star.'

Hugues has not come, I thought. He is at war with Raymond and there has been no truce. That is very sad ...

'I can see a tall knight who looks like you, dressed in black and silver. He is pitching his tent by the spring. He's wearing a star ...'

All this hubbub had silenced the persistent grasshoppers; some hesitantly started up again in fury or timidly answered one another. At last I was able to go to sleep.

When I awoke, the sun had changed sides in the sky. Bernard had not moved. He heard me and brought me some milk, then took up where he had left off.

'The stone is suspended over the foundation while the noblemen are standing around the apse. Farther off there is a group of humble people, a mass of brown, dark red and grey. The craftsmen are standing next to the lay brothers; you can hardly tell the difference between them in spite of their coloured insignia. Our brothers are following the bishop, falling into the places they are to occupy ... In the middle, almost underneath the stone sit the count and his standard bearer, next to the abbot and the bishop.'

'What are Paul and Benoît doing?'

'Don't worry, they're standing in the right place to supervise the laying. You know, the whole scene looks like the Last Judgment ...'

'"The first shall be last," say the Scriptures.'

'The abbot is reading the parchment with three seals. They are putting it in a metal casket ... the bishop is blessing it ... a deacon is putting it into the hole we carved out for it. Master Paul is closing the little slab and sealing it up ... The bishop is coming forward, handing the trowel to a deacon and blessing the stone; the abbot is coming to bless it too ... the count is on his knees, praying ... everyone is standing up ...'

I heard a mighty 'Te Deum Laudamus'. Bernard went on, in a choking voice, 'The stone is being lowered; Master Paul is holding out the hod; the bishop is leaning over, spreading the mortar ... he is giving the trowel to the count, who does the same ... the abbot is coming towards them; he is taking the trowel from the count's hands, kneeling down in front of the foundation, spreading the mortar very carefully ... the stone is coming slowly down, very slowly; Brother Pierre and Brother Tiburce are helping to set it in place. It is finished, the stone's in place! They are forming the procession, walking down the axis of the nave ... coming up again through the north aisle ... every few steps the abbot is stopping to show the bishop and the count the places where the pillars are to stand, which we chalked down ... they're going through the cloister door ... following down the galleries.'

So I could see it all though I was confined to my mattress. The untiring Bernard was still telling me what was happening as I lay with my eyes closed, listening to the sounds and the chanting. By evening I was feeling better, and joined Bernard by the door. Torches and lamps lit up the bottom of the valley. The wind had dropped, and a warm south breeze was sweeping the thick smoke of the torches over to the other slope. Sitting side by side, we watched the end of the ceremony, which now seemed to possess the tragic aspects of the pagan sacrifices of ancient Rome—the blaze of silks and other cloth, the sparkling flashes of armour and precious stones flaring here and there in the valley. Banners and flickering flames were gently blown away, and suddenly fantastical beasts appeared out of the darkness to dissolve in a strange ferment.

Bernard left me to go and eat. Later, as I was following the halo of white habits winding over our land in the candlelight to leave blessings where it passed, a great ghost came to keep me company. Thirty years of absence were made good in a single moment. Two children who have issued from the same woman can never forget. We told each other about our own lives and the lives of our people with the trust of blood relations. Hugues has gone to sleep on my mattress, wrapped in the folds of his great cloak, and I have been writing for hours. I can still pick out the lanterns of my brothers as they make their way by various short cuts to Florielle. I can hear the barons as they continue their feasting, singing to the accompaniment of their musicians, gambling and fighting among themselves. My seigneur in black and silver is breathing softly.

St Sergius, seventh day of October

The days are too full. Today everything went wrong. After a month of tiring work uncovering a bed of stone, Paul found it to be unusable. Apparently the stone is too hard and liable to flake after frost, and is flawed as well. According to him it is 'every plague and leprosy rolled into one'. We examined it closely. In my opinion we shall be able to make use of it. We can either turn it to account inside the less important rooms or for building the mill. Paul angrily opposed this scheme with a volley of arguments. I had to give him his way, so we shall be abandoning this bed and setting to work elsewhere. Luckily, we are ahead of schedule.

We have had two days of torrential rain. The east wind, which blows where it pleases, has torn away part of the roofing of clay, pine branches and poor-quality planks. Rain is coming in all over the place. I have tried to stop up the holes with a mixture of chalk, sand and clay just to get us through the winter. I think it will hold. If not, two lay brothers will have to patch up the roofs, taking their labour from some other work for several months.

Benoît has come to trouble me with more bad news. The water in the stream, which is usually so well behaved, has risen;

according to Benoît, former high-water marks give every indication that it may reach the upper level of the cloister. It seems incredible, but I shall go and have a look. We hardly managed to put in four hours' work today. The workshops are in a mess, and we cannot use them because repairs are being carried out there. In the dorter, the mattresses are soaked, there is mud all over the place and we stand and shiver like wet dogs.

St Brigid, eighth day of October

It has stopped raining. Everything has been washed clean and fresh, and our forest looks like new. About midday the sun was so hot that some end-of-season grasshoppers thought that summer had returned. My leg is so purple and inflamed, and the veins so swollen, that I am afraid it will burst; the pain is violent above the knee where I burnt it.

St Denis, ninth day of October

My work progresses; the plans are nearing completion. The strong, warm wind brings ugly clouds with no kindly whipped-cream roundness in their tattered dirtiness. And as for the stream and the roofing—I fear another storm while we are still in full equinox. The heat is stifling, the flies are biting and the animals are excitable.

One day I am hopeful, the next depressed. Just give me a month's respite for my leg. 'After that, you can do whatever you want.'

Matins. In the evening the large clouds disappeared to make room for a black ceiling of thunder and lightning which overwhelmed and engulfed all other differences in level. The site no longer stood at the bottom of a valley but in the middle of a great plain. If the steeple had been finished, we would not have been able to see the top of it. Disaster struck after Compline. My chalk-clay mixture was still too fresh and fell in flakes of mud all around the buildings—a few moments later there was no shelter anywhere. The exhausted lay brothers shivered in their sleep. After an hour of it they went and sat against the walls where they were out of the wind, and huddled together. Some of them, protected from the cold by the warmth of a body on each side, fell into a heavy sleep. Together they formed a heap of weary, muddied flesh alternately soaked and sticky.

We three were having a struggle in the workshop. Having covered the plans we stuck strips of linen over the planks of the roof with resin. We finished just in time. Half the hut was under cover when the storm broke over us. Economy and the abbot will have to be disappointed, since in the end we just had to use linen and resin to mend the roofs.

Lauds. Just after Matins, Benoît assembled all the lay brothers and sent Bruno to wake the craftsmen. The water was rising and endangering all the embankments, on which we had expended months of work and three hundred yards of good quarry chippings. The stream has become a torrent. This valley must be cursed! There is no water in the summer, and in the winter we get floods. I have forgotten my chest and my legs, all my aches and pains. Faced with this disaster, I have regained a fast pace and unexpected energy. I went up to watch the men working. They were battling against the current and against the uprooted trees which we had to be on the look-out for when the lightning flashed, for they appear without warning and can fell a man and carry him away. The men were tying down these fruits of misfortune with ropes, breaking them up and stripping off their branches so that they could be of use to us. It is an unequal struggle, but I am still hopeful. A dike just half a yard high would be enough. I have had all the available wood brought down. The mules were driven frantic by the thunder and reared up, injuring themselves in the total darkness which followed each dizzy flash. Then the blood began to flow, streaming from the torn hide at flanks and crupper. How was I to make those frenzied beasts understand, so that they would stop wounding themselves with their burdens? I shall wait, and write, so that I do not lose my patience and go down to order the chapel to be demolished: just an hour. At daylight I shall be able to see better.

St Florent

Brother Simon ran away last night; he was a stubborn man but worked like no one else I have ever known. Ever since the lay brothers had tried to rebel, this man of a hundred strokes of the discipline had clung to me like an animal. He would clean our workshop, lime the floor, carry the water and turn my mattress — all that over and above his own work. He no longer had any trust in his brothers and lived in the cruel solitude he had prescribed for himself. He must have left us at the moment when the lay brothers were finally abandoning the dorter. I do not remember having seen him in the vivid green light of last night. I had intended to take him back to Cîteaux with me one day. Alas, no one is either surprised or upset, so I shall be the only one to miss him, to love him for his purity and narrow-minded pride.

The water is still rising. The squalls have been succeeded by dense, vertical, senseless rain; it seems to have set in like the rain decreed for the Flood. At Vespers I shall decide whether or not to demolish the chapel, but for the moment we are busy keeping the torrent under control. Our work has been responsible for a slight shift in its path, but we have lost the foundations we dug under the north wall of the refectory. I gave orders to shore up that particular piece of work a long time ago; last night I did some more shouting about it but it was too late, everything must have caved in. If we can just save the upper part under the cloister gallery the damage will be halved. If I have to choose between that and the chapel I shall not hesitate, it will have to be the chapel. Writing helps me to relax. What could I do, anyway? Go and watch the lay brothers running from one breach to another, contemplate their ludicrous efforts? I know that it would only take another few inches to carry everything away.

Sext. After Tierce we had a battle to make some soup, and lost. The rain quenches our fires before the water comes to the boil. The prior had to distribute all his bacon and all his wine. We bolted down the raw vegetables, just lukewarm, with damp bread. What are we going to do this evening? If everything has been lost we shall come and take shelter here. There will only just be room for us to stand, but at least we shall be dry. I am going to have a big fire lit.

Benoît has come to tell me that the rain is letting up, that the wind is veering to the north. The water has stopped rising, indeed is tending to fall, and the current is less powerful. The prior wishes us to go down to the chapel where all the craftsmen are assembled.

Midnight. In the dark I fell over and my leg burst open. It is less painful, but what a hideous sight!

St Placid

In the space of a few hours, the mistral has dispelled the rain and clouds, and dried most of the mud. The craftsmen carpenters are on the roofs sticking on linen cloth. Luc has gone to Florielle to beg for some of the precious stuff. The prior has entrusted him with a letter which should help greatly to persuade the abbot. Benoît has gone to Fréjus on the same errand. The order of the day is first to roof the workshops and then to finish with the chapel. Afterwards we will protect the resin-stuck cloth with roofing planks. We do not expect to finish before the end of the year. Nevertheless, in a few days we shall be able to sleep, eat and work even under the most violent storm. Even our gentle Provence has her angry moods. We have learned a hard lesson, but we shall turn it to good use. The flood water has subsided into the stream, which is now hardly any higher than usual. It seems a long time since all those people came for the laying of the first stone, and yet only seven days have passed!

Work on the site was resumed after Sext. We did not get up until very late, but now that our muscles are warming again we are going on with the excavation of the rock. This particular work moves slowly; the number of strokes falling here must be unimaginable. The south wall of the church is set into the earth to an average height of five feet along its entire length. This way the thrust of the arches will be absorbed and rendered harmless at the point of maximum danger. Carrying away rubbish in hand-barrows is wasting our time, and though I have been trying to find a satisfactory method as an alternative, to my vexation I have not managed to do so. The incline is not steep enough for us to build a smooth slope.

Jean has had a trench dug all along the line of the pillars on the south side of the nave. The lay brothers were loath to do this kind of work because they did not understand the reason behind it.

'Instead of tapping and scraping at surface level,' he said, 'I am pursuing the same method as Paul does in the quarries, with a trench first and then an attack on two fronts with a pick and a crowbar.'

'Give me a demonstration.'

He had been waiting for this moment for a long time, but was not sure whether to start before the whole trench was completed. I insisted. He gave his orders and the men hurriedly brought the necessary implements, sought out the faults, drove in the tools, braced themselves against billets wedged between the walls and, all heaving together on command, prised up half a cubic yard of rock in one movement. In less than an hour the whole of one side had been loosened and the stone extracted and rolled away.

'Why didn't you explain your scheme to the lay brothers?' I said. 'They would have set to work with a better grace.'

'I prefer to take them by surprise. I have noticed that my method works on other sites. After this I shall be able to ask them to make the most overwhelming effort and they'll suppose in all confidence that there is some piece of craftsmanship waiting for them as a reward. Often that is in fact the case, but sometimes there is only the labour to be done and no satisfaction. I prefer, whatever the case, to keep my secrets to myself. All in all, productivity remains higher and giving orders easier. A man has more respect for our decisions if he is not aware of their outcome.'

'Perhaps you are right. For myself, I would rather not surprise anybody, but give the impression that whatever knowledge and experience I possess is first and foremost ours, and will then become theirs.'

'Everyone does as he thinks best. You are giving me a lecture — but are you sure that you are right? I am not very important, only a foreman. I spend all my time with the men. If I don't keep my distance a bit, I sink in their estimation.'

St Edward, thirteenth day of October

*Homer believed, then, that a truthful man is different from a
liar and that the two cannot be confused.* (Plato, *Hippias Minor*)

My mattress is clean, and every day I set it neatly up against the
east wall with its head to the north. The lime and earth floor is
spotless; I have it lime-washed every morning to increase the
reflection of light; I have one window facing north, three facing
south. In the evenings, my door in the east wall, which is rarely
closed, lets in a most warming light. Our trestle tables are
positioned north to south. The originally unadorned stone of our
walls has now been plastered and whitewashed and we can draw
on them whatever sketches we may need for the site. The corner
hearth enables me to heat water for medicinal purposes ... and to
wash myself! I am living like a well-to-do citizen with several
servants. When my kidneys, my chest and my leg combine to make
me feel dizzy, I stretch out on my mattress; it gives me a great
sense of well-being. I settle my accursed leg on a cushion to support my thigh. There is something going on in the small of my
back which makes me feel hot. When my chest hurts, I make
believe that it is not so bad, just moving slightly to limit the con-
tractions or dodge them altogether, to calm the burning sensa-
tions when they become too intense. At such times, I can only
wait until I catch up with myself and I say to myself, Quietly now,
I am coming.

I smile at some trivial thought, good memories or bad, or else
I become anxious, painfully aware of some awesome call from the
void. I tell myself, You will get no ideas today.

Luckily, I have the ceiling, a panorama from my mattress to
distract my attention: a crude, untidy, primitive ceiling, full of
visions, shapes and holes. Its complex of thick planks, splashed
mortar, straw and branches is a wild world open to the discoveries
of an idle man. It moves from bird of prey to man, from man to
monster, from monster to labyrinth, from labyrinth to caves,
from caves to abstraction and thence to dreams. All I can see now
is a mosaic, impressed in fierce colours on my lowered eyelids,
luminous with sparks and variegations. Finally, the continuous
renewal and shifting of shapes is exhausted as my imagination
falters, falling into dull geometric figures or the depressing

uniformity of seed-beds. I open my eyes and I know that I have gained an immaterial peace.

When I was a child, my elder sister, Josephine, used to draw that way. What began as a horse would finish up as steep rock faces, underground caverns, coats of mail, helmets, a dead tree, jewels, amethysts bedded in crystal, pikes, furs or silken cloaks. I used to love watching these concrete shapes turn into meandering lines, angles and abstractions. Any subject matter would disappear into a fabulous backdrop, a magnificent annihilation of the concrete. Then the observer, cured of his obsessions, would retrace his steps. As his feelings took him, he would leisurely re-create in his visions the helmets, pikes, caves, horses ... *ad infinitum*. Those drawings with their statuesque designs have survived as dreams in my adult life.

Inactive as I am, forced to lie on my back facing that impossible surface which is as flighty as a shadow, I end by succumbing to tiredness; the sleep of pain. I know that the moment has come. I still make believe that everything is all right and say, 'Don't worry, just wait, it will all happen because you have given it all due consideration; you know what you want, you know the size of it. So wait for the feeling you are going to achieve.' Then, in the midst of sickly and recurrent details, of hair like skeins of translucent silk, reflections distorted by the concentric ripples of water which reach for the flawless mirror's calm—I see myself coming. I am filled with a wild sense of joy, the joy of the feline creature as it leaps on a sure victim. I have been waiting for myself and now I am coming. It is a miracle among my everyday troubles. Subject to this new feeling of vigour I can forget my pain, and fall on to my back with the real world turning upside down around me. I go towards the table to meet myself—we are united to live out our common joy.

St Luke, eighteenth day of October

> *I am Alpha and Omega, the beginning and the end, the first and the last.* (Rev. xxii 12)

And in this cloister there is Christ.

The plan of the cloister is governed by an outline. Its origin is in the spring and there also is its result. Echoes from the pavilion of the lavabo reverberate throughout the composition. The hexagon, the way the outlines are constructed, axes and diagonals, the modules and the arcades are the beginning and the end. The cloister is their mother origin and also their final meeting point.

The pavilion to be built over the spring is complementary, additional matter, but the freedom of its shape and dimensions has determined all other proportions. Alpha and Omega — the theme I decided on a long time ago. I wanted the outline to seem disturbing at first, and then purified and inspired. Starting with the shape of a hexagon, the offspring of obtuse angles, which I settled on because the plan's basic irregularity demanded it, I have multiplied the corresponding proportions from echo to echo, reverberating the reflections off one another until they formed a unified whole. I wanted the symbol of God and of Christ to remain the cloister from century to century. I am certain that one day a dove...

Bernard, take care to remember and never change the slightest line as you put my plans into execution. Exercise the utmost strictness and precision. In case our plans are destroyed one day or stolen from our workshop, you must learn the following by heart.

The cloister is composed of two right angles and two angles which together make 180°. The diagonals are parallel to two sides of the hexagon. There should be a straight line running from the axis of the lavabo's south bay, through the intersection of the diagonals, this line being, first, parallel to the east gallery and, second, ending in the axis of the third arcade on the south gallery, counting from west to east. The axis of the same south bay and of the pavilion is, first, parallel to the east gallery, and, second, ends in the axis of the third arcade on the south gallery, counting from east to west. There should be two straight lines running through the pavilion in the axes of the south-east and south-west bays and ending in the fourth arcade of the east and west galleries, counting from the north. The position of the four arcades on the north gallery, two each side of the lavabo, is determined by symmetrical lines drawn from the two columned bays of the lavabo towards the north-west and the north-east respectively. To be more precise, the axes of each columned bay should end in the centre of the pillar between each pair of arcades on every side of the lavabo.

And above all, never forget that the cloister will be the last part to be built, since it is the least necessary part. If you feel that death is approaching, then bequeath what I am leaving you to someone else. You know the other drawings well enough and I have no doubt that you will always be able to reconstruct them from memory, especially those for the church.

Whichever way one turns one's eyes from the living spring, one will be conscious of the presence of God and of Christ. In contrast to the dark half-shadows, the galleries will form an atrium of glaring light to this luminous cave, glittering with its sixteen rustling fountains. The mystery of the sun takes precedence over the mystery of water. The massive columns, the thick pillars and the oculi of the symbol will filter and carve an endless variety of sunlit patches. The heavy cyclic lace-work, painfully realistic in its multiform abstractions, is an illustration of the Passion.

St Lydia and St Maglorius, twenty-second and twenty-third days of October

From dawn to dusk I am conscious of a thirst to live, to work and to love all around me. Even in the mist the site looks bright, with the craftsmen and the young lay brothers working briskly at the start of the day. At Sext the hours of gloom begin, and then the light turns its back on us and the shadows assume a livid, leaden hue. Sitting in the workshop or the chapel, I wait for time to pass. I am waiting for the evening light, the prelude to the never-ending night. This evening the moon will be full; it will light my walk so that there will be no danger of my falling. I shall be able to walk along the half-cleared foundations, imagining the start of walls, columns and pillars. On every site there comes a time when one can visualize the future. And if such moments are prolonged or stand altogether still with a total stoppage of work, one becomes even more aware of them, since the unjoined sections of wall and the archless columns look more and more dismal. Ruins are only beautiful when they show us the remains of their previous complete existence. An unfinished building cannot lay claim to the beauty of ruins. Thus, these moments on the site are thrilling only inasmuch as they are part of progress, of a continuous and steady development. Their many different aspects start with the laying of the first courses of stone and end in the vaults as they shut out the sky for ever. No time is closer to the master builder's heart than the day when the first wooden frames are set up, squared on the last vertical courses. These struts immediately outline the curve, fulfilling the intention of a drawing which has been no more than a geometric figure for so many months and years.

I have walked around sites for nights on end before work there began. The sky was usually oppressive, the ground sodden. I was glad to get back to my hut, take a hot drink and dream of things to come. This evening the dark sky is peaceful. There is such a tranquil mixture of warmth and moistness that the only feeling in one's body is an awareness of airy existence. I look forward to watching the rising of the full moon with the utmost pleasure. I think I know why: it is because this evening it will rise at a reasonable hour with an immeasurably bright light. Yesterday's moon was not fine enough and tomorrow's will bring incipient regret. I sit waiting at my table until Bernard and Benoît have gone to sleep, spying on them and listening like a thief. When I am quite sure that I am left alone, I shall open the door wide and lie in wait for the light. The moon has no dawning, it rises suddenly, from one moment to the next. I shall go off and visit the site by night.

I remember stumbling in the doorway and making a lot of noise, then thinking, my brothers are in the first, heavy period of sleep, they will not have heard anything. I made my way to the building plot without taking the short cut; after all, I had all the time in the world. The site loomed into view like a wide clearing of bright sunlight in a forest. The rock broke the surface, tracing white streaks, while the sandy ground, scratched, trampled and uneven, lay waiting for the morning when a fresh series of blows was to impress on it the superior right of man. And the land knows that these blows cannot be halted. Even unyielding matter has been no protection for it. Men decided, 'It shall be here'; whereupon trees were felled, the thorny undergrowth burnt, any loose soil dug up and the rock laid bare to be carved with the pick. Now I could see the various levels outlined. I was able to walk up an unmistakable nave, sit down in the middle of the transept, facing the apse, and pause for contemplation in that light which renders clear and distinct the spaces reserved for future blocks; those blocks which will enclose and divide up the normal way of life of our Order. The serenity of our sedentary way of life will be truly founded in this, our chosen valley.

Later on, our venture will seem quite natural. A house of men or of priests is at home in natural surroundings; it adjusts itself to the lie of the land whether it be forest, plain or valley. Its existence is justified by the road which winds towards it from afar. It reigns over the fields, a shelter for man and beast. It is made in the image of the law established thousands of years ago, namely, that a man comes to a place, tills the land and builds a shelter for himself, his wife, his children, his men and his domestic animals. However, just as in this spot, every human settlement has its origins in a choice. We follow the direction of a path, taken either intentionally or by chance, and are led to a certain spot which is part of a whole environment. There we say, 'This is where it shall be. We will enclose a portion of this space between walls, organize our lives inside them and, confining ourselves to this area, we will spend each day cultivating and maintaining this little space that we have taken from nature.' So, in his valley or his plain or on his peak, man occupies the land, clears a piece of earth or rock and shuts in the impalpable. This land is to be a home, a different, important world, sought out by man to be his place of defence, where he can take shelter and turn his mind inwards. After the providential cave, the hole hollowed in a tree, or the tent of animal skins filled with the stale exhalations of his wild beast's body, man began building artificial shelters. Then he began to want these to be beautiful, powerful or monumental, and in this way his mind became so full of the importance of his house that it swallowed his sense of sight. Even at a great distance he could see the house and would say to whoever happened to be with him, 'Look, you see behind that hill, that little stream of blue smoke floating into the sky—that's my house.' Mentally he is already there, behind his shutters, by his bed or sitting at his table. Amidst all the fascinating variety of nature, the only place that counts for him is that transparent veil, an illusion. He may travel all over the world, comparing sizes and differences, but his thoughts are full of the idea of returning to rest and happiness. His hopes are centred on an object fifty feet long, thirty feet wide and fifteen feet high, or ten or twenty feet larger if he is a king; not much, in any case, in terms of space, but almost everything in terms of his heart.

I stretched out my legs, laid my head back on the warm, sandy ground and there, in a sky so bright that the little stars had been scared away, I could see corners, pillars and arches as though they were outlined by fire. Once again I have lived through the history of a building site, bare and unadorned as it stands. This patch of cleared ground is destined to bear the body and soul of the instrument which binds us to God. This place will be the thoroughfare of the white habits which, in their encounters and minglings, have accumulated for so long that if their woollen thickness were heaped together, they would weigh more than the walls. If we held back the sounds of our chanting and then all burst out singing together after a hundred years, the noise would bring the vaults crumbling down, and the murmuring of prayers would be like the sound of thunder. I was lost in thoughts of this kind when I saw two habits falling from the sky quite close to me. After a moment of fear, I heard familiar voices. 'Come, elder Brother, you will catch cold. It's not very sensible to lie here on this wet sand with your injured leg.'

I was ashamed to have been caught in this way and thought it better not to try to explain. They helped me to my feet. Gradually, with just a brief sentence and a word here and there, I managed to win them over to my own brand of madness. Far into the night we went tracing the apse and locating the pillars of the nave and the walls. Benoît would stride about, measuring the distance between the principal points, while Bernard, with his arms stretched out, would shout, 'I am the line of the wall at the end.' To keep up the illusion we climbed one by one up to the inclined plane of the cloister. We knew that our estimates were meaningless and our measurements inaccurate, but we went from one room to the next, outlining with broad gestures or with lines in the sand and nail marks in the stone a particular angle, door or pillar. I taught them how to play. Tired, we stretched out side by side with our hoods drawn down and our hands in our sleeves like statues on tombs.

Above us the sky was white and flat, and not a hundred feet overhead hung a cloud of fixed, motionless black shapes, with great, outstretched wings chiselled like long fingers at the end, and thick necks under flat heads and pointed beaks. This blackness hurt my eyes as much as the whiteness, and I swayed about in space like a falling leaf, which rises, twirls and flutters. My dizziness frightened me and I did all I could to bring myself under control. Just as I was digging my fingers into the sand, the flock of crows suddenly came to life. I was paralysed. I could feel my back stiffen and I heard the shrill bells sounding Lauds. The cold air woke us completely. Meanwhile, the flight of winter birds, which some call the birds of misfortune because of their association with corpses, flew away on the wind screaming harshly.

Three monks, older by one day, returned once more to their positions as masters of the site. We went sternly to meet the first arrivals as the men went in twos and threes to their allotted posts, with sagging features, stiff limbs and a heavy tread. As they came level with us, the Antoines, Tiburces, Nicolases and Pierres hailed us with a slight gesture or a resigned smile. At dawn life is incomprehensibly hard, and the reasons behind the work are forgotten. Their faces expressed the fatality of slaves. It is like this every morning; our lay brothers are not men but wretched puppets jerking on the end of strings held from above, with damp crumpled tunics stiffened by grease and grey with mud, the conventional garments as worn and soiled as the still-sleeping souls inside them. Their noses drip, their necks are muffled in rags, their hidden hands conceal numbed fingers, scarred red or grey, or sores which will not heal until next spring. For myself, my doubts and wounds are like the one on my leg; hideous to look at, but covered by the folds of my habit. That is why I am the master and why they acknowledge it. Like them, I am suffering from all the confusion of the early stages on the work, only it is my duty to conceal the fact.

Later, when we had forgotten about our escapade, we went to see the stone-dressers, carpenters, quarrymen and labourers, Antoine, Nicolas, Bruno, Pierre and all the others, agile and flexible now and healthily brown-skinned, using their muscles and their minds with skill. Every day, activity takes them in hand again. The three of us went everywhere together without separating. We took several decisions, made endless improvements and solved some outstanding problems. There are times like this when everything seems to be moving forward by leaps and bounds, times which one remembers for a long while afterwards. Perhaps one of my brothers will say, 'You know, elder Brother, it was that Monday when you decided to abandon the middle quarry and stopped them felling trees too far away from the site, and sacrificed the two great oaks, and agreed that the level of the refectory was still too high.' I shall know that his underlying meaning will be, 'You know, it was the day after that night when we played at building in the moonlight.'

St Anthony

The day before yesterday was like any other. The sun rose at seven; there was no wind and no rain, and it was cold enough to stay like that for some time. The men started work before seven, when the early dawn gave them just enough light to see their hands and resume interrupted tasks.

Shortly afterwards we began the meeting in our workshop. I had intended it to be on the first of November, but on reflection there seemed no good reason to delay it, especially as my leg was now becoming an ugly sight. The men arrived one by one, not seeking any explanation, but sitting down around the table, yawning. There were Jean, Paul, Étienne, Edgar, Antime, then Bernard and Benoît and finally old Gabriel, who always looks like a barn-owl exposed to bright sunlight in the mornings. The plans were set out in front of me. It was the first time any such meeting had been held and, though my own attitude to the proceedings was serious enough, I was aware that sitting around a table at the beginning of the day made the craftsmen uneasy and hypercritical. I spoke for a good hour. Every word or phrase that I uttered, whether to one group or another, weighed heavily on them. They were quick to understand what I was saying and tried to follow the pattern of my thoughts and the path of my hands as they described the curves of arches or denoted weights and quantities.

It was our attack on the work site; each different trade was discussed in turn. There were shouts of 'Absolutely impossible!' 'Difficult!' 'We'll see!' Problems were raised and each man was required to give his own answer. Bernard and Benoît took notes, and Gabriel followed the list of topics to be dealt with. The installation of machinery and gathering of materials on the site was scheduled for the following day at dawn. In the end the craftsmen began to say what they were thinking. Some of them were even more forthcoming than I had hoped they would be. I was very pleased, for I knew that such discussions usually make people extremely exacting and intransigent. Men like these are used to moving within their own spheres, and are hardly inclined to fall in with plans where everything is common property. By nine the meeting was drawing to an end. Time had not dragged for anyone; indeed, the initial yawns of boredom had given place to yawns of hunger. We did not open the windows or the door until everyone was hurrying back to his post. The air in the room, which was thick with the smell of men, flew out like a symbol of the accumulation of our thoughts to fire the workers to action. Accompanied by the prior, we made our rounds as night was falling. The lay brothers were sullenly tidying up and putting things in order. Our secrets had been well kept. I think they imagined that during the meeting we had laid down stricter rules for the storing of materials, which was often carelessly done, and for cleaning the store room, a job which was continually being postponed. We had been surprised when Luc and Antoine went off about midday, leaving the animals. To rest the mules, even for half a day, is quite an event. About midnight, Bernard and Benoît finished drafting memoranda for the craftsmen and for us. Three gangs of men were drawn up to tackle the hard labour, with a total force of thirty-one—thirty excluding the brother kitchener. Paul was to remain at the quarries to keep an eye on work there and to make sure that good stone was chosen, Antime was to stay at the forge, while Joseph was not given any specific duties. Gabriel had a tiring time ahead of him. I thought of him lying sleepless in that tunic which was too long for him, busy counting, losing count and starting again—real torment. I sent my young brothers to bed and waited as the night grew colder, straining my ears as if they were eyes towards the window over-looking the road; waited for something to happen which would decide everything. As always, I heard the sound of wheels first, then voices and, much later, the horses' hooves. I counted two of them first, then four, and then, as I continued counting, I began to build up a picture. There were eight wheels, two carts and a wagon. Trembling with joy, I called Luc's name when I caught sight of the lanterns on the Field. He came straight up, slipping and falling, running headlong up the steep slope and forcing his way through the thorny undergrowth, thick and tall as it is. Though he kept stumbling, his progress was not slowed, and finally he gave himself a mighty shove with his hands and landed in front of my window. His long, horse-like face looked even redder than usual and seemed to trap all the light from my lamp, which was standing on the sill. If I do not speak to the lay brothers very often it is not because I do not wish to, but because, in the normal course of events, there is never anything to bring us directly in contact.

'Well, Luc, I see it went well. Are you going to tell me all about it?'

He was out of breath and spoke in jerky phrases. 'At Florielle ... I gave the cellarer your note ... he left me ... I was beginning to get pins and needles ... when ... I heard them harnessing up ... it seemed reassuring, I left Antoine there ... "Come and meet me at Tourtour at the Julliens' house and hurry up while you're about it ... " so that was all right as well ... They even lent us the carter for two days ... then we had a drink while we were waiting for Antoine ... It was pitch dark when he arrived, apparently our brothers had been piling questions on him ... he didn't know anything ... had to leave their pangs of curiosity unsatisfied ... Then I was afraid of getting back too late, we ran like thieves with the animals steaming, and on the way we caught up with the Mathieus going home to Saint Antonin ... and it so happened they were leading the wagon ... I took a quick look at the mules, they'd just done a day's work but they were still fit, so I said to myself, "It'll be hard going, but we'll make it" ... So the whole business started at the roadside. They looked at us and then at our animals, white as if it had been snowing ... "You drive them hard, Luc" ... and so on and so forth ... Oh dear this and oh dear that ... in the end, just to be friendly, we followed them to the farm ... we sat down at table, had a bite to eat and a glass to drink, and started on at them again. When I'd managed to make them laugh I knew we'd won ... '

'What? How did you make them laugh?'

'Oh, you know, it's not very difficult, just talking about ourselves, that's all it needed ... we had a bit to drink. Well, as time went on, the old man started on a long speech, but I wasn't worried, they hadn't unharnessed, you see, and I said to myself, "If he wasn't willing, he'd have stabled the animals." And then his wife comes from Carcès, she knew me when I was a baby. It was just that he wanted to make us sweat a bit. We began to talk nonsense; that pleased him no end, but he was a good fellow. In the end he asked us, "How long?" "Four days," I said. All right. Then he wanted to give us everything, straw, fodder, the lot. "Go on, Luc, take some more, don't worry, but take care this evening! Not too fast, don't flog them into the ground and don't start them working before nine o'clock tomorrow morning. I don't want you to turn them into Le Thoronet monks." That must have been because of you.'

'Obviously. Well, good work, Luc! Unharness them, rub them down and put them in the stable; then sleep through till eight, since we can't make promises about tomorrow. Keep one animal for me, the quietest one. I shall need to be moving about.'

He had certainly drunk a bit, Luc, or they would probably not have got Mathieu to lend them the wagon. But where's the harm in that?

The site was really something to be seen yesterday. Anyone who did not know would have thought that there were over a hundred of us. There were wagon-loads being drawn down from the quarries and the sawmill, and up from the forge and the store room. The gang of men under Jean were putting everything in its allotted place. He was walking about with his plans in his hands, measuring and marking out on the ground where the piles of stones, machines and wood were to go. We shall start building on the north wall of the church and on the corner with the apsidal chapels at the east. The two crabs are laid out there together with the poles, and, along the line of the wall, as close as possible to where it will stand, the stones. Gabriel was running after them, book in hand, making sure that nothing had been forgotten. Edgar was setting up poles, getting ready to build the first platform of the scaffolding. We would not need it for another ten days but we had decided to make this one sign of our new channelling of efforts. Seven months of preparatory work were descending on the site. Tubs were being filled with smoking lime, tools being laid out under shelter and their unused handles branded. The timber was arriving in the shape of squared logs, poles, planks, ladders, levers and framework for the fifty-foot crab. Carts from the forge toiled painfully up, apparently empty; slowly they were unloaded, and the sagging boards of the cart deck sprang gradually back into shape. Racks, set up for the purpose, were being filled with nails, rings, rivets, bars, pails, trowels, picks and shovels — six months' noble work on the part of Antime. Even after three journeys there still seemed to be as much again to be transported. From the workshops they were bringing rope, thongs, pulleys, mortar hods, hand barrows, wheels and rollers.

Luc and Antoine made a few trips with just the animals whenever they were made useless because the carts or the wagon were standing still; in this way any gaps in movement were used to transport lighter objects. The fruits of seven months' labour are bulky and heavy. It took us more than a few hours to move the stuff around. But the site was gradually being furnished and generally taking shape. By the end of the day Edgar's ten poles were pointing up towards the sky. Any of the teams who were ahead with their work lent a hand wherever they were needed. Meanwhile, the stone was a long time in the coming. Harder than iron, it stood firm against our efforts, tearing the skin and crushing the fingers. Some blocks took four men not only to load and carry them but also to unload and stack them. Our work on the stone has hardly begun and yet already two lay brothers have been cut to the bone and a mule killed. The stone is thirsty for blood, goes for the eyes of the dressers, wears away their strength and drains the water from their bodies. It is killing my brothers. Yesterday, the first stack could not be called tall, nor long nor broad. Even so, this stone has claimed the attention of more than half the men, and if the animals could barely walk by evening, the stone alone was responsible. This first day, everything was a game. The cheerful disorder of the moving gave way to a more encouraging orderliness, in which everything took up a limited amount of space and looked neat and tidy. But the stone was not so accommodating; it took hold of Paul, made a slave of the prior, made heavy work for the strongest, and disheartened the most skilful. The mules were uneasy, and pondering on the downward trip, they would grow restless at the quarry and at the site while the men were laboriously tilting the blocks with cautious, pre-planned movements. Ours was decidedly unlike other kinds of stone. Even with our experience, both Paul and I were greatly disappointed by the end of the day. We had not made half our predicted progress. Then it was time for supper and the sleep which had caught up with all of us by the time we took our last mouthful. The men fell into bed without even saying their last prayers.

The round began anew this morning. I had to give up my mule and drag my leg around again, but my presence was not so necessary any more. Our festival ended with the slow carting of the stone. But another one is beginning, for the marking lines have been stretched two by two, one to each face of the wall. Two crouching lay brothers draw the measuring chain between them while, in the middle, Jean is holding the plumb-line over the angles, axes or edges. Others are tracing a line and a cross in the fresh lime which has been carefully spread and smoothed over; but, mark my words, there are no games involved now. All these actions are disturbing. The craftsmen, who were so proud yesterday as they brought their booty and provisions, now eye this serious little man with respect. They are getting his hut ready and fixing a desk for his plans, fitting up the tiny building which is to be their confessional and torture cage of the future. Until now, Jean has been just a little craftsman who clambered over the rock with his three ropes, his level and a handful of fellow labourers, doing the work of a simpleton or an animal. We others, the master of trees, the master of forges and the master of stones, and myself, the master builder, looked down on him, since he was in charge of the least skilled workers. In future, however, the workshops will lose their privileges as one by one they become subordinate and bow to the will of the foreman of yesterday. Tomorrow he will be saying, 'I shall want twenty lengths of planking, twelve poles, some nails and iron rings and twenty yards of rope.' Everyone will jump to it. There will be no question of the stone being kept waiting in the dresser's gauge when it is to hold up a wall or an arch. At first things may be difficult for Jean, who is used to respecting the orders of others, but I know that he will change before very long. As director of stone-laying and masonry he will hold the key position of authority, responsible for the whole site. Antime may be proud, Paul arrogant and Étienne dignified, but they will bend the knee; for they will have made promises as yet unfulfilled. Whatever problems and difficulties they may have will lose all interest. From now on the site will be uppermost in everyone's mind. We shall have to beware of betraying any signs of anger or insubordination to Master Jean when he speaks contemptuously and says, 'Now we can see what you really are. Promise after promise, it's easy enough to make them! What I would like to know is what the hell you are *doing!*'

I have been waiting for this moment. It marks a new phase, and one to which I have been directing all my efforts – getting the site in motion. I shall have my share of awkward moments, too, when Jean comes to this hut and says, 'I must have that detail, Master, you are holding up my work.' And if I admit my own inadequacy or indecision, he will only add, 'Fair enough, but you can imagine what my boys will say when I tell them tomorrow that the chief hasn't finished drawing his pictures! You can all just stand there with your arms folded or go back to bed. I shan't be able to sleep, I'll be so ashamed.' But all that is nothing: trifling difficulties, trivial wounds to one's self-esteem; just a moment of depression. The site is getting on and nothing can stop it. At last the day we have been waiting for has come.

This evening the animals could not go on any longer, so we stopped work after Vespers and went about in full daylight to contemplate our achievements. We walked around the Field, as contented as villagers strolling around their village square, proud to be able to look at the first row of stones set there for ever. But the great day could not end without some incident. We heard the clumsy steps of a horse starting up the slope and turned to see who the new arrival was, glad that some traveller had come so soon and could tell the district what we had done and more besides. But it was only a donkey, so heavily laden that it hardly knew what its feet were doing any longer. Farther off we could see an old man bent double under his pack. 'Joseph' –

the name ran shivering over our lips like a sigh. We had forgotten Joseph for three days, thinking he would be happy enough making his tiles, turning and firing his pots. But Joseph was not looking very happy, not at all happy, in fact. He walked past us without a greeting, without saying a single word, rounded the bank and led the donkey over to the stack of stones where he unloaded two baskets brim full of cakes of clay. Then he picked up a plank and two logs which he arranged firmly over the cakes like a wall. Judging by their number, they must have weighed at least two hundred pounds. The poor animal began to look like a donkey again. The man and his beast then walked down to the stream, where Joseph threw his pack into the water, untied it, soaked his cloths and loaded the donkey up again; then they walked back up to the site and Joseph carefully wrapped the cloths around his wall of clay. Finally he took about thirty tiles out of the bottom of the baskets and put them together in the shape of a roof to protect the clay from sun and rain. None of us felt much like laughing; in fact, I was nearer crying. As he left, without halting his donkey, which was already trotting off towards some imaginary manger, he flung at me, 'In case you ever happen to need my clay in a hurry ... I thought perhaps Joseph might just as well come and ...' Nobody heard his final words, which were lost in a sob.

St Simon, twenty-eighth day of October

The abbot insisted on seeing my leg. I uncovered the sore and he looked at it for a long time. I told him how it had come about but he merely shrugged his shoulders. I realized that he had been alerted by the prior. He seemed bored by his inspection of the site, and as he left me, said, 'You cannot remain in that condition; that sore smells bad. I'd rather you had leprosy; then, at least, the immediate danger would not be so great.'

I made excuses, explaining that I had not had time to look after myself properly. I had my reading, the plans and the building to attend to. 'Now everything is in place, I can go away for a month or so without worrying.'

'You're mad,' he replied. 'I shall see you soon.'

St Narcissus, twenty-ninth day of October

Florielle has admitted a Knight Templar who is to come and inspect Le Thoronet and ask my advice about the commandery he wishes to build a few leagues from here. This is good news.

St Quentin

The Templar has only come to tend my wound. He examined me and then said, with an odd expression on his face:

'Your abbot is convinced that you purposely inflicted this injury on yourself; I want to know why. Tell me, how did it start? What did you do?'

I told him the whole story right from the beginning, told him how I had neglected myself. He did not believe me and persisted in his questions. I had nothing more to tell him. Did he really come all that way just to ask me questions? The abbot could have done it just as well. He did not give me any treatment for my leg, nor did he bring me any relief. I shall have to go, go back to Cîteaux. I do not want to die on this site.

All Saints' Day

Tomorrow, after Prime, the Templar is to amputate my leg.

All Souls' Day

Offer up my suffering ...

St Hubert, third day of November

At last I slept, in spite of the savage dogs, the cruel foxes, every imaginable ferocious animal, all biting endlessly at this limb of mine which is already gnawed by gorging insects.

My shaky life is torn between dreams and unconsciousness; it is a pendulum, exciting my heart and emptying my brain in its perpetual upward swing. I am being crammed with milk and honey and with warm blood.

St Catherine, twenty-fifth day of November

The Templar came this morning, looking strong in the folds of his wide cloak. I would like to see all noblemen look like him; clad in iron and cloth, with a cross and weapons. His mount is lean, an Arab horse which is said to be able to cover twenty leagues without stopping to drink.

I feel so weak in his presence that I begin to think, in the strange way of youth, that he is a score of years older than me. After examining my dreadful stump, he stayed to talk to me. From the moment when I began to exist again, the sound of conversation has been echoing round my hut for hours on end. It is in this that the mind, before the body has even begun to try, seeks its lust for life, thrusting forward like those plants which impel their impatient and disproportionate stems out from the darkness, towards the light of the sun.

St Severinus, twenty-seventh day of November

Since I started wanting to live, life itself has been wooing me. After a month of almost total isolation, during which the sounds of the site and the quarry have been my only companions, and my three brothers and Jacques the Templar have only been coming on their missions of pity to talk about my soul, my body and the precariousness of my life, the men are beginning to climb the path to my hut again. Death has missed its mark and is going away. The craftsmen are coming back. The healthy smell of action is entering my hut again. The door opens and a gust of the mistral sends our plans flying. There is a man standing before my bed. He is a little embarrassed and, blowing into his hands and keeping well over by the fire, he comes out with the usual phrases about my healthy complexion and recovery. No one manages to escape without saying, 'You'll soon be on your feet again,' or, 'You've still a fair amount of running around the site to do.' The ones who realize what they have said are abashed. I find the words to comfort them for their tactlessness, using the same phrases again myself. After the conventional preamble, their problems take over again. I can no longer count on the slightest discretion from them. The emergency has gone on for too long. In their eyes, it is time for me to live the life of the site, offering the only capabilities I can still muster—my mental strength. To them, this does not count as work. They think of it as a game because I can do it lying in bed and because it does not make me hungry. They are prepared to admit that the drawing takes a certain amount of energy, but even then they estimate the work involved as being only relative. It is the patience needed to make delicate sketches which calls forth their admiration. As for the rest, they really think that everything they come here to get is their due, since, as chief, it is my job to give advice or explain what is wanted. Anyone can be chief, but the man who has become one, whether by luck or by chance, must stay on the job. His brain is needed: it may be a poor thing, and of secondary importance, but it is needed. The master builder gets certain ideas into his head, flights of fancy, not like other people; and the craftsmen have been chosen to satisfy his whim. Well, every man to his own trade. When the building is completed, any devotion, indulgence and obedience involved will become matters for common pride. This was the way we had to go about it, and this is the way we have gone. The name of the monastery may be on a banner, but who will have woven and embroidered it? Who will have trimmed the wood for the staff? The craftsmen. Any attempt, by the chief, then, to recall his arguments or do down former sceptics would be to inflict a cruel humiliation and tarnish the brilliance of those lovingly embroidered letters.

Sitting awkwardly on the edge of a stool, the preliminaries over and the practical or technical questions dealt with, my visitors start to gossip, telling their stories, speaking too much ill of one man and too much good of another. It is from this kind of small talk on a work site that we can very often extract the truth of a matter. What a jigsaw puzzle of pieces there is to put together, and how cautiously I have to select the pieces, too. Paul's exaggerated way of speaking provokes fears of imminent crises; yet, if we were to act on his words immediately we would miss the embracings and the peals of laughter which follow an hour later. Equally, ignoring one shrug of the shoulders from Edgar would provoke a troublesome disagreement which might go on for weeks on end.

They hope to see my return to the site. Any wishes they may all express to see me 'running around' soon are not empty words. They miss my passionate speeches, my outbursts of anger, my words of praise or moments of silence. They have realized that both harshness and affection had their uses. A site cannot be run on forbearance or understanding, otherwise it crumbles. Anyone who is slow to curse, wound or make demands is only allowing the building to suffer. Unfortunately, to do all this well the chief has to mull over his ideas and weigh up the consequences before giving vent to anger. If he is young or new to the job, he will be extremely cautious. Let it never be forgotten that a master builder is followed everywhere by his own legend. The men on work sites form an almost universal brotherhood; stretching mouth to ear across the country, they transmit reputations, idiosyncrasies and weaknesses. We think that we are winning or losing whereas we are judged by the ever magnified rumour of our merits, or our faults, which pursues us from two hundred leagues away. Success or failure really lies with Pierre or Jacques, foster-brother to Paul or cousin to Joseph, craftsmen in stone or wood. In any case it is very hard for men who only 'sweat with their grey cells' to win the love or respect of men with calloused hands. And as for arousing admiration, there is not a hope of it without the twenty flames of the legend bearers and their trumpets. Generally speaking, the safest thing is to be content with a kindly tolerance.

The general gossip of these last two days has prompted me, after consideration, to have a talk with Benoît and Bernard. The former has long been fully responsible within his special field, but until now he had never acted on his own initiative. The insignificant words we have exchanged every day have, without our realizing it, set to rights many blunders or over-hasty moves which have been arousing steadfast hatreds during my month of absence. Bernard, though unsurpassed in his ability for drawing and layout, is betrayed by the contempt he has always shown for the practical side of the different crafts. He demands the impossible, which is often, none the less, very close to some simple application of technique. Moreover, he thinks that he alone possesses the key to certain imaginary secrets, and makes mysteries of them accordingly. For some perfectly modest explanation he will substitute a sermon of abstruse vocabulary which irks these men on the site, who are admittedly slow, but full of sharp good sense and a wit which is easily moved to mockery. Though he is essentially a good and simple person, Bernard turns his simplicity into a ludicrous cloak and arrogantly drapes it round himself for fear of being unfaithful to my wishes. Benoît listens to him, and then, for some unaccountable reason, goes even further, transforming some decision which is often clear and simple into a dilemma of obscurity.

I may have been wrong in inviting both them and Master Paul to see me at the same time. I thought that his unpolished, frank and sensible criticism would help my young brothers to understand their task. The confrontation was helpful; and if in the course of the meeting I was unlucky enough to hear some notes of discord, we nevertheless learned something from the experiment made during my absence, and were able to put it to constructive use.

The upshot is that I have arranged that after my departure a meeting of the elders should be held every morning, to which both lay craftsmen and lay brothers are to come, and which is to be presided over by Bernard and Benoît. Their time will soon come. Decisions will be made about the jobs to be done and the difficulties involved, as they would be in a chapter. Any differences will have to be dealt with and ironed out, either through discussion or by some word of authority. There will be time allotted for the expression of all assent and dissent, though any private remarks are to be clamped down on, however well intentioned.

Master Paul played his part as critic admirably, speaking with sincerity but not without a certain deference to my brothers. After he had gone, a harsh but edifying argument took place, which allowed me, or so I hoped, to make a final ruling on the question of my succession. Benoît was the first to express his dissatisfaction.

'Why did you invite Paul to join in our discussions? After this, he won't want to obey me any longer!'

'Have you or I ever given orders to Paul? For my part I have always yielded to what he really wanted. Paul has done just as he pleased from the start. As far as I know the orders he was given fell in with what he considered necessary.'

'A craftsman is a craftsman,' said Benoît, frowning, 'he is there to serve and not to give advice. I contend that his intrusion is a nuisance. It will be unlucky, humiliating and damaging to the authority you have established here which stands so firm and independent. Too many are asserting themselves on this site, too many differences of opinion are being heard. As you lie there in bed you are becoming kind and indulgent. You think you can set up an assembly to replace you. Well, let's try it! And you'll see that the beetles we are now will change pretty quickly into silly butterflies.'

'I would like to turn your analogy against you, Benoît. Remember your own inadequacy, and your partner's. You will only be beetles for as long as you are harnessed together, and then you make the best team I have ever known. And to use a comparison, as you have done, do not forget that a pair of mules has to know what it is pulling or what is pushing it along. The reason is that otherwise the cart will run you over and crush you. Your load is the advice the craftsmen give you, which will make up for the experience you lack and the brake that snaps. I can assure you that, unknown to them, men like these have been governing me all my life. It was not until I had watched them and adjusted myself to them that I began to make demands. I would listen to their order and then, after analysis, merely notify them of it. My only merit lay in choosing the right time to do so, if I was able. As for government by assembly, that has existed all the time, as you know better than anyone. Have I ever prevented you from speaking or criticizing or taking part in all my affairs? I have always allowed the widest possible scope for discussion so that I could be sure of acting under general agreement rather than making a command which might be foolish or harsh. I had recourse to authority only in order to carry on with something which had already been settled and accepted, to strengthen the feeling of continuation which is essential to any action once it is under way. You are confusing authority with tyranny, Benoît.

The one is the result of advice, often requested in all humility from the man who is later to put it into practice. The other is like asking for some impossible order to be carried out. Do that three times and you lose a man's respect for ever. A team of builders is like an anarchic society. The men recognize the most extreme among them as their chief, the one who defends the thesis that man is free and who is capable of breaking down any form of coercion, whether it is the result of incompetence or of a nascent sense of protection. How is that to be done, you may ask. Well, have you never noticed that for us a command is a service demanded by our obedience? It is our obedience which dictates, compels and constrains. The mason turns to the stone-layer, the stone-layer to the labourer, the labourer to the carrier, the carrier to the stone-dresser and the stone-dresser to the quarryman. Is it our fault when a link in that chain is broken? Yet there are ten pairs of accusing eyes threatening us and making it imperative that we repair the defective link immediately. Why did we discuss you today, children? Since I began to win back my powers of speech from the suffering that made me dumb, and cleared my brain from the clouds of pain, I have been receiving complaints from Edgar, Paul, Jean, Étienne, Joseph and Antime. And all because Thibault, Luc, Pierre, Tiburce, Antoine, Nicolas and the others have been looking at them critically or mistrustfully. All these anarchist builders are demanding as their right that I return to the enslavement of authority. Benoît, my Brother, why change your ways, when everyone is happy with you as you are? For a long time you have been the only person to mitigate the force of what you call established authority. Your lightness of touch has worked wonders. The position of chief has turned your head. You must know that a man is not chief because he bears the title, but because of the duties he performs; no one makes any mistake about that. As for fearing Paul and the familiarity of his criticisms, you must realize that they will carry weight only if they are justified. Don't worry, then, since you consider your powers of reason superior to his. Haven't I been the object of numerous attacks during the four years we have spent together? Here alone we have undergone the lay brothers' revolt, Joseph's gibes, and the doubts of the Chapter. Am I despised because of it? Have I lost my position? What are you afraid of, Benoît?'

'The end of your reign, elder Brother. Though I have learned much from your kindness and generosity, I feel as though I am standing in front of a gate with three locks. Bernard holds the key of the lowest, I hold the highest while you are taking the middle key away with you when you leave us.'

'Parable for parable: force my lock, open the gate and hang your keys on one single nail, then everything will go on as well as ever.'

I am not anxious. These two young men are happy only when they are together. I do not think they could ever leave one another. This evening I heard them going to bed, then talking and laughing, but I did not knock on the wall as I usually do.

St Andrew, thirtieth day of November

I know thy works, and charity, and service, and faith, and thy patience, and thy works; and the last to be more than the first ... I have set before thee an open door, and no man can shut it. (Rev. ii 19, iii 8)

The hooves of the Arab horse hit the road with a regular thud. As they follow the footpath, the beats falter for a moment, gather impetus and dash up the slope. The horse scrapes away the soil and pebbles with its shoes, under the thrust of its hocks. As it passes through the copses, only muffled sounds reach me, and then grow more distinct after the first bend in the road. As it rides down, an echo doubles the sound of trotting. I can hear another leap and more effort as it crosses the spring. There is silence as the waterlogged embankment absorbs the sound of weighted hooves. Then the uneven beats scale the last slope, starting uncertainly on the direct ascent with its steep terraces and moving more swiftly, keeping time with each other as they reach level ground, draw near and finally halt. There are sliding sounds, rattling, the rubbing of leather, sharp pawing on the ground interrupted by pauses to whisk the flies away, and the snorting of nostrils. Rings, bits, curbs, tinkle faintly but clearly with brisk movements of neck and withers. I can hear the tired man dragging his legs awkwardly. The door opens and the rider appears, stooping, his neck sideways, his face, pale but clear-eyed, tilted downwards. Jacques the Templar has come in.

Every day for a month I have waited for his visit. At first, when I was delirious, I would think I could hear him and see the door open; but it was only my fever. Only my sense of smell remained true to me. It was when I could smell leather, oil, wool and the coat of a heated horse that I knew I could open my eyes without being disappointed.

'Greetings, Brother, I have come to have a gossip. Let me have a look at your leg.' We talked together like friends. Later Benoît came in, and he stood there waiting until I gave him a questioning look.

'Four peasants have come,' he said. 'The prior has made them welcome, discussed terms with them and put them under my charge.'

'What can they do?'

'Nothing for the building site, and not much more when it comes to making *bancaou* in the winter.'

'You have some ideas, I suppose, Benoît?'

'I suggest sending one to work with clay, two to the wood-cutting and the fourth to either Antime or Joseph to work with one of them.'

'Why do you want to get rid of them?'

'To prevent any lapses in discipline.'

'No, Benoît, I would rather put them to work with the lay brothers. Left alone, they won't be very productive and their labour is expensive. I wish to put them under Paul and Jean so that they can follow our men. Make sure that there is nothing to exclude them from our way of life, as far as both work and discipline are concerned. I suspect that Brother Pierre will force them to say their prayers and that they will feel as though they're our brothers that way.'

'But they're laymen!'

'They're Christians too! Chapel should bring them some calm if not exaltation. Off you go.'

When Benoît had gone, Jacques said to me, 'As a master builder you are perfect; you become straightforward again. As a monk you make everything complicated. Let me tell you something – I don't care for Benoît. He is too much like some of our sergeants who are only as good or bad as their captains are. Left to their own devices, they are loathsome.'

'You are wrong. Benoît is the best site chief I have ever known. I have been watching him for three years now, and apart from a few blunders, all recent occurrences, his management is greatly appreciated.'

'I do not agree. He does not seem open-hearted to me, but full of jealousy and pride. When you aren't there he looks about him in a curious, contemptuous way. Your good Bernard will have a hard time if you carry on with your idea of leaving.'

'Let us talk about something else, if you don't mind,' I said in irritation.

'I went and looked at the site yesterday.'

'What changes have you noticed over the last month? Everybody tells me about their problems but no one says how the work is progressing.'

'The swallows do not dance round the scaffolding poles any more.'

'Now that's very important ... thank you for telling me.'

'I don't know anything about it, you know. As far as I can see it's all moving very fast. One section of the wall is over fifteen feet high already, but what a business with those stones! It will take you years to finish it. One of the skilful lay brothers, Tiburce, has begun a rounded chapel on the east side; each stone is being dressed again on the spot. It'll be a long job.'

'We have the time. Next year we shall have a harvest to reap and from then on we won't be a liability. In two years we shall be able to help support Florielle.'

'And what about paying the craftsmen and buying their supplies? All the tools you have to buy that you cannot do without? Jean told me that at the present rate it will take seven or eight years at the very least.'

'Next year we shall have some kind of income from bartering our tiles. The craftsmen won't stay here; the more skilful lay brothers will take their place. As far as the time we take is concerned, Jean is mistaken. We now have a considerable stock of stones, but in a few months' time we shall be reduced to the daily yield of the quarry—about a quarter of what we are laying now. When we reach the arches, there will be yet another delay as dressing, laying and assembling the stone will be so difficult. As long as we are working near the ground with the stone under our hands, the work will move forward fast, but one day the masons and the layers will have to leave the site to prepare a new supply of stones. That will be a severe setback.'

'I understand. But why must you have so much precision in your stones? If you were to use them in undressed blocks, it would go very quickly, wouldn't it?'

'As a surgeon you are perfect. As a monk your arguments are simplistic!'

He seemed not to have heard me and went on, 'I saw one wall which was very thick and over a hundred feet long. In some places it stands two feet high, and in others fifteen. Space has been left for two doors at the same level and two very fine arches. On both sides of the wall is a first course of stone to indicate eventual pillars, three on one side and seven on the other. Two of these seven are broad and five are narrow and deep. On the east side, the returning angle of the wall thickens so much that I was able to lie full length on it without either my head or my feet showing beyond it. That's where I saw Tiburce and Pierre. They have marked out two semicircles and, with just three workers to help them, they are racing against time in order to reach the level of the arches by Christmas. On the curved side they are laying polished stones and cementing them with lime. On the other side they have already set a row of very large blocks, splendid to look at, rough-hewn on the visible faces and very smooth on the four fitting sides so that the joints can hardly be seen. Can you recognize your site from my gibberish?'

'Yes, I can see it. I haven't dared ask anyone to describe it to me with any feeling in case I seemed too soft-hearted. I have only been told the daily quantities, the points at which work has been begun and the effects of regularity in laying stones. I can see the five pillars of the cloister arcades with the two massive corner pillars, and the three pillars on the north side of the nave with its main wall broached by the cloister door; I can see the transept wall and the passage to the sacristy, the two apsidal chapels, all of them finished up to the level of the arches for Christmas.'

After a pause, Jacques went on, 'They're very beautiful, you know ... those stones. Tiburce and Pierre explained to me that it was you ... that nobody wanted to, believed that ... it would be magnificent ... The chimney seems to be smoking. I'll get the fire blazing or else it will affect my eyes too; I should have done something about it before ... Will you ever be able to leave this site?'

'Never, with my heart! But I want you to help take my body to Cîteaux, and very quickly so that it gets there warm.'

Look, Templar, I take back simplistic.

'What will your abbey be like?'

'The most humble and the most moving in the Order.'

'Are you so sure?'

'I love what I am doing so much at the moment when I first conceive it. All my life I have thought in this way. When I have finished something I often go out of my way not to see it again.'

'You know that, and yet you can start all over again?'

'I always have hope.'

'You are mad, strange. I didn't imagine the joys of the master builder to be like that: seeing one's thoughts and feelings made concrete. I am someone who struggles against suffering with no other effect than to take away what God has given. I thought that the creature, man, had a better lot.'

'Be glad, Templar, that every evening you can say, "I have done what was strictly necessary, I have given care, I have healed, I have contended with death. My hands are instruments of pity and mercy." '

'Thanks, you old idiot—I must go now. Night falls quickly at the end of November. I don't know where the moon has got to and my horse has no cat's eyes. I can see that you're sound of mind, you may go on thinking for hours. Lately I have been reluctant to ask you, but now that you are going to leave us, I can say it—I need advice, plans. Can you help me?'

'Gladly.'

'I have my commandery to build. Before you go, talk to Bernard about it, and sketch a few drawings for him. Quite simply—we haven't any money, and soldiers, you know, have no idea how to build. If you could plan some massive masonry, thick enough to stand up to anything, a rough surface, unpolished and irregular, that's the kind of thing I like. Draw a fine outline, you know, like a man-at-arms standing in the middle of a great, bare plateau, with his cloak and his sword all part of the shape. You think I have set ideas? You're smiling, you're mocking me.'

'No, I have simply come to the conclusion that you were lying.'

'When?'

'When you said "I don't know anything about it." '

'When I'm with you, I stick my neck out.'

'Good, tell me all about it, and then be off with you. The moon is only half full and it will rise late, and I want to work. By tomorrow I think I'll be able to show you a plan.'

'Really, so soon?'

'You have told me everything. Your monastery is you, I could draw it from life. You must write your life story, the story of the horseman and the brothers, talk about your horses, your weapons and your books.'

'I'll send you a copy of our Rule, but you are right, I shall describe my house, give you the measurements of the rooms. Oh, you know — nothing grand!'

As he sat there, setting down his ideas with some difficulty, my heart beat faster. Less than an hour later, he handed me a single sheet of paper covered in large writing.

'Early tomorrow morning', he said, 'one of my brothers will bring you the Rule your Abbot of Clairvaux made for us.'

In one great movement which swept the whole workshop, he wrapped his huge cloak round him. He took both my hands and added, 'I am coming back after Vespers to sleep here. You don't mind? We can either talk or be quiet. Make a sketch that I can understand.'

He helped me to get up to show him to the door. He sprang lightly into the saddle and rode cautiously down the stepped terraces. After thirty yards he stopped, turned in his saddle and shouted, 'I forgot to tell you: the shape of our house, you know, when we mark it out on the ground, you see what I mean?'

'Yes.'

'Three sides, a triangle, you know?'

'Yes.'

Now it is midnight and I am working on the house for the Temple. Tomorrow we'll start making drawings with Bernard's help. Once more, it is good to be alive.

St Eligius, first day of December

My departure has been settled. Thanks to my brother Pierre and Jacques the Templar, the abbot has allowed himself to be persuaded. With rest, the gradual healing of my wound, and a compulsory and plentiful diet, I am gaining fresh strength. I shall be leaving in tranquillity and peace. Perhaps there are long months of happiness lying ahead at Cîteaux. I shall end my days as a true monk.

The Templar will be coming with me as far as Lyons, then some of my brothers will take charge of my litter. There is a peaceful journey before me, free from danger. If all goes well we shall be at Cîteaux for Christmas.

Vespers. I have informed Bernard and Benoît of my departure. After a touching scene, they gazed at one another for a long time, aware of the magnitude of their approaching responsibilities.

Compline. It looks as though the fine weather has come to stay. Bernard feeds the big fire in our workshop and the flames give out so much heat that we have opened the door on a moonless night. He is drawing the three-sided commandery, just a small building, as the Templar means to complete it in less than two years; it will be a man-at-arms standing on the plain with his great white cloak, his cross and his sword.

Advent Sunday

Sire, I give thanks to Thee that Thou hast fulfilled my desire. Here I see the beginning and the cause of all things. And now I beseech Thee, grant that I may depart this earthly life and enter the heavenly. (The Quest of the Holy Grail)

Bernard has been helping me take my first step. There is no second one. We pass our days writing, drawing and making notes. My younger brother, both proud and wretched as he is, is impressed by the number of instructions I have to leave. Benoît, who is less affectionate, comes every day to consult Bernard rather than me. He does not realize that I am hurt by this. Despite my lecture, he is full of his new importance. I sit up in bed, sketching details, profiles and plain mouldings. We have nearly finished putting the commandery into shape. Jacques is excited by the speed at which we are working. He wants to start building straight away and hovers round the site hoping to steal Edgar away from us, since he can, of course, turn his hand to anything. If the prior so wishes, we could lend him his services for a few months. This evening we had a discussion with Bernard about building the farmhouse and the mill. He insisted on my making the plans but I refused and said, 'You will start on the studies for these buildings alone. They are the little brothers of the abbey just as you are my little brother.'

He hid his face in my shoulder, and for a moment I held him tightly. I think, as he does, that he is more a son to me than a brother.

Now that everything is drawing to a close, as far as I am concerned, I am thinking back over my life. I have preferred to act, to do whatever was useful and effective; this is the cause of my remorse. I am haunted by a nostalgia for the work I have accomplished, which adds to my regrets as a master builder. Now that I am about to leave it, I can look at this abbey and the other works I have completed in my life as a builder. Of the qualities of my most recent work I am certain; yet when I was about to leave the others they too aroused feelings of confidence that were just as deep. If I had had the time and the brains I would have liked to devote myself to building a single monastery or church. I could have studied, observed, kept in check and returned to the numerous steps I regretted, so as to obtain undeniable perfection. Perhaps it would have been at once a more selfish and a more generous way of working, more humble and more proud, more fruitful and less useful: how do I know? There is always one reason to confront another. Truth is always equally divided between truths.

I had a wealth of ideas which I have squandered. I have burned up my gifts running from one place to another. I envy those artists, painters or sculptors, who tirelessly cover one piece of work with another. How do they know when they have achieved true beauty? How can they daily destroy the creative impulse which inspired them the day before? It is a mystery to me.

Others will make ten studies, similar in form if different in inspiration. And this preliminary work allows them to concentrate the good qualities of the earlier works into an eleventh. Is intensity preferable to quantity, then, should it be compared to the superiority of contemplation over action?

That soothing enthusiasm of mine has been my welcome enemy, for through it I have produced many works with a blameworthy self-confidence. I have always been a naive creator, vain and touchy. I have believed in the inspiration of the moment as if I had been given a series of shapes on the mountain that I might construct them on the plain. Later I became harshly and relentlessly critical, saying, 'Are you sure that you had reached such heights when you thought up that one?' But how can I build while I'm continually mocking my emotions; while I'm full of self-doubt, continually procrastinating? In any case, it is too late now; there is no point in my inner conflict.

St Barbara, fourth day of December

The prior is displeased because my two disciples can no longer agree about anything. Benoît had given some order, whereupon Bernard came along and gave a counter-order. Jean complained about it to the prior: 'Whom am I supposed to obey when the master isn't there?'

'You'll have to decide who is going to be your successor,' Brother Pierre told me.

'You can understand my reluctance, Prior. Why not wait and carry on with things as they are? It was not a serious incident, their friendship goes deep. When Bernard and Benoît are united and working together, they can manage the site. Divided they count for nothing.'

'It is causing us a certain amount of anxiety. The abbot is worried. He said that in his opinion Bernard is the obvious choice for your successor; Benoît will never make a master builder. This kind of building can only be entrusted to a man of sensitivity, and this requirement will apply until the end of time. He went on to say that experience, knowlege and practical application are bound always to depend on the imponderable. Woe to the architectural form if sensitivity is constrained, and woe to the man of sensitivity if he neglects or is ignorant of knowledge, experience and application. As far as I am concerned, I am very much afraid that you put too much trust in letting events take their course. Both the site and the management of the site must be planned with due consideration, and not in the sentimental wish that the frail friendship of men will hold good.'

'I cannot entrust that role to Bernard. I have only given a part of myself to each of them.'

'While you are here, they are conscious of your weight. Their friendship, kindliness and mutual forbearance rest entirely in you. If we remove the third side of a triangle, all we have left is two converging and diverging lines, just an angle. At the moment the abbey needs a foundation for the future, the third leg of the table, the third pillar of the Temple.'

'Prior, will you agree to be patient? We have reached the point where the task of the most important angle has been completed; now we have to follow up by maintaining a balance between feeling and fact. I am certain that you are the only one to take my place at the apex. I would have liked this to have become established by tacit agreement after my departure. Until now you have allowed me to encroach upon your office as supervisor of works. Neither Bernard nor Benoît alone, let alone the pair of them united for ever, will be able to overlook your position as Abbot of Le Thoronet by procuration. You allowed me to perform your duties out of tact and because you recognized the need for efficiency; but that particular episode is drawing to a close and we are starting on a new venture. Do me a favour and don't say anything to our little brothers who are so dear to me, not until the evening after I have gone, when you can quite simply tuck your mattress under your arm and go and sleep in the workshop in my place.'

'The abbot had the same happy idea, Brother, he sees this as the best solution. He has already written to tell me his reasons. I can only approve them with regret, for I fear that the Spirit that warned me may have less success in bringing about an understanding between our brothers. But I am quite willing to try the experiment.'

Our conversation was interrupted by Jacques the Templar.

He realized that he was intruding and turned to go, but the prior would not let him.

'I have come with some good news for you: we are leaving the day after tomorrow on the Feast of St Nicholas, in the morning.'

I was stunned. 'I can't leave so soon. I am not ready.'

'You must, I have things to do. Besides, I am concerned about your wound. I don't want to hand over a corpse when we get to Cîteaux.'

I had spoken without thinking, with a distress in my voice which showed how hurt I was. The prior was ill at ease and Jacques did not know what to say. In an attempt to take my mind off things, I suppose, they sat back and began to discuss the building of the commandery. I was terrified of their leaving, and for the first time I tried to stop the hours passing. I had not been expecting to hear that piece of news this evening. It seemed like the refusal of a pardon to a condemned man at a time when he is still living in hope. At that moment the rest of his life is like the contents of a cup which he wishes to drink slowly, savouring it with great intensity. He can already see the bottom, but carries rashly on so that the liquid spills over his lips, paradoxically wanting both to make an end of his apprehension and to cling on with his whole body.

I knew it: as long as I was not able to see the lights of Cîteaux at the end of my journey, I would continue to draw out these painful days or try to stop them passing altogether so that they would not drag me along with them.

The prior was the first to tear me away from my thoughts. 'What are you going to do tomorrow?'

'I don't know. I still have a lot of work to do. I wasn't expecting this, I still have so much to say.'

I couldn't suppress my sadness. If we had been alone, Pierre would have let me continue, but the presence of the Templar seemed to force him to play his role as my superior and forget our friendship.

'It will be none too soon, Brother,' he said. 'We thought you were ready. We can hardly allow for negligence on your part. You do want to go, don't you?'

'You can make a choice,' added Jacques, 'there is still time. I shan't carry you off against your will. It is basically a question of where you are to be buried.'

'No, it's all right as it is. I want to go back to Cîteaux.'

'What are these instructions you have to leave,' resumed the prior, 'and whom for? What have you forgotten? Is our abbey going to suffer from all this?'

'Nothing, Prior, nothing has been forgotten. I have either left written notes or drawings of everything that has to be done. The abbey can suffer only at the hands of others, I am leaving it to you complete. But, as you know, one is always fearful.'

'A Cistercian! Fearful? What are you afraid of?'

'Why shouldn't one confess to fear?' interrupted Jacques. 'We Templars know what it means. We are men more often than we are priests, and in battle we cannot always keep the cross of Constantine before our eyes. Rather, the weapon that will pierce us sends disgusting shudders through our bodies. So perhaps his fear, like ours, is the fear of a man.'

'Thank you for coming to my defence, but the word "fear" was not altogether accurate. I am uneasy, Prior, about the dressing and laying of our stones. I am uneasy about the rivalry between my disciples and the naive simple-mindedness of Master Jean. I want my drawings to be followed. This is my last work and I have put so much into it. The triangular shape made by the diagonal across a square is behind the whole building. It defines the projection of the roofs of the nave and aisles below the steeple, and determines the height of the apse when the base of it is placed across the width of the church. When the apex of the triangle is placed in the centre of the oculus, that is to say, over the line of the nave's semicircular arch, it controls the height of the side arches. In the cloister, the design of the twin arcades depends on this angle in conjunction with the number five. And there I want this angle to be made concrete so that the arch-stones of the oculi and the lesser arches are always joined on the lines connecting the three centres. I want the stones making up the greater arch always to have five sides and the diameter of the column to be one fifth of the arch's breadth, as the diameter of the oculus will be. And that diameter will be equal to the radius of the lesser arches, which, multiplied by five, will give you their height ...'

In this way I described the many aspects of the building to the prior, apologizing for not giving practical or logical reasons for my wishes in most cases. Then I spoke to him about the craftsmen and the lay brothers, listing each one's faults and showing how, with guidance, these could become good points. Finally I spoke about our materials and the deep-rooted connections between them and the way they could be adapted to become shapes and bases. As he listened to me, the prior was weighing the effect of my words on Jacques. He must have been thinking that my frequently obscure way of speaking explained my previous attitude to this stranger to the Order. Not knowing of the conversations which Jacques and I have had, the prior wanted to safeguard our dignity and show of decorum. My digressions put him at his ease again. He replied, more gently:

'But, Brother, we have your drawings and we shall respect them. I have followed you, watching and listening. I have said that I shall be your successor. When Bernard and Benoît give any orders, I shall be able to tell whether they are giving voice to your wishes or theirs. If, one day, some new suggestion is made, I shall be able to feel whether they are carrying your thoughts through or departing from them. So your problem cannot lie there, and if we are to put an end to your ... uneasiness, may I ask whether you are sure that you weren't nervous about overlooking something, some vital instructions, perhaps, or perhaps there is something even more serious?'

'Nothing in particular, Prior.'

'Now you must admit that it was difficult to confess to that.'

'You Cistercians are beyond me,' broke in the Templar. 'I don't want to butt in, but you always conduct your arguments with one foot on the staircase to heaven. Prior, you think that your brother has now wound up all his doings properly and that he has only to withdraw into prayer and taste the joys of the monk's vocation in order to prepare for eternity. At first he is very moved and takes refuge in learned elaborations on the triangle and pentagon, using them as an excuse for his confusion. He is almost in tears, standing there with one foot on the staircase and his crutch on the ground. He presents himself as a good servant of the Order, scrupulously setting forth his corresponding anxieties. Good God! Wouldn't it be better just to look at this hut? Here we are, not with a monk, but with a man who has been planning, organizing and supervising for more than twenty-five years. Look, you lunatics, even the crucifix is hidden behind his drawings. We are soldiers three-quarters of the time, and that way we remain men. That does not make us superior, I grant you, but it does help us to recognize weakness and believe that it is fatally necessary. It is useful, I tell you, to be able to detect it. Before he managed to take hold of himself, he spoke of fear; if he really wants to confess it to you, Prior, I am pretty sure he knows what it is, that fear of his. You can see the meaning of it here, in this place of work which sums up a whole life.'

Surprised at first, Pierre had closed his eyes, but he was listening and, without looking up, he replied: 'Why are you so anxious to tear us away from the convention and dialectic of our Cistercian Order? I want us to remain in all things on the same level as an Order which strives to be at the level of God. You, old soldier, are holding us back on the earth to speak of our contemptible sufferings and probe our emotions. Leave us our stage on the ridges of Sinai. As a Cistercian prior, I am watching over the nobility of our dialogue, keeping it removed from the human. Now you, you are lying in wait for some sign of weakness from us. This evening his weaknesses interest you because you are a friend and want to help him with your rough and ready sentimentality. You hope he will weep, so that in his shame he will turn his tears to laughter and be comforted by the usual mundane means. For you, true contact between one spirit and another lies in the hand which clasps a shoulder or grips it affectionately. This is no time to try that method with him. You would be only too glad to stay here alone with my brother and teach him how, as a man, he can regain serenity, the courage which comes only from pride and makes superficial heroes, men who are only in control of their bodies, but are mush inside. As a man-at-arms you offer a breastplate. We Cistercians know how to go naked; thorns may tear at our skin, but our souls are in perfect balance. And this is the way we shall remain truly invulnerable.'

'In my case it is more simple, my friends! You are quarrelling over the invalid that I have become, a man enfeebled by suffering. Your reason, Prior, and your logic, Jacques, have nothing to do with the way I am feeling. I really am afraid, afraid of dying, because I have more love for life than hope from the hereafter.

My decision was made in a rational moment — I often think like a Cistercian. I am protecting myself against loss of life. I knew that to stay here would be to die like a man. One day I shall pass away here among my friends and my craftsmen, without noticing it, in this workshop, sitting at this table, perhaps, or on the site or lying on my bed giving orders to the masons. That way I shall leave the land of the living in an unspectacular death, as everyone dies. My decision to leave was in accordance with Pierre's way of seeing things. As a monk I was going to break loose from my quarter-century of professional work so that I could go naked in search of balance of mind. But this evening, whatever you may say, wish or do, I am merely a wretched man who has had some bad luck. My decision was still only an intellectual speculation, nothing concrete. Can you see the difference between "in a week" and "the day after tomorrow"? Well, I can. Don't count on me to be heroic either inwardly or outwardly. I could have prevented your quarrel by answering Pierre quite frankly and saying, "What am I going to do tomorrow? I am going to say goodbye to my life, to what I hold most dear, to the site. Tomorrow is the day I die." I gave you your cue, Prior, out of friendship. I know that is what you like. You have won your faith, I have lost mine. If I have stayed a Cistercian it is for the sake of what I shall be leaving behind tomorrow. Now go. You can see I am well below what you two would offer me — human courage or divine invulnerability. You know, there are times when one doesn't force one's gifts. Words are only the expression of a comedy in which none of the characters seems real. This evening let me be; my thoughts are too tied up in what the pair of you disdain, surrendering to the current, the memories. Good evening, my friends. I give you leave to go in your peace, whether it is real or assumed. The day after tomorrow I shall be ready, I shall be playing my part as you wish, I hope.'

St Sabas, fifth day of December

> *Before the light disappears, we pray you, O Creator of all things, to keep us in your care.*

Nine months ago today we came to Provence. Tomorrow I am going back to Cîteaux. I shall read the inscription over the door for the last time: 'Hail Holy Mother, under whom the Cistercian Order gives battle.' A knight of the Virgin, his mission accomplished, seeks his pitiful reward—to die surrounded by his brothers.

Night has fallen swiftly, bringing me despair in my loneliness. I had intended to spend this short day gorging myself with visions, filling myself with memories so that I might achieve some serenity on this last evening. But it was wasted effort; left to myself, I felt lost. Before making up my mind to return to these few remaining pages to write something, anything at all, I wandered about in this hut, from my bed to the hearth, to the table. I looked over my drawings but my head was empty and my throat tight. I dragged myself along the walls, hopping like a locust on one leg, trying to remember when and why I had scratched out those drawings. The cup is empty. Jacques will be coming at about the ninth hour to load me up like some object left at the side of the road.

I have been leaving sites all my life but always happily, with some fresh plan in my head. And then, quite often, I was only leaving for a few weeks; I was going to more pressing tasks. This evening it is not the same. When I reach the end of the journey there will be nothing more, nothing to await the good will of fate and that hereafter of which I am so afraid, surrounded by my brothers.

This morning Bernard dressed me. For the first time in a month I am wearing my habit. Yesterday, after my two friends had left, Bernard brought it to me. It was clean and mended, like new. Hanging on the door it looked very beautiful, with the luminosity of thick and frequently washed material, soft and sculptural at the same time, milky marble. This morning I was happy, conscious of the pleasures of my first excursion. Supported by the two brothers, I got to the door and breathed in the cool softness of the thin air. The sky was blue as it is in spring, with lovely white clouds, just the right number of them. I went round to inspect everything. The walls are rising; it is all as it should be. It seemed strange to me, the bustle and hope, all the activity and the conscientiousness of these people building their church. It is their business, not mine any longer. I am abandoning the work which I love more than God. A moment ago, cowardly, I prayed. I think I was crying without shedding a tear, leaning my forehead against the cold wall. I said, 'You understand, my God, it is Your house and Your church also! Put Yourself in my place! I cannot leave it without a qualm, it is not possible; I have become more attached to this place than to any other, all of me. But here I am, sick, and I have to let go before I have seen the end.' I muddled everything together, feeling the uncomprehending pain of the mortally wounded animal. Now I feel more dignified, more sure of myself and my movements, and I can remember all the details, buried deep at the back of my eyes.

I shall never see the quarries again, the way the stone is extracted with pick and crowbar, the way the soaked wedges, carefully placed in round auger holes, suddenly split the block apart, and the way the stone is cut up on the spot, then dragged on rollers to the dressing area. I shall never know the worry of the daily inspections again.

'How much yesterday?'

'Four clean cubic yards quarried, one dressed.' That was a good day.

'How many stones yesterday?'

'Six cubic yards of crumbling rock, all rubbish! And as for the dressing, we hardly managed half a yard.' That was a bad day.

My heart will no longer beat the way it used to when Master Paul said, 'Give me ten more good lads and in a month we'll be dressing five a day.'

He did not really believe it; nor did I, but we were happy enough just to talk about it to give each other pleasure.

What a reassuring sight that chaotic amphitheatre was! The lay brothers, armed with mallets and chisels, carving out straight and curved edges, cutting out grooves, sorting by thickness, making up stockpiles, numbering the special stones; then loading the blocks as the layers asked for them, by the heaps of waste they crush with the sledge hammer to fill up foundations or the insides of walls. Nothing must be wasted, even the poorest material goes to make walls for the fields, and the chippings always end as great piles of sand.

I can see five or seven of them sitting on the ground with the block between their outstretched legs, their bare arms tanned and coated with dust. The precision of their movements makes their muscles stand out in a regular rhythm like quick panting breaths.

Their eyes, wrinkled and diseased, are fixed attentively on the block of the moment, which is just like yesterday's, tomorrow's, every day's. Their faces, bowed into dust-grey beards, follow the movements of hands plaited like rope around the handles of their tools. It is disheartening work, for each day carries away the stones of the day before; the heaps melt away, yet remain untouched. As I pass by, the movements become more rapid in an accentuated zeal which takes the place of a greeting. I have often thought about this reaction of theirs. Anyone who did not know everything it implies could imagine that it meant almost anything: dread, the fear of punishment. I do not deny that this fear exists in some places, but on all the sites where I have worked I have been conscious of something different, impossible to define in one word. Nothing ugly or base, in any case, but a surge of good will, cheerful energy, like actors before an audience they like, or oarsmen who strain as they come into harbour. Their arms are raised, the mallet comes down on the chisel they have positioned so well and the chips fly away in splinters. From the first blocking out to the end, the breadth of movement alters, the space between the chisel and the hammer diminishes and the rhythm changes to one tenth of its speed. And that is how it goes on, for months and years, one yard a day, every *good* day.

I gripped my little brothers' shoulders in my hands. We looked at one another before taking in for the last time the strips of space before us, the searing light over the countryside and the sharp sounds, the smell of flint.

Some internal wound, dark and black-blooded, was tearing at me as my red blood pounded the fear of the morrow. What do my brothers believe? And the craftsmen and lay brothers? Your master has a soul too, open to the slightest breath; he is a mere child, an adolescent. How do they think I let the light in, caress the shape, bend in love over the material, and speak to the arches? And yet all my life I have tried to make others believe that I was firm, cruel, indifferent to suffering, strong! I was kneeling on the ground, weeping, when I suddenly laughed and said: 'Come, Benoît, come, Bernard, drag me to the sawmill. I have seen enough of this rubbishy stone. It is your turn now!'

The trunks and branches are carried, rolled along the ground, stacked according to species, then chocked up on billets. There were my trees; not many really fine, straight trunks. They are all marked with the date of felling, then they have to dry for several months while awaiting the saw. Then we set up the scales, mark out and cut off timber for squared logs and members for frame-work according to length and shape. The finest quality wood goes to the joinery. The thicker branches and the tops of the trunks are barked with the adze and used as scaffolding timber. The load-bearing poles are chosen from the thin, straight trunks. All the waste—bark, chips and small branches cut into logs—is carefully collected and sent to the fire. Wood is scarce, and the kiln has a voracious appetite what with lime, tiles and a furnace to be kept going for years.

As usual, the area was scented with resin and incense, but I thought I could hear the complaints of a saw and the dull sound of axe strokes. We have wood enough. That has been one of my great anxieties since so much is needed in construction work.

Going down towards Joseph's den, I had to stop for a while. My arms are not strong enough to support very much walking and when I am upright there is pain from my wound.

The warm wind of rain was rising and beating down the blue smoke. The ashes keep their twig forms, living and intact. They hover over the chimneys, then float away and scatter, the little souls of the fire which will escape year after year from hell, a hell with a good smell of pine faggots, resin and bread-making.

The kilns are under construction. The little provisional kiln has been in operation from the beginning, but the accursed thing is completely ruined because the brick was not properly fired. Here we burn the limestone we quarry from the cave, thus saving the open quarry stone and enlarging Joseph's workshop at the same time. Each block which falls into the fire increases the space. The old potter is already working under cover, and by next year the floor space will be large enough for him to dry his tiles under shelter, safely in the warmth.

Joseph is not happy about the omnipresent lime, which is harmful to his clay. He has had serious trouble with the first batches of tiles, which were all wasted and broken. In future we will separate the two products. Then later we shall start working the rock in the galleries and there will be no more trouble. The building of permanent kilns is taking quite a time, since we are making them out of twice-baked bricks, crushed and mixed with raw clay; a lengthy procedure to which we can devote little time. We have already sent one lay brother to work in a quarry a league away from here. I have been there only once in six months, on the day we brought the vats of water. Since then Benoît has told me that the operation is moving forward briskly and six vessels have been filled with an oily mud, strained of sand and impurities. Each week Luc sets off with the red clay that has been skimmed off the vats. Joseph's store is full, which means that there is three months' supply. Soon we shall be able to retrieve our man for the main site.

I am still thinking as if I were going to stay. The memories I came to collect are just so many plans for the future. Even so, it really was a farewell tour. On the way to the site we paid a visit to the blacksmith. Our universal man did not stop work as we approached because his bar was red and malleable, rapidly being flattened in a shower of sparks. There was a smell of sulphur, of burnt hoof, of leather, of sweat, of scorched hair, of soot, of ashes, of horse dung and of molten lead. A blacksmith's forge is always tidy and clean in its own way, with its anvil polished and the tools neatly hung between pairs of nails on the wall, its earthen floor sprinkled and swept each day. Antime looked like a pagan god with his great beard as he went on striking without seeing us. This man of leather is being sulky with me. Like a dog he can scent my imminent departure. He has known since the moment the decision was taken, just as he knows when an animal will kick, when the iron is flawed, when the lead is about to melt and when the iron will harden without going brittle. He knows, too, that without him everything would come to a standstill. The animals would not be able to walk, the wheels to turn, the stones to reach the scaffold planking nor the water to reach the abbey. The trees would remain in the earth and the blocks in the ground. The sullen man continued to strike. I wanted to say, 'Stop grumbling, try to understand: you must; I am counting on you, you devil of a smith; the site is not me any longer, it is all of you!' But the sweat ran down his cheeks and trickled into his beard, sweat or tears from smarting, reddened eyes, or something else, not worthy of him, which he wiped away with the back of his hand.

We made a detour through the workshops which stood empty

and dead in the fine weather. On rainy days they are full of different noises, squeakings, thuds and grating. When they are lifeless, these rooms look as if they had been abandoned months ago; yet tomorrow, perhaps, they will look as though the work never stops. Each stranded tool will find its hand, so that the plank may be clamped, nailed, grooved and assembled. Waste fibres will be twisted into ropes; all these amorphous lumps will become wheels, handles, pulleys, pack-saddles, sledges and harnesses. This whole world was my life. To speak of it and evoke it gives me a sense both of pain and of relief, like the scab pulled off by one's nail. This evening I need to re-live my impressions. I had kept the site until the end, seeing in it the final object of all these disparate and often mystifying exertions; the site, where men are more proud, more assured and more free. Down in the quarry the men are like slaves, at the sawmill independent, at the kilns joyful, and at the workshops rushed and busy. Here they are proud. The other men are servants, these are masters.

I was like a curious passer-by who stares in astonishment. I wanted to say, 'What are you doing here? Why have you abandoned these trenches to stagnant water? What are these shapeless heaps? Why are these vats full of some turgid, smoking stuff? How do you know what to use this stone for, this one that is one foot by two, or this one which is irregular and crooked, or this one, finished on five sides and rough on the sixth?'

Imagine being that intruder who had wandered into our valley, suddenly thunderstruck to see stone being torn out of the ground by that great claw which grips when the rope goes taut. Like him I have watched the men at the windlass, watchfully following the path of the block as it leaps up and stands out against the dark blue sky with its sharp and dazzling edges. And then the three ant-men above who finger the stone, examine it, handling it cautiously, turning it, and gently, with a slight movement of the finger, leisurely steer it. Magically, the block comes to rest in its allotted place, and the wall seems none the higher for it, since the stone has filled its space discreetly, as though nothing has happened.

'And why are you plugging the joints with that clay? And why are you pouring grey water from that bowl into those funnels?'

All this kind of work is laughable, just little everyday jobs.

Tireless efforts are rewarded as are those of pitiable insects. One says, 'At this rate, never the ant-hill, never the bee-hive, never the wall.' Yet there are already two yards, next month there will be four and one day the traveller will come back and say, 'Well, well, finished already, that didn't take them long.' He will not have witnessed the work in the mud, the rocks in their hundreds of thousands being painfully dressed over the years, the stone which stands firm against their desperate strokes. He will not have spared a thought for the burning lime, the mangling wheel, the snapping ropes, the stifling heat, the sandstorm which stings the eyes and pushes a man off his balance, the drenching rain, the clumsy, blue hands, the frost which destroys yesterday's work, the human error which builds only to pull down again and the forgotten tool that falls and kills.

The work on a site lasts longer than a war and is less inspiring. Its battles are the dangerous work patrols which set out every day. But victory is certain, the victory of the Virgin's bouquet, nailed up there, at the tip of the steeple, at the blacksmith's cross. Some day it will come, after a long time. Meanwhile men die every year, men leave the game, and few of them will see the victory. I am leaving, it is settled; but one day may the Lord allow me to come back and hear the greeting of those men, from the clay of the foundations, to the iron of the cross, who will finally have seen victory without death.

This site, my last site, brings them all back to me. I can see them like ghosts in the mist, peaceful beneath the snow. They appear rosy and unreal in the breaking of dawn at Lauds. They are pure in the true morning sun at Prime and Tierce. They look sad, weary and dusty after noon at Sext; desolate when the men abandon them at None, serene in the golden light that stretches endless shadows at Vespers. They are flattened by the dusk, their masses melting together as they array themselves in the uniform grey of farewell at Compline. Then, Matins, and they wake under a lurid moon, haggard like us and simplified in the extreme. They are the brightness of light and the void of darkness, immaterial like night itself, the colour of the shroud.

I can see those sites again when they were at the same stage as this one today, the moment of promise. The children of architecture are beautiful at any age. I have adored them in frail infancy. I have trembled for their childhood illnesses. I have given them their first lessons in space. I have been hurt by the early adolescence tearing them away from me.

I have left the muffled sounds of the site behind. The sight of the first stone courses remained imprinted on my eyes for a long time. Everything is just as I was hoping, 'not numbed by any mortar that one can see'.

We stopped at the spring to drink the clear, cool water. If I were a pagan, then I think water would be my goddess, revered so much the more here because she is more precious than pearls. It is her miraculous powers that have enabled us to put our monastery in this blessed countryside, which nevertheless dries up for eight months of the year, during the time when the crystal sounds of liquid and the grasshoppers' indignant whisperings celebrate their providential marriage.

Since everything ends with a balance sheet, I am leaving these few notes about little deeds and characters. It sums up the story of the birth of an abbey. The essential part is over; now it is time to persevere. The day of ideas is ending; when I leave, the world of action goes too.

The abbot will remain at Florielle, die there, no doubt, after a life of struggling — and why? First to establish the reign of justice through the hand of iron, then to create centres for prayer which are, in our opinion, saving a world too laggardly in its penitence, too eager for vice or lack of belief.

One fine morning, the craftsmen will heave their tools and their clothes on to their shoulders and walk off to another site, to obey a new master.

Bernard and Benoît will go on to the very end, as far as the setting-up of the cross of iron; then they will be chosen to assist the master builder at Senanque or Silvacane. Later still, Bernard will take the road away on his own, his back bent and his face as dull as old parchment; small wrinkles will have come to pucker his skin and remain there. Then he will have his own obsessions to satisfy, his own principles to give shape to in three dimensions.

The lay brothers, each different from the other, will remain lay brothers. In the course of mentioning them I believe that I have described or named all of them. If I have omitted one, or ten, of them, then it is among the unmentioned that the most deserving are to be found; the brothers of whom one says nothing because they have stirred up no scandals, been behind no remarkable deeds. Yet they have been everywhere in the early days of this site. There must have been some among the thirty-odd men who were freeing Poulide, or dressing and manhandling Master Paul's blocks, or moistening Joseph's clay, or holding Master Antime's iron bar, or weeding Brother Bruno's vegetable garden or coiling rope for Master Jean's great crab. These nameless, horny-handed people are the men who do not speak. Labourers or craftsmen, they continue to build, waiting for the trench six feet by two which will swallow the grey cowl first of one, and then of another, to be trapped between the forgotten worms of the earth and the worms that are within each of us. Between these two, swarming over their prey, the cloth will crumble away in no more time than it takes the sun and the rain to efface the name from the wooden cross.

I shall be their memorial, like Philippe the tortured or Thomas in his agony beside the stone. I shall live long, thanks to those of them who did not calmly pass away but died in full health and vigour. And then I shall be the abbey itself. There will be a picture of me leaning on Paul by our walls of stone. We shall be those who depart but do not die. The memory of the news that we have gone will be lost in the vagueness of the distant past. So long as our bodies are not seen lying stiff and straight, the smell of our corpses will not be noticed by the men who stay behind. They will say, 'I think I heard of his death some years ago, but I should not be greatly surprised if he were to turn up walking on his one leg,' not surprised either to hear Paul bursting into laughter behind a bed of crumbling, frost-flaked stone.

That is the advantage of the one who departs. At first his disappearing is limited to the turn in the road and does not positively exist until the memories of him are worn out. But if he planted something more than lettuces, a domestic tree for example, or a stone set up at the roadside, he will not die for those who stay behind, for the ones who, one day when discipline is relaxed, will tell stories round a fire on the site or a chimney-corner in the warming house. One wet, cold day when the sky makes it futile to stir from where one is, when shoes as soft as tripe, sucking quietly at the feet, will take a lot of drying before they harden again — on this, and days like it, the departed ones will return through the mouths of the old men and founders. Out on the almost completed site, the young men, the new ones, will be listening to the beginning of the story. 'Fifteen years ago next March, we were working on the foundations for the store room, when ... ' Their eyes will be lost in the flames, dreaming, while the leather oozes its grease and the tunic fronts smoke.

'And what became of this knight Jacques?'

'Oh, he is quite an old man. He does not come this way any longer since the abbot died ... '

Or perhaps, 'He was lost at sea. He set off suddenly in pursuit of the Moors at the massacre of ... '

Or perhaps, 'He caught the "evil" in his practice. He was seen a long way away from here, walking all alone towards the East ... '

'Will he recover?'

'With him, you know, anything can happen. He was a terror, that Templar!'

The limp, warm bodies will lean, hunched, over damp backs. The 'He was a terror, that Templar' will fall into their gathering and behind the heavy door built in days gone by, by the tall Étienne, they will hear the Arab horse go by, and in the silence left by someone like Tiburce a wooden leg will walk across the cloister and a rough voice will suddenly cry, 'Rotten stone! That's my burden, my misfortune! Take my stone from Fontvieille, where it's as white as goat's milk!'

Compline called to me this evening like a knell. Out of fifty, God has chosen this one to strike me down: Adieu, Le Thoronet; be the fulfilment of my life, since you have taken it for yourself!

The banners of the King advance, mysterious shines the Cross whereon life has suffered death and by its death has brought forth life.

(Venantius Fortunatus)

'And the King commanded and they brought great stones, costly stones and hewed stones, to lay at the foundation of the house ...
(I Kgs. v 17)

On St Nicholas's day we were waiting for Jacques the Templar. At times like that when there are so many things one would like to say, silence falls over the men. Every thought, assessed in advance, looks superfluous or useless, so one says nothing.

Though the heart may try to speak, the head is empty. All one has left are the trite remarks which hide one's emotions and make the time pass. Resignedly, the prior and I were looking at the site, which has taken on a fresh aspect from this viewpoint since the night wind carried off all the old leaves from the oak tree at one go. Paul and Bernard were muttering over our most recent drawings. Down the slope from the site the lay brothers were digging a trench. Suddenly they all gave a great shout and ran towards the church. The men who were taking up stones left the scaffolding and rushed to meet them. There was a confused bustle of fear and curiosity, then, all together, they ran down again to crowd round the edge of the excavation. Pierre asked me what was going on. I answered, 'Someone must be hurt, there's been an accident. It must be serious!'

They ran off, leaving me to try to balance on my crutch, but I couldn't take a single step; my wound was one mass of pain. After what seemed like a very long time, the prior came back up to me and mumured breathlessly, 'Simon!'

The evening before, during my tour of inspection, I had told Jean to drain the flooded trench before winter. Bernard commented that he had been asking for the same thing to be done for a long time. Jean replied that Brother Benoît had told him to wait until next spring. I was annoyed, and decided that the sooner it was done the better. If they had listened to me the last time, the trench would have been shored up and safe from the havoc of the flood. They immediately began to bail out the water and mud. The men did not go down until the earth was firm enough not to let them sink in too far. Victor, Jean the lay brother, Lambert and Nicolas were at work with shovel and spade. Nicolas was pulling out a boulder when he realized that it was in fact a clump of marsh grass and began striking at the roots so that he could cut it out. Suddenly Lambert pointed out the 'thing' to Nicolas, who gave a yell, got out of the hole and ran, with the others close behind him. There was a head sticking up out of the bottom. Simon had been engulfed as he stood there, and now he was reappearing: Simon, the one we thought had run away, the lay brother of the hundred strokes of the discipline.

In the darkness, I had cried out, 'Shore up the trench! It is bound to fall in!' I had not made an issue of it as too many things were claiming our attention elsewhere that night. I realized that my request would go unheard. No one can have taken me seriously but Simon. He must have gathered his tools together by the light of the flashes, saying to himself, 'I will go. Simon will obey the chief; the chief is right, he is the only one who is right, Simon knows that. I will go and shore up the trench and to-morrow he will say, "Simon has saved the excavations single-handed; he's a real man, is Simon!"'

We discovered the props, the planks, the nails, the saw and the hammer, everything he would have needed. They were all laid out tidily on the bottom ready for him to set calmly to work there under the rain, only three yards from that wave of mud licking angrily at the lip of the trench. Ten feet below, Simon had arranged his tackle between two thunder claps. When he had assembled the first crossbar and begun to set it in place, the side of the trench nearest the stream collapsed, holding him fast under a ton of clay as he stood there with his arms out towards the north supporting the props. I wonder if Simon cried out. Probably not; he had no further love for the brothers who had betrayed him by persuading him that God, the Order and the promise were three different things. Then he must have waited in silence while the water rose to engulf him. When the mud finally reached his mouth and his blood-shot eyes grew dim, his last thought was probably for me. I do not mean to put myself in the position of God in Simon's last moments, but I had known him in all his simple devotion. God was the chief, and it was for him that Simon had been propping up the abbey in the solitary little task which was so much his own.

Some of the men lowered their eyes before the swollen body. Simon's face contained none of the tranquillity of death, but, staved in by spade-strokes, it stood as a true symbol of his recent past. Pierre the prior has covered him with the community's first cowl. I was glad that such an honour should fall to Simon, for I loved him. It is for that reason that I have delayed my departure, to wait the two days necessary to put him in his grave.

I had my own ideas on the subject of Simon's funeral. He would not go to join Thomas in our cemetery; his destiny was different. For me he was the prop of the abbey. I had little difficulty in convincing the abbot and the prior, who agreed that he should be buried in his excavation. This evening we closed his water-tight sarcophagus which we had embedded in the thickness of the foundation. He was laid with his head to the east, along with his hammer, his nails, and his cross-shaped prop. Later another cross of stone will be built into the bond of the north wall of the refectory.

The service was held after Vespers under cover of a darkness which had overtaken us before the end of the day. The storm which had killed Simon had returned to take part in his funeral, together with the dangerously rising stream. The chapel was so dark that we had to light torches, and the incense flew out through the lattices to climb high on the great wind and turn the rain into a blessed shower of fragrant water.

Four lay brothers carefully bore Simon's body. The bier was protected from the rain by a canopy of canvas. Four other brothers kept the tomb dry. These honours fell to the first lay brothers to come to the site, the eight and the three of us, that was all. A shelter, the privilege of a dying man, had been erected for me and I shared it with the abbot and the prior.

Everyone performed his allotted duties with befitting love. Though Simon had been despised in life, his merits were re-discovered in death. The men had worked in driving rain for two days to clear the trench, shore it up and build the foundation. Then they had had to hollow out an enormous block, fit a lid for it to within one tenth of an inch, lower the whole lot on rollers by hand and position the monolith on the bottom.

I leaned towards the prior and said, 'Pierre, you were worried about the future of the site, but now you can see that you have nothing more to fear. Its past rests firmly on three ordeals, three sacrifices — the martyrdom of Thomas the holy and of Philippe the tortured and the devotion of Simon the simple. I wanted to build you the third pillar at some distance from the other two; the first is behind the choir, the second in the brush and the third supports the abbey wall.'

When it was all over, I was carried back to the workshop on Simon's bier, under the same shelter of canvas. On the way there, I murmured, 'May God, who has enabled us to build an abbey together, bring us all together again one day, monks, lay brothers and craftsmen, without forgetting one of us. May our gifts, our virtues and our vices all be put in one bag so that we shall be able to say, "Together, we have built Thy house." We have put everything into the common cause so that together we may be worthy of the same reward, and undergo the same punishment. Any man who has brought much to the cause has achieved as much as the man who has not, for together each of us has given his entire strength and his entire heart.'

The abbot and the prior settled me on my bed. Later, Jacques the Templar came to see me. We are to leave as soon as the bad weather has cleared. All four of us talked about the site. Edgar is leaving us to build a house for the Temple. Paul often speaks of going home to Fontvieille; he has grown thin and yellow-skinned and his hair has turned white. He is nearing the end. The rivalry between Bernard and Benoît is obvious. It is time for me to go so that the prior can get the new order settled, or jealousy will turn into hatred, of that I am now convinced. So we part sadly to leave with anxious minds.

I, Brother Pierre, prior, remember these words: 'Thy God, whom thou servest continually, He will deliver thee.' (Daniel in the den of lions: Dan. vi 16)

The storm had returned, more violent than ever. Lightning struck close by and for whole seconds the noise was completely deafening. With a certain amount of trouble, I got out of bed and dragged myself to the door. I opened it with difficulty, by sitting on the floor, pulling at the door in my haste and bracing myself with my back, finally rolling half over and, despite my clumsiness, getting it open. Then I hoisted myself up on to my leg by taking a firm grip of the thick door frame.

I had been alone for some time and was about to go to sleep when I heard the distinct sound of an incipient quarrel. I should have knocked on the wall straight away, as if I were just calling them, but I wanted to find out what was on their minds. After some harsh words they continued the discussion in undertones and I thought it was all over. Since the day before yesterday, when Simon's body was discovered, I had known that Bernard and Benoît hated each other. Suddenly I heard shouts and the sounds of fighting. I sat up in bed, heard their door open, then slam shut and hurried footsteps coming round the corner of my hut. The pair of them were grappling with each other on my doorstep. I could hear the sound of blows and bodies scraping against wood. I called out, shouted an order.

I hopped over to the door and, holding on to it, opened it wide. They were on the ground, locked savagely together and panting like animals. In the dazzling light, I saw Benoît rearing up to strike with some weapon, a quarryman's callipers, I think. Bernard clutched to Benoît to protect himself and they rolled away about twelve feet. In my confusion I forgot about my stump and took a step forward, but there was no ground on which to walk. As I collapsed the pain was so fierce that I lost control of myself and tears of anger or of agony ran warm and salty down into my mouth. The icy rain was falling on to the back of my neck and streaming down my back. Dragging myself along by my elbows I got within reach of a foot and then an ankle. I pulled at it, holding on as tightly as I could, but it shook itself free. My whole body was tossed away, my stump hit the ground and I let go. I saw Bernard running away, up towards the quarries with Benoît chasing after him. I shouted at them and called their names but the thunder of the storm and the rattle of the rain made a mockery of my voice. I dragged myself back to my door, but once under cover I became extremely concerned and decided to go down and look for help.

I covered the first part on my elbows, as the ground was flat, but when I reached the first step on the stairway my unsupported thigh fell over the top. I waited for the excruciating pain to end, then made my way towards the second step, realizing that I would never be able to bear the shock thirty times over. I turned sideways, my body flat along the top of the step, and tried to roll inch by inch to the next step, supporting myself on my left hand and arm and using the other as a balance to stop me falling. I tipped over with my right arm caught under my back. The stump caught on the edge of the step, rebounded and came down again.

I was considering going back to the warm safety of my bed when I heard a terrible scream from above me. I set off again, this time on my buttocks, dragging my thigh, leaning on my hands and pushing against my heel. I hoped to make fast progress this way. As I came to each step, I put down the good leg first and then my buttocks. Lastly I propped up my stump, placed it cautiously on the foot of the step and crept a little farther forward. Unfortunately, the storm had passed over, and I found myself plunged in total darkness. I groped my way, anxiously waiting for each distant flash of lightning, and managed to reach the thirtieth stair. My habit was soaked with rain and weighed me down so that I was in a state of near collapse. I had not noticed that the course of the stream had become a torrent. Getting down the slippery bank was easy enough, I just pushed myself down head first with my heel. Suddenly I found myself up to my hips in water, breathing in mud and water in my panic. I thrashed about and managed to get my head out of water on the far side. I was stuck in the freezing torrent, where all I could do was vomit, moan and call out. It took some time to climb out because the folds of cloth, heavy with slime, hampered my movements. Then I had the insane idea of taking off my habit.

It had not occurred to me that my stump would then be naked and that the exposed wound would be open to the friction of earth and stones. My true Calvary began. On that mortified thing, secreting some filthy liquid, were raw nerve ends which caught on the slightest roughness. After about one hour I had travelled a hundred yards. Then, as I dragged the mangled stump along, I made no more progress for I lost myself in the darkness and landed up in the brush. The whole thing was becoming impossible. I could have begged for death. It occurred to me, however, to take off my tunic and make it into a padded dressing which I could wrap around the stump. This task took an infinite length of time because I kept catching myself on the thorn bushes which completely surrounded me. I took off the soaked garment as well as I could and pushed it down so that I could put it under my thigh, fold the flaps over and pull it tight, using the sleeves to tie it. Then I tried to get out of the thorn brake by pulling the stems of the briars. A searing pain made me realize that my tunic had been caught on the thorns. All protection was gone, I was completely naked except for one shoe. I called out, but my shrill cries faded and disappeared into the thick night and the rustling of the water that fell and flowed. I struggled with frantic, uncoordinated movements to leave that prison of branches. I clenched my teeth and said, 'You must get out or die,' and tugged with all my strength. I renewed my efforts a moment later. By a glimmer of light which I took for a belated flash of lightning I suddenly caught sight of the Field below the great bank, the beautifully flat Field, the broad path of the lay brothers sloping gently down to the huts, the chapel, the prior's door; in short, life! I could imagine Bernard and Benoît being looked after, saved, punished and forgiven. I could see their friendship being rediscovered after its trial, my little brothers supervising work on the site, my children. I was conscious of a deep sense of joy, a wild surge of hope. I stretched like a worm pursuing its way to reach the crest of the bank. Without weighing the risk, I hastily let myself roll down the slope.

I must have regained consciousness soon afterwards. Some kind of sticky liquid was flowing from my forehead. The storm was coming back over the valley. In a flash of lightning I saw the stone which had been waiting for me, that stone which had rolled down from above to welcome me with a corner sharpened like an axe. By another flash I saw which direction I should have been taking. I stretched out on my back to let the rain wash away the blood which was blinding me, then, with my head to one side so that I could keep one eye clear, I resumed my easy progress, putting down heel first, then buttocks and then the palms of my hands. In my earnestness I had passed the bounds of pain. I counted to ten, lay down to get my breath back and set off again. The distance across the Field and the path was a hundred yards. I counted eight, then six, then just two but I could not manage to get up again. I was twenty yards from the chapel, fifty from the lay brothers' dorter. I chose your door, Prior, and there, under a deluge of rain and in the incessant din of the thunder, I crawled along on my back, then on my side, curling up and stretching out slowly like a larva.

If it was my head wound which put me to sleep, my stump woke me. My eyelids were stuck down with blood. I no longer knew where I was. I painstakingly scooped some muddy water up in my hand and bathed my eyes. No sooner had I unstuck them than they filled with sand. I still could not see. Whimpering like a puppy, I groped around me. I was so near the end after so much suffering, and I was stranded. I then began to cry; the tears gushed out and I could see. I had three yards to go but to me they seemed impassable. I moved forward inch by inch on my belly, touched the sill and began scratching, then tapping. It was then that I remembered: on stormy nights, you always slept with the lay brothers. Lying there with my face to the ground, the cold cut me to the marrow. Then, gradually, I began to feel at ease in the rising of an icy wind. The pain left me, as God had left me; as you had.

Later, the excruciating vision of my little brother Bernard lying up there, hurt and wounded, perhaps even dying like me, came back to me. I was completely helpless and stretched out my arms with my hands clasped together. Something brushed against my fingers, once, then twice, something like a furry animal. I was no longer alone. There was some animal, as numbed and pitiable as myself, alive out there. I might be able to warm the little creature, cherish it and save it. I grasped the sopping hair in both hands and pulled it towards me, close to my heart ... It was the rope! The bell-rope!

Now you must be able to hear it! It is still ringing in its steeple. I can see a kind of door opening on to brightness. 'What do you seek?' 'God's mercy.' *Salve sancta parens, sub qua cisterciencis Ordo militat!*

Supremum vale, Daniel, saint and prophet.

Faithfully recorded, this last narrative ends the journal of our brother, master builder of the abbey-to-be. I have written this in his workshop.

BROTHER PIERRE
Prior of Notre Dame de Florielle at Le Thoronet.
Eleventh day of December, eleven hundred and sixty-one.

Notes

PROVENCE

In the twelfth century, Provence formed part of the Holy Roman Empire and belonged by inheritance to the Bérenger family which ruled Catalonia. In 1160, the year before this story begins, Raymond Bérenger II, known as the Younger, had won a decisive victory over the Balzes in the person of Hugues II (the husband of Anna, Viscountess of Marseilles), who died in 1172 in Sardinia. The rivalry between the two families resulted in unending battles for dominion over Provence, known as the Baussenque Wars. In actual fact they began in 1129 and continued until the end of the thirteenth century. They originated in a quarrel over an inheritance. In 1110 Gilbert de Gevandan was assassinated; he had married the Lady Gerberge, heiress to Provence and a descendant of Boso, King of Cisjurane Burgundy (brother-in-law to Charles the Bald), and of Louis the Blind (died 911). Gilbert and Gerberge had two daughters, Doulce and Stephanette. The elder, Doulce (died 1129), was her mother's favourite and received Provence as her dowry when she married Raymond Bérenger I, Count of Barcelona (died 1131). The younger, Stephanette, married Raymond Balz (died 1150). From then on, Provence became a fief of the Catalans of Barcelona. The powerful Balz family found this unacceptable. They reigned at Les Baux and were descended from Count Leibulfe and from Pons I (died 954). The name Balz had legendary origins; the family claimed descent from Balthasar, one of the three Wise Men, whence their escutcheon: gules, a star argent. Taking the view that Stephanette had been wrongly deprived of her share of the inheritance (according to feudal law, Provence should have been equally divided between the sisters), Raymond Balz, her husband, claimed her rights on the death of Doulce and his brother-in-law Raymond Bérenger I. In 1161 the opposing champions were cousins: Hugues Balz II (eldest son of Stephanette and Raymond Balz) and Raymond Bérenger II, the Younger (grandson of Doulce and Raymond Bérenger I). Guillaume the monk (a Cistercian master builder and hero of this chronicle) was the younger brother of Hugues. A third Balz, the youngest, subsequently founded the Avelline branch and carried on the Baussenque Wars. The Bérenger and Balz families offered protection and financial support to the Cistercian abbeys of Provence.

THE SCHISM

The schism was the most important political and religious event of this time. In 1159 Frederick Barbarossa, Emperor of Germany and suzerain of Provence, had supported the candidature of the antipope, Victor IV, and had him elected by the clergy of his own party, in opposition to Pope Alexander III, successor to Adrian IV and elected by the anti-Germanic clergy. In 1160 Frederick summoned all those bishops who favoured Victor IV to the Council of Pavia. Following this council, the Kings of France and England, Louis VII and Henry II, had Alexander proclaimed legitimate pope by their own bishops. The Balz family supported the emperor and Victor IV, while the Catalans sided with the kings and Alexander III. The schism came to an end in 1162 with the victory of Alexander over Victor. There is a record of the accession to the bishopric of Rheims of Henry of France, brother of King Louis VII in 1161. Henry was a personal friend of Alexander and his chief supporter against the antipope, Victor.

THE ABBEY OF LE THORONET

Le Thoronet was a Cistercian abbey in Provence, in the commune of Lorgues, begun in 1160 (restored and almost entirely preserved).

The community did not settle at Le Thoronet when work started there, as was the custom when an abbot was chosen by a mother abbey to found a new monastery. In fact, the monks had been in the area since 1136, at Notre Dame de Florielle, twenty-four kilometres away from Le Thoronet, east of Tourtour, on a Roman road. They did not leave Florielle to occupy the new abbey until about 1176. From 1160 to 1176, then, Le Thoronet was merely a building site where the lay brothers worked under the supervision of a master builder. The Abbot of Notre Dame de Florielle, who was superintendent of the project, came to Le Thoronet only to keep an eye on the work and to maintain discipline among the monks. The abbey of Le Thoronet is one of the finest in all Cistercian architecture, and though the design of the church does not follow the strict tradition of the Order (having semicircular chevet and apses instead of the flat chevet), the monastery as a whole is a fine expression of the simplicity and austerity inspired by St Bernard.

THE CLOISTER AT LE THORONET

Frequent mention is made in this work of the unusual layout of the cloister as an irregular trapezium. Archaeologists have remained silent on this subject, apparently accepting that, for reasons which are obscure but fairly common as far as Romanesque architecture is concerned, this anomaly is the result of the altered alignment of the store room built on to the west wing of the cloister in the thirteenth century. We do not share this view. The first precise drawings of plans and elevations of the abbey of Le Thoronet were made by the author, thus enabling him to analyse for the first time the various guide-lines, whether intentional or fortuitous, which suggested the construction from the outset. It seems certain that the oldest building, at least in its basic structure, is the cellar. It was probably intended to be used as a provisional chapel or as a dorter. Later, a change of scheme or of master builder led to a new alignment of the church, now facing exactly east. Hence it is possible to arrive at a rational explanation for the unusual design of the cloister: having decided to preserve work already started beneath the original building, the master builder was forced to contrive ground plans of particular intricacy. Thanks to these, the solution he chose is astonishing in effect. Working from a predetermined shape, both in plan and in elevation, the master builder has created a masterpiece of harmony. Apart from what we have in the plans themselves, and the hexagonal form of the lavabo, the proofs confirming this thesis are numerous.

THE CISTERCIAN ORDER

The name is derived from Cîteaux, the first Cistercian abbey. The Order was founded in 1098 by a Benedictine, Robert, Abbot of Molesme, whose intention was to return to the strict Rule of St Benedict. In the beginning the Order was the centre of amazing vigour and roused great enthusiasm. Towards 1110, however, the austerity and privations of monastic discipline diminished the number of vocations and the monks were decimated by sickness. But when, nearing the limit of human endurance, they were about to give up the fight, Bernard of Fontaines appeared with thirty Burgundian gentlemen of his family. It was early in the year 1112. The virtue of these powerful, devout noblemen gave Cîteaux a fresh start, the true beginning of the 'Great Adventure' of the Cistercians. In this narrative we frequently find the man who was to become St Bernard, called by various names: Bernard of Fontaines, Abbot of Clairvaux, Holy Abbot, Great Abbot, Bernard, Abbot of Clairvaux. The sanctity, activity and political skill of the saint made it possible for him to exercise a major influence on all the important affairs of his time for forty years. Though he was continually battling for his cause, any setbacks which befell him were few and far between. Thanks to him the Cistercians remain the greatest builders of the twelfth and thirteenth centuries, because of the original quality of their Romanesque and Gothic abbeys. The Order expanded throughout the Christian world. In 1153, when St Bernard died, there were 343 Cistercian abbeys in existence. By the end of the thirteenth century, nearly 1,500 abbeys had been built, including convents for women. When one considers that some of these abbeys held over 1,500 monks or nuns, and that such houses stood in every country from Scandinavia down to southern Italy, from Brittany across to the far side of the Danube and even in Palestine, one begins to have an idea of the considerable part played by the Cistercians in twelfth- and thirteenth-century Europe. The decline of the Order from the fourteenth century onwards, the wars of religion, the Revolution and the passage of time have prevented the preservation of many an architectural masterpiece. Nevertheless, numerous churches and abbeys are still intact or have been restored.

THE LIFE OF A CISTERCIAN ABBEY

Foundation

The first abbey to be built was Cîteaux, which is the mother house of the Order, *par excellence*. From the first quarter of the twelfth century onwards, five mother houses gave birth to all the Cistercian communities: these were Cîteaux, Clairvaux, Morimond, Pontigny and La Ferté. It was by sending out 'swarms' that the Order organized its foundations. When an abbey had become sufficiently strong, the Chapter appointed an abbot to found a new community. He would then leave the mother house, a daughter or grand-daughter of Cîteaux, in company with a few monks and carrying the materials necessary for religious services. They would proceed to the appointed place and immediately set about making a provisional settlement, usually built of wood, which they could use until permanent buildings had been constructed of stone. The place had to be isolated. Further imperative requirements narrowed the choice of site: water, either a spring or a watercourse; land, to assure livelihood; and materials for building — stone, clay and wood.

Plan

Each abbey was laid out in conformity with an invariable plan, and on principles dictated by simplicity and poverty. The centre of the plan was the cloister. The church, which was the most important single feature, generally had its chevet oriented to the east. The earliest Cistercian churches were plain, rectangular buildings. Later the Latin-cross plan with flat chevet was adopted. The cloister abutted on a side aisle of the church, usually at the north. The living-quarters were arranged round the cloister. At the end of the north transept stood the armarium or library, and the sacristy, next came the chapter house (the community's place of solemn assembly), then the entrance, the parlour, the dorter stairway, the monks' hall, the warming house, the monks' refectory, the kitchen, the lay brothers' refectory, the cellars, the store room and the lay brothers' dorter. On the first floor of the east wing of the cloister, next to the church, were the abbot's lodgings, and next to them the monks' dorter. This dorter communicated directly with the church by a stairway running down one corner of the transept, and with the east gallery of the cloister by another stairway. Opposite the entrance to the refectory a lavabo was installed for the washing of hands. In many cases, it stood in a pavilion which projected into the cloister garden. The enclosure and the galleries were open only to the monks; lay brothers and laymen would be invited there only in exceptional circumstances. Women were not admitted, and one abbot was severely punished by the General Chapter for having received a Queen of France, Marguerite, consort of St Louis. On Sundays the lay brothers could be present at the monks' assembly, looking on from behind two windows arranged one on either side of the entrance to the chapter house. The architecture of Cistercian abbeys does not seem to have been subject to written rules. St Bernard left no definite instructions, though his virulent attacks on the extravagance of certain churches and of Benedictine monasteries imposed a contrary style. He strove to exclude any form of decoration likely to prove distracting or expensive. This is why there were no carvings, statues, decorated windows, or wall paintings in Cistercian buildings up to the middle of the thirteenth century. Their architecture was designed to provide for living quarters and for religious observance to the exclusion of any useless or precious objects and any superfluous elements such as steeples, towers or other structural complications. Obviously, the absence of rounded shapes in the plans, notably those for the choir and apsidal chapels, was chiefly due to the desire for economy and efficiency.

Internal Organization

The abbot was the head of the community. He had no superiors but had to render his annual accounts to his mother house when the General Chapters were in assembly. It was he who appointed the monks who were responsible for various offices, though under his overall supervision. The prior was his second-in-command and his deputy in case of absence. Next came the master of novices, the sacristan, the precentor, the infirmarian, the cellarer, the hosteller and the porter. Not including the prior, all these offices were of equal importance. However, it was the cellarer who played the dominant role in the economic, administrative and financial life of an abbey during the time of its foundation, providing for its material needs and later providing for the material needs of the community and its continuing prosperity. In addition, he supervised the lay brothers, gave orders to the craftsmen and artisans and bargained for purchases. He was, at one and the same time, master builder, steward and man of affairs.

The Rule

At the foundation of a religious Order, the Rule prescribed the regulations in their entirety, for spiritual and material life alike. The Rule is complete in every detail: it contains timetables, services, prayers, authorized books, chants and so on, as well as discipline, dress, food, medical attention, etc. Nothing seems to have escaped the notice of the men who wrote or perfected it.

The Monks

When a postulant presented himself at the door of a Cistercian abbey, the porter would ask him, 'What do you seek?' and he would reply, 'God's mercy.' He then passed through the doorway. At Cîteaux, above this door, were written the words, '*Salve sancta parens, sub qua cisterciencis Ordo militat.*' The Cistercian Order was dedicated to the Virgin. Her cult brought a special gentleness and affection into this strict confraternity. After he had been admitted, the postulant became a novice and was given into the care of the monk responsible for novices. One year later to the very day, he pronounced the vows of poverty, chastity, obedience and stability, and received the habit and tonsure (few monks entered the priesthood). At the ceremony, the abbot would say, 'May the Lord cover you with this garment of salvation,' and then, 'Which is the highest commandment of the Law? Thou shalt love the Lord thy God with all thy soul, with all thy heart and with all thy might.'

Once he had pronounced his vows, the Cistercian monk began his religious life; a life of the utmost harshness and strictness, of silent prayer, physical and mental labour, privations and voluntary corporal chastisements. The longest work days began well before sunrise and were governed by the canonical offices until nightfall. Thus, from Lauds till Compline the monks shared their lives with one another and were subject to all the obligations which the Rule laid upon them. They slept fully clothed on straw mattresses in common dorters, never undressing at all. They had to keep their shoes on and be in continual readiness to proceed to the church or to their work at a moment's notice. All their gestures were prescribed, right down to the way in which they made their way to the latrines with cowl drawn over face and hands crossed over breast.

The monks wore a habit, a long white woollen robe with a cowl. Their other garments consisted of a tunic, drawers, stockings and leather shoes.

Their food consisted of vegetables, dairy produce and bread. Meals were taken communally in the refectory at about noon and again at about seven in the evening. In Lent, one meal only was provided, in the evening. Wine was forbidden; after 1150, however, it was alternately refused and permitted, though in minimal quantities.

The monks were clean-shaven and their hair was cut several times a year. Hygiene was virtually non-existent; only the twice-daily washing of hands was compulsory. As part of their medical care, the monks were bled four times a year, in February, April, June and September.

The death of the Cistercian monk was an occasion for solemnity. When the death throes began, every monk would leave whatever he was doing to be with his dying brother.

The Lay Brothers

The lay brothers were untonsured followers of the religious life, regarded by the monks as their brothers in religion. Their conduct, their tasks, their religious observance and their whole way of life remained independent and separate from that of the monks. Thus they had their own refectory, their own dorter and their own place at the lower end of the church. Like the monks, the lay brothers bound themselves at the end of a novitiate, pronounced the religious vows of poverty and chastity and made a promise to obey. They were not subject to the major Rule of the Order, but to a minor ordinance called *The Usages and Customs*. In the daily life of the lay brother, moreover, everything, compulsory services, prayers and so on, took a simpler form so that he had more time to work with his hands. For the cloistered and contemplative monk, manual labour was regarded more as a matter of principle than a matter of necessity. Consequently economic activity and prosperity depended on the lay brothers. They were farm labourers or workmen, usually living on a farm or a work site where they were supervised by one of their own number who was also responsible for them, though they took their orders from the cellarer.

The Usages and Customs set out, with a precision similar to that of the Rule, the various obligations to be carried out by these domestic workers of the community. It contained timetables and prayers, sections on food, garments and medical attention.

Their day, too, began before sunrise, when, after prayers, they worked until nightfall, ending their day in prayer. They ate two meals a day, but were not subject to the strict fasting of the monks. Their rations were increased by extra allowances when they were working: the pittance, which consisted of fish or meat, and the *mixtum*, an extra meal of bread.

In the early days, the lay brothers wore clothes like serfs': a tunic, a scapular of varying length, a leather belt, drawers and shoes. In 1161 they were given the cope, a long robe less full than the monks' habit and made of brown or grey woollen cloth, with a cowl. When they were working they also wore gloves or mittens. In contrast to the monks, the lay brothers wore beards, while their hair was cut short. They were known as 'the bearded brothers'. Although they were under a rule of silence, they were allowed to express themselves to make their work easier. Their general hygiene, medical attention, bleedings, the fact that they were never to undress, etc., made their physical life very similar to that of the monks.

To make up for the inadequate amount of sleep in the summer, the lay brothers were authorized to take a siesta or short afternoon sleep after the midday meal. In some circumstances the afternoon sleep was also permitted to the monks.

Many important facts have been omitted from this short account of the life of Cistercian communities in the twelfth century. The reader is advised to consult *L'Architecture Cistercienne*, Vol. I, by Marcel Aubert.

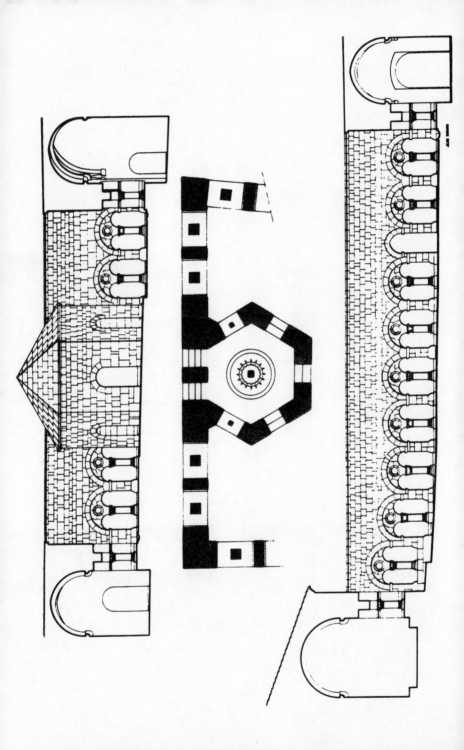

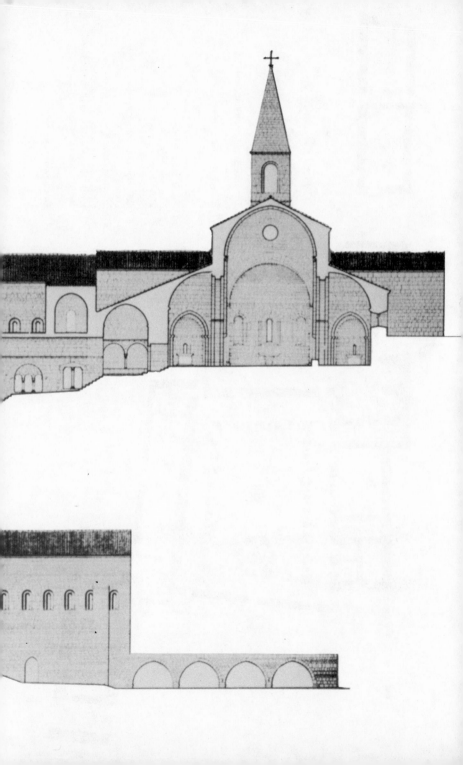

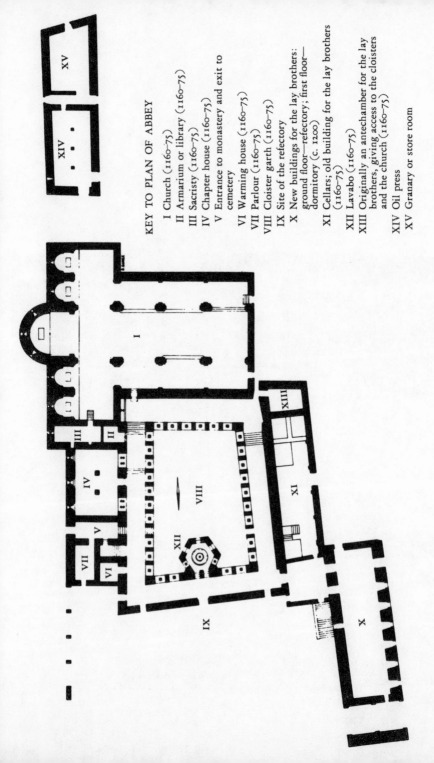

KEY TO PLAN OF ABBEY

I Church (1160–75)
II Armarium or library (1160–75)
III Sacristy (1160–75)
IV Chapter house (1160–75)
V Entrance to monastery and exit to cemetery
VI Warming house (1160–75)
VII Parlour (1160–75)
VIII Cloister garth (1160–75)
IX Site of the refectory
X New buildings for the lay brothers: ground floor—refectory; first floor—dormitory (c. 1200)
XI Cellars; old building for the lay brothers (1160–75)
XII Lavabo (1160–75)
XIII Originally an antechamber for the lay brothers, giving access to the cloisters and the church (1160–75)
XIV Oil press
XV Granary or store room